St. Patrick's Gargoyle

Katherine Kurtz

ACE BOOKS, NEW YORK

This is a work of fiction. Names, characters, places, and incidents either are the product of the author's imagination or are used fictitiously, and any resemblance to actual persons, living or dead, business establishments, events, or locales is entirely coincidental.

ST. PATRICK'S GARGOYLE

An Ace Book / published by arrangement with the author

PRINTING HISTORY
Ace hardcover edition / February 2001
Ace mass-market edition / February 2002

Visit our website at
www.penguinputnam.com
Check out the ACE Science Fiction & Fantasy newsletter!

ISBN: 0-441-00905-0

ACE®
Ace Books are published by The Berkley Publishing Group, a division of Penguin Putnam Inc., 375 Hudson Street, New York, New York 10014. ACE and the "A" design are trademarks belonging to Penguin Putnam Inc.

PRINTED IN THE UNITED STATES OF AMERICA

10 9 8 7 6 5 4 3 2 1

For Mobi, Tiger, and Kat,
who are very fond of gargoyles . . .

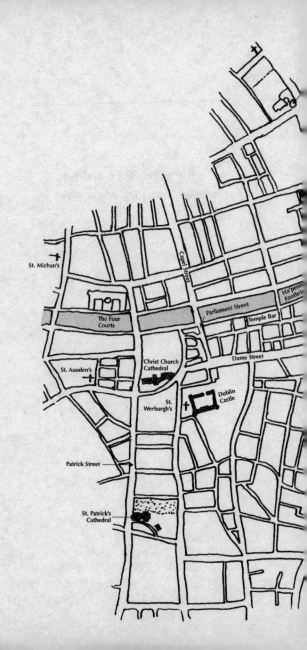

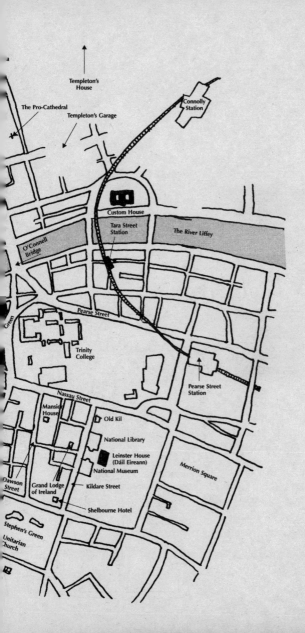

Templeton's
House

The Pro-Cathedral

Templeton's Garage

Connolly
Station

Custom House

Tara Street
Station

The River Liffey

O'Connell
Bridge

Green

Pearse Street

Trinity
College

Pearse Street
Station

Nassau Street

Mansion
House

Old Kil

National Library

Leinster House
(Dáil Eireann)

National Museum

Merrion Square

Dawson
Street

Grand Lodge
of Ireland

Kildare Street

Shelbourne Hotel

Stephen's Green

Unitarian
Church

Chapter 1

In the bitter cold of a late December night, the gargoyle's sharp gaze scanned restlessly over the deserted streets of Dublin. Not far below, the clock in the tower of St. Patrick's Cathedral began to strike midnight. The sound of the bell reverberated on a breeze brittle with the promise of snow, skittering among the city's chimneys and across frost-kissed slate roofs. Very soon, the rhythm was picked up by other clocks elsewhere in the sleeping city.

Revelling in the music that sang freedom, the gargoyle stretched batlike wings and gave a snort of satisfaction. From his lofty vantage point behind the tower's stepped Irish battlements, invisible from street level, he had guarded this part of the city for centuries. Only once each month, when the moon was dark, did he customarily descend from his windswept eyrie to prowl among the shadows.

The clock in the bell tower finished striking midnight, and the gargoyle flexed his wings again, breathed a deep gargoyle breath, and exhaled. As he did so, dense shadow sighed from the stone-carved jaws—darkling manifestation of a gargoyle's true essence—and he plummeted toward the pavement below, only slowing with an abrupt *whoosh* of suddenly extended wings as he touched down gently instead of splatting on the pavement. In less than a blink of an eye he was hidden in the soft-edged shadow of a frost-glittering buttress, casting a glance around to see whether anyone had witnessed his descent.

The street was empty and silent, just the way he liked it, with snow flurries dimming the electric glow of the wrought-iron light standards along Patrick Street, which fronted the cathedral. He had much preferred gaslight, though he needed neither. Furling his leathery wings, he turned to skulk along the side of the cathedral, ghosting from shadow to shadow. Catching a hint of movement in the back of a frosty window, he briefly bared his teeth at it, but he knew it was only his own reflection.

The old churchyard and adjoining park afforded far less cover than the looming bulk of the cathedral, but they were also deserted at this midnight hour. Vigilant nonetheless, the gargoyle streaked above one snowy footpath in a blur of speed and plunged into the murky darkness of St. Patrick's Well, scaly wings bumping and scraping against the ancient stone as he fell.

The chamber in which he landed was redolent of pigeon droppings and the foul, dank smell of stagnant water, littered with rubble and the refuse generated by humans—

empty soda cans and cider bottles and paper trash. Ignoring this evidence of mortal sloth, the gargoyle squeezed through a series of drains and ancient culverts to emerge in the system of medieval tunnels that still connected St. Patrick's with Christ Church Cathedral, Dublin Castle, and St. Michan's Church, on the other side of the Liffey.

Down the close, musty passageway he sped on his midnight errand, the tips of his close-furled wings striking sparks whenever they brushed the low ceiling, talons scuffling hollowly against the stone underfoot. A creature of the night, he could see well enough in the inky darkness, but as he passed beneath Dublin Castle and approached his destination, the light-limned outline of a door beckoned, and a distant murmuring sound grew gradually more distinct.

He pushed open the door to a barrage of agitated voices and the fierce, ruby-glowing gaze of more than a dozen other gargoyles milling in the vaulted chamber beyond.

"Hey, Paddy, we were beginning to worry you'd be late," one of them called, to murmurs of greeting and agreement from several others, as they all began to take their places along rock-cut tiers like a small amphitheatre.

Late, indeed! As Paddy settled between the venerable Christ Church gargoyle, known as C.C., and their colleague from St. Audoen's, another very ancient church, he reflected that in all the centuries he'd been guarding St. Patrick's, he'd never once missed or even been late to the monthly conclaves that all duty gargoyles were obliged to attend.

Beside him, the St. Audoen's gargoyle resumed harping on his usual complaint—one that was certainly justified, if grown somewhat tedious through repetition, since nothing could be done about it. A few years back, the crypt of the church he'd guarded for centuries had been turned into a Viking heritage center—an outrage, so far as its guardian was concerned. The old synod hall at Christ Church had suffered a similar fate, now housing a tourist venue called Dublinia. The gargoyle of St. Audoen's hadn't yet been turned out of his living, because the building was still standing—and since it was the only truly medieval church in Dublin, the city fathers were unlikely to simply knock it down—but guarding tourist attractions was hardly in the same category as guarding sacred buildings. All the gargoyles were increasingly concerned about the conversions.

"It's the foot in the door, I keep telling you," the St. Audoen's gargoyle was muttering under his breath. "'Lo, Paddy. First they take over the crypt, then it's a chapel or two, then it's the whole lot! I just don't understand the big fuss about Vikings. The Vikings were terrible people. They raped and pillaged—especially, they pillaged!"

"I never liked Vikings much, either," the Christ Church gargoyle agreed. "Back in the old days, we used to give 'em what-for! Remember the time I turned a Viking into a puddle of putrid flesh?"

"Did you really?" said the relatively junior gargoyle who guarded the Four Courts, sounding both eager and scandalized, as several of his elders rumbled acknowledgment.

"Before your time, kid," said the gargoyle from St. Werburgh's, not far above their heads. "You civic gargoyles'll never see the kind of action we used to see in the old days. I say the rot set in when the Georgians stopped putting gargoyles on churches!"

"It was before that," said the Trinity College gargoyle.

"I blame it on the Reformation—Luther, and Calvin, and that crowd. No proper sense of how things ought to be, and no sense of humor!"

"Yeah, but at least the Protestants still remember it's supposed to be the Church Militant," said the gargoyle from University Church, an elegant Roman Catholic edifice over on St. Stephen's Green. "My building's all right, if you like Byzantine decor, but you look at most of these modern Catholic churches—not one goddamn gargoyle! No bell towers, either. How do they expect to defend the faith?"

"Good question!" one of the Church of Ireland gargoyles agreed. "People think those little pointy spires on our bell towers are just for decoration. Boy, would *they* be surprised if they knew the things were surface-to-air missiles!"

"But will *He* let us use them? No!" the St. Audoen's gargoyle pouted. "I liked things better when He was an Old Testament God, and we were His avenging angels. Why even bother to call us the Church Militant anymore?"

"Yeah, and most of these new churches don't even *have* bell towers, much less missiles," said another. "Or, if they do have towers, they've got *electronic bells*!"

"Not at St. Patrick's, we don't," Paddy pointed out with pride. "We've got a full ring of *real* bells—*and* missiles! Back when they were making all that fuss about the city's millennium, my bell team rang a full peal of Grandsire Caters. That's more than five thousand changes without a repeat! Took a good three hours. Now, *that's* ringing."

As several other gargoyles agreed that the feat was, indeed, something to be proud of, two more gargoyles burst through the door, engaged in an angry and animated disquisition.

"It's this modern generation: they got no respect!" one of them was saying. "Somebody said some cherubs in the churchyard saw the whole thing—but these days, nobody's gonna pay any attention to a bunch of naked putti!"

"Yeah, but what're ya gonna do?" his companion replied—a tough old gargoyle from the Presbyterian Church in Parnell Square. "Street punks! Lager louts! They litter the streets with empty cider cans and cigarette butts, and scribble graffiti on the walls—*illiterate* graffiti—*and* they throw up on the sidewalks, and piddle in doorways—"

"I know what *I'd* do, if I ever got my hands on the culprits!" the first one grumbled. "In the old days, we would've set their piss on fire! St. Michan's used to be a damned decent place."

"What *ever* are you talking about?" the Dublin Castle gargoyle demanded. "What's happened at St. Michan's?"

"Where've *you* been?" one of the new arrivals asked disdainfully, as he flounced into his place.

"At my post!"

"Let's don't *us* fight," the second newcomer said. "You know the vaults under St. Michan's?"

"Of course."

"Vandals broke in and trashed the place a couple of nights ago."

A horrified chorus of "No!" greeted this revelation.

"Yeah, got pissed on cider, busted up some coffins, set a couple of fires—even roughed up that crusader mummy who made it back from the Holy Land."

"But, that's disgraceful!" said the Trinity gargoyle. "All apart from the disrespect for hallowed ground, that's where Bram Stoker got his inspiration for the crypts in *Dracula*! I remember when he was writing that. I used to watch him pacing back and forth in Trinity Yard, mumbling under his breath about vampires. 'Course, everybody knew he was a little strange. . . ."

"Well, what are we going to do about it?" asked the very practical gargoyle from the Unitarian Church on St. Stephen's Green. "Didn't anyone notice anything suspicious?"

"Who can tell, with tourists all over the place?" another grumbled. "Over at St. Andrew's, they've turned the place into a damned tourist information center. I spend my days having my picture snapped by hordes of Spanish tourists! Or French, or Italian, or—God help us—Germans. At least the Brits and Americans speak the language—sort of."

"At least you aren't overrun by crazy people dressed like Vikings!" the St. Audoen's gargoyle muttered darkly.

"Let's get back to the point," said the somewhat officious gargoyle from the Lord Mayor's residence at Mansion House. "I don't think any of us are particularly pleased with recent trends in building conversions, but we've all had to adapt to the times."

"Yeah, but there's a limit," said the Christ Church gargoyle.

"That's right," the St. Audoen's gargoyle agreed. "Who was the bright spark who thought of putting a Viking heritage center in one of the oldest churches in Dublin? The city fathers spent *centuries* trying to keep Vikings *out!*"

"Hey, it costs money to maintain these old buildings," the Mansion House gargoyle pointed out. "For the most part, I think the city planners do the best they can. Think of all the great old buildings they've *saved. We* don't have to worry about filthy lucre, but humans do."

"Yeah, bean-counters," said a crusty old gargoyle from north of the Liffey.

"Now, wait just a minute," said the Custom House gargoyle, who called himself Gandon, after the building's architect. "I, for one, am rather grateful to the bean-counters."

"Yeah, you would be," said St. Werburgh's gargoyle, whose building was falling down around his ears. The Custom House was regarded as the city's most important architectural jewel, sited between the last two bridges on the Liffey, just before it flowed into the sea. Burned in 1921, during the Troubles attendant upon Irish Independence, and subsequently rebuilt, it recently had been the focus of further loving restoration entailing some six years and several million pounds.

"We're straying from the point again," said the Mansion House gargoyle. "And I really don't think we should be so hard on the city planners. *Despite* their many faults," he emphasized, glaring at the others to silence the incipient grumbles, "they save a lot of our homes, when they take on restoration schemes. Restoration is *always* preferable to demolition."

"And *now* who's straying from the point?" said the gargoyle from the Dominican Priory in Dorset Street, not unkindly.

"Yeah," said a crusty old gargoyle from Collins Barracks, which recently had become the new home of the National Museum. "And who wasn't doing his job when St. Michan's got trashed?"

"I hardly think we need to go casting blame," said the exceedingly proper gargoyle from the Catholic Pro-Cathedral in Marlborough Street, a stately classical building whose design required that no trace of its gargoyle be visible from the street. "St. Michan's hasn't had its own gargoyle for centuries. He got reassigned when the Georgians tore down the old church and rebuilt on its foundations—went off to Paris, as I recall. In any case, it's hard to have proper gargoyle security on a mostly classical Georgian building—and we *are* spread awfully thin. We all do the best we can."

A stout gargoyle from atop Leinster House, seat of the parliamentary chambers of the Daíl and the Seanad, gave an exasperated sigh. "We aren't going to get anything done if we don't stop bickering among ourselves and making excuses."

"Yeah, just like the government," Paddy muttered, to snickers from the Trinity gargoyle and the little stone monkeys from the front of the old Kildare Street Club, who rattled their pool cues against the stone floor and made rude noises.

The meeting continued for a while longer, still plagued by periodic interruptions, but eventually a stepped-up neighborhood-watch plan was agreed upon and the gargoyles dispersed. Paddy spent the rest of the night prowling the streets of Dublin, for only in their shadow-forms did gargoyles have this mobility, and then—except in unusual circumstances—only for the twenty-four hours immediately following the monthly conclaves.

He ranged among the shadowy back streets and alleys of the city until nearly dawn, watching for evildoers and occasionally spotting another gargoyle on similar patrol, but the increasing snowfall was keeping most people indoors. The clock on St. Patrick's was striking seven as he approached—and saw the flashing blue lights of an ambulance and several garda cars pulled to the curb outside the south door, which was standing open.

Keeping to the shadows—fortunately, still plentiful at this time of year, even at seven o'clock—Paddy eased his way closer into the shelter of a buttress to get a better look at the people clustered at the back of the ambulance. Young Philip Kelly, one of Paddy's favorite vergers, was sitting on the back bumper and holding a compress to his forehead, while a uniformed garda wrote things down in a small notebook and an ambulance attendant applied a bandage to Kelly's hand. There was blood down the front of Kelly's dark purple cassock, and one eye was swollen shut.

"They took a couple of silver alms basins from beside the high altar," Kelly was saying. "Probably would've got more, but I guess I interrupted them."

"Valuable, I take it—these alms basins?" the garda said, looking up.

"I'll say. Irreplaceable. Really big and heavy, with Georgian hallmarks. And they'll probably be melted down for the silver."

"Afraid you're probably right. Anything else missing?"

"I don't know. I didn't have time to notice. They were here when I came to open up for Morning Prayer—two guys. The dean is on his way."

"I don't suppose you saw which way they went?"

"Oh, I did, indeed: right up Patrick Street, heading for

the North Side. Car was an old red banger. Afraid I didn't get a reg number."

That was all Paddy needed to know. He was really furious that punks had dared to mug young Kelly—and in the church, no less! And how *dare* they steal things from *his* cathedral?!

Restraining his indignation, he streaked up Patrick Street toward Christ Church, determined to find the red car and its occupants before it got too light to move around freely. The sky was brightening already, despite the snow, so he would need to hurry. And if he'd had no luck by midnight, it would be a full month before he could alert his fellow gargoyles—unless, of course, he called a special conclave, which wasn't often done. By then, the thieves would be long gone.

He met the Bank of Ireland gargoyle coming out of Christchurch Place, and summoned him briefly into the roofless but elegant ruin of St. Nicholas Without, to brief him about the break-in before heading on through Temple Bar. The Bank of Ireland gargoyle might be a fussy old busybody, but from his rooftop post atop the graceful building that formerly had housed the Irish Parliament, overlooking College Green and the entrance to Trinity College, he saw and heard just about everything that went on in the center of Dublin. He would have the word out to the other gargoyles as quickly as anyone.

Across the Ha'penny Footbridge and eastward along the quays Paddy sped, stopping briefly to confer with the river-god heads who graced the arches on the O'Connell Bridge—who grumbled at being disturbed—then heading into O'Connell Street itself.

There, on a sudden whim, he paused to inquire of the Anna Livia statue reclining in her fountain—the "Floozy in the Jacuzzi," as the irreverent were wont to call her, or sometimes "Anna Rexia," for she was very thin. (Dubliners were wont to bestow irreverent nicknames on their city's notable landmarks, and had given rhyming epithets to many pieces of popular street sculpture. Across from the Provost's House in Trinity College was a life-sized bronze statue of sweet Molly Malone, her name immortalized in song, who had "rolled her wheelbarrow through streets broad and narrow." She was known as the Dolly with the Trolley, or the Tart with the Cart. Over near Liffey Street, the seated statues of two weary shoppers had been christened the Hags with the Bags.)

Indeed, little Annie did look more like a good-time girl than the noble goddess of the Liffey, more interested in good *craic* and a bit of a knees-up than in stringing together two thoughts in a row. But she'd been civil enough, the few times Paddy had spoken to her—not a gargoyle, of course, and no more mobile than the orators' statues lined up along the center island of O'Connell Street, or the classical statues adorning the Four Courts complex or the General Post Office; but they were only meant to Watch, after all.

To his delight, little Annie had seen something.

"Yah, there was an old banger came zipping past me and then off toward the station," she said. "Ran the traffic signals and nearly hit a milk truck."

"What color was it?" he demanded.

"Red, maybe? Yah, I think it was red."

With a nod of thanks, Paddy headed off in the direction of Connolly Station, threading his way through the warren

of elderly buildings that once had been a very fashionable
part of old Dublin. The dawn was fast approaching, the
shadows fading. He would have to go home soon, or go to
ground.

He ventured down yet another alley that ended in a cul-
de-sac, and was turning to head back out, when something
caught his eye through a chink in the bricks of an old,
dingy building with a padlocked garage door. He did a
double take and leaned closer to peer through the chink.

It was a gargoyle he had never seen before, silvery and
still in the dim light that filtered through a couple of grimy
windows, crouched on the radiator cap of a shiny black car
of antique vintage. It had beady little ruby-glowing eyes,
and tiny webbed wings swept back from its scaly shoulders, and it was holding the top of a heraldic shield. The
shield was enamelled in red and white.

Vintage cars were hardly anything new to Paddy, of
course. He had witnessed the evolution of the motor car
from the very first horseless carriages, and still saw cars
like this one at weddings and such, coming and going at St.
Patrick's. But almost all the others he'd seen with a double-
R radiator badge like this one bore hood ornaments of
graceful females trailing diaphanous garments behind
them like wings. Not once had he seen one with a gargoyle.

The sound of footsteps on the pavement beyond the
building sent Paddy zipping through the chink like a
squeeze of liquid shadow, to peer warily back through the
opening as a white-haired old gentleman in a green waxed
jacket and tweed cap came tap-tapping up to the padlocked
garage doors, using a furled umbrella as a walking stick.
Above rosy cheeks and white moustaches, blue eyes twin-

kled with spry good humor from behind old-fashioned wire-rimmed spectacles. He looked a lot like the Father Christmas in the window of the Brown Thomas store in Grafton Street, only without the beard. His breath plumed in the cold air as he hooked the umbrella over one gloved wrist and fumbled in his pocket for a ring of keys, then bent to unlock the doors.

Quickly Paddy retreated to the sheltering shadows behind a leaning stack of dusty old shutters, as one of the doors screeched open far enough for the old man to enter. He made not a sound as the man turned on lights, deposited umbrella and cap on pegs above a tidy workbench, then lit a gas heater and filled an electric kettle from a tap above an old sink. After that, the man removed a small carton of milk from one of the waxed jacket's capacious pockets, stuffed gloves and keys into another, and set about making a cup of tea.

While the man was puttering, his back to the old car, Paddy tried to get a better look at the little gargoyle. But the man soon returned his attention to the car, humming contentedly under his breath as he walked around it and sipped at his mug of steaming tea. When he set the tea aside and began wiping down the car's brightwork with a soft yellow flannel, starting with the little gargoyle, Paddy could contain his impatience no longer.

"Where'd you get that gargoyle?" he demanded.

Chapter 2

The old man whirled at the sound of the unexpected voice, looking for its source.

"Who's there?"

"You heard me," Paddy retorted. "Where'd you get the gargoyle? I need to borrow it."

"What?!"

"I need the gargoyle."

"Who *is* that?" said the man, reaching for a large spanner on the workbench behind him. "Damned kids!" he muttered under his breath. "You come out *now,* or I'll be calling the guards!"

"Ah, now, don't be doin' anything rash," Paddy said calmly. "I can't come out. I'm a gargoyle."

"You're a *what*?"

"I'm a gargoyle."

"Right. You come out right now, where I can see you!"

"That wouldn't be a good idea."

"I'm warning you—"

"You don't want to see me."

"Why not?"

"You wouldn't believe what you saw. You'd be terrified. We're ferocious. Did you hear about the guy who saw one of us and his hair turned white, and he died three days later?"

The man blinked, clearly brought up short by the question.

"No," came the cautious reply.

"Well, that was a long time ago, but that's what happened. Believe me, you really don't want to see me."

"Who is that, *really?*" the old man ventured. "Séamus, if you're after winding me up again, it isn't funny."

"It isn't Séamus, and I wouldn't wind you up about a thing like this. I need your help. I only want to borrow your gargoyle."

"What for?"

"I told you, I'm a gargoyle," Paddy said patiently. "We guard buildings—churches, mostly. It isn't easy, especially these days. Did you hear about what happened at St. Michan's a couple of nights ago?"

"I seem to remember seeing something about it on RTÉ," the old man allowed, slowly lowering his spanner. "Didn't vandals break into the vaults underneath the church?"

Paddy snorted. "Lager louts! They busted up some

coffins, roughed up one of the mummies, set some fires—left the place a mess! Cider bottles and cigarette butts everywhere. You a Templar?"

"A what?"

"A Templar, a Templar," Paddy said impatiently. "The shield on the gargoyle—isn't that a Templar cross?"

"No, Knights of Malta," the old man said, lifting his chin proudly. "I'm a Knight of Malta. And that's a gryphon, not a gargoyle," he added, pointing. "But my name *is* Templeton," he conceded.

"Knights of Malta, Knights Templar, Knights of Saint John, Knights of Saint Lazarus—they were all crusaders, weren't they? Who can keep track? That mummy who got roughed up at St. Michan's was a crusader."

"Was he, now?" Templeton sounded skeptical, but also faintly amused. "That'll be a pretty good trick, seeing as how the present church only dates from about the seventeenth century."

"Hey, don't be so hard on the old guy," Paddy replied. "Maybe he went on a later crusade. Besides, tourists like the crusader story. Without them, the whole church might be crumbling around his ears—or what's left of his ears. Not that his rowdy visitors much cared . . .

"But, that's not my department," he went on. "I've got my own problem. You say you're a knight. How'd you like to put your knighthood to the test right now? Your own private crusade: help me right a wrong."

"What kind of a wrong?" Templeton asked, a wary edge to his voice.

"Well, not a very big wrong, in the grand scheme of

things," Paddy admitted, "but if you let bad guys get away with little things, soon they're trying really nasty stuff. There was a break-in where I work, over at St. Patrick's. Sure, that's a Protestant cathedral, and you're R.C., if you're a Knight of Malta, but I'm not particular where I get help. Thieves stole a couple of big silver alms basins—nice Georgian stuff. But what really has me steamed is that they roughed up a friend of mine. He says they got away in an old red banger. An informant tells me they headed in this direction."

"An old red banger, you say?" Templeton echoed.

"Yeah, you see many of those in this area?"

"Well, it's a common enough color. . . ."

"I know that," Paddy said flatly, exasperation tingeing his voice. "Maybe you can help me find it, then. Make it your ecumenical gesture for the week. I'll put in a good word with the gargoyle over at the Pro-Cathedral. Heck, he can probably put a bug in the Papal Nuncio's ear, get the good cardinal to sing your praises to the Holy Father, next time he's in Rome."

"Are you mocking the Church?" Templeton asked, drawing himself up stiffly.

"Mocking the Church? Of course not! Where would I be without the Church? Out of a job—that's where! Mind you, it isn't like it was in the old days."

"You've got *that* right," the old man agreed with a snort, warming to the subject. "Too many changes, if you ask me. I don't miss the Friday fish, or hats on the women, or even the Latin—but when it comes to long-haired priests wearing hippie beads, and guitars instead of organs, and young people dancing barefoot in the church—

"And your Protestants have got *married priests!*" he added, flapping his yellow duster in the direction of his visitor's hiding place. "And *women* priests! What do you think of *that*?"

"Well, gargoyles don't eat, so I wouldn't know about the fish, but I kind of liked the Latin, and the hats," Paddy allowed. "I still see some nice hats at St. Patrick's, especially at weddings. Funerals aren't what they once were, though."

"What about the women priests?" Templeton persisted, challenge in his voice. "I didn't see Our Lord ordain any women."

"Strictly speaking," Paddy said mildly, "I didn't see Him ordain *anybody,* man *or* woman. Still, maybe women priests aren't a bad idea. After all, women know about setting tables, and serving a nice meal. They helped with that Last Supper, you know. And they're into vestments. I like vestments."

"Well, they can *sew* the vestments, or *iron* 'em," Templeton muttered. "Just keep 'em off the altar."

"But they're really good at making celebrations," Paddy pointed out. "Especially weddings. How many weddings've you been to?"

"Oh, thirty or forty, I suppose."

"Well, I've seen thousands. Believe me, if it were up to men, there wouldn't even *be* weddings. They'd be out gathering the nuts and berries, or whatever it is they do these days, while the women keep things ticking over at home.

"But the women want celebrations. They want the big dress, and the flowers, and the music, and the bells and smells, and everybody dressed up in their Sunday-best, including the priest. So, all in all, women priests ought to have a better handle on stuff like that, right?"

"Well . . ."

"They should let the priests get married, too. How're they supposed to help married people sort out their problems if they don't know what they're talking about? They can't, that's how. Get the women into the act!"

"I suppose you could have a point," Templeton allowed. "But the Church's teaching—"

"Hey, I don't have time for theological debates; I get those from the Trinity gargoyles all the time. Can you take that little guy off the car?"

"Well, yes, but—"

"Would you please just do it, then? It's getting late."

"Late for what?"

"I need to get this wrapped up by midnight, and I can't go out in the daytime."

"Why, are you a vampire or something?"

"Of course not. I told you, I'm a gargoyle. I'd scare people."

"So, why have you only got until midnight, and why—"

Paddy's snort of exasperation caused the shutters sheltering him to rattle alarmingly.

"Will you quit with the questions? You sound like those kids in the choir, always asking Why! I told you, I need to find the punks who broke into my church and mugged my friend—and the longer it takes, the less chance there is of getting back my silver."

"But—"

"You're impeding a gargoyle in the performance of his

duties," Paddy said stiffly. "Now, would you *please* give it to me?"

He thrust a taloned forearm into the light in unmistakable demand, its iridescent scales shimmering flame-dark within matte-black shadow, fire glinting from talons as long as a man's hand. The old man gasped and backed up hard against the side of the car, crossing himself.

But when the talons only clicked together several times in obvious impatience—though that, in itself, was frightening enough—Templeton groped his way warily to the front of the Rolls Royce, eyes never leaving the arm, and carefully unscrewed the car's mascot. As he nervously polished its red and white shield with his yellow duster, a second taloned arm emerged beside the first, both upturned to receive the little gargoyle. Templeton flinched and started to hold it out, but then he snatched back his hand and bravely stood his ground.

"I want to see you first," he said boldly.

"No, you don't."

"Yes, I do. You come out where I can see you, or I'm not handing it over."

Paddy heaved a forbearing sigh. "What's your Christian name?" he demanded.

Templeton gulped, then stammered, "F-Francis."

"Francis," Paddy said. "Saint and confessor. Well, Francis, you're beginning to piss me off, and that isn't a good idea. Your middle name wouldn't be Thomas, by any chance?"

"Thomas?" Templeton repeated blankly.

"For Saint Thomas, 'doubting' Thomas. Francis, do you really, *truly* think I'm not a gargoyle, with *these*?"

He flexed his talons again, more deliberately menacing. Templeton grimaced, flinching back a little, but he also lifted his chin even more defiantly.

"Those could be—well, arms from a rubber monster suit!" he blurted.

"You *are* the brave one, aren't you?" Paddy murmured. "I really don't want to scare you."

"So, I'll be scared. I've been scared before."

"I do wish you'd reconsider."

"You heard me." Templeton hefted the little gargoyle. "These things are expensive. You might not give it back. I want to see who I'm giving it to."

With a resigned flash of his ruby-glowing eyes, Paddy moved fully into the light. The old man gasped and half turned away, shielding his eyes with the hand holding the gargoyle mascot while he crossed himself again with the other, his rosy cheeks draining of their color.

"See? You think I'm frightening," Paddy said.

"Well, of course! I've never seen a gargoyle before."

"And you still haven't. That takes a black mirror. We were avenging angels, in the Old Testament. Then the New Testament came along, and we got reassigned. These days, we mostly guard churches. But with congregations getting smaller, our job is getting harder. People don't pray enough anymore."

The old man dared a glance back at his visitor, still cringing, but he was starting to recover a little of his color.

"That's what they're always telling us at Mass. The Holy Father says we should pray more. I guess maybe you and I agree on *that,* at least."

"Yeah, the old boy gets it right most of the time." Paddy

flexed his talons toward the little gargoyle again. "Can I please have it now?"

Templeton came just close enough to hand it over, jerking his hand back nervously as the talons closed lightly around the silvery form. But as he skittered back to a safer distance, closer to the car, he did a double take.

Reflected briefly in the car's polished black door, just as his visitor ducked back into the sheltering shadow of the shutters, was not a darkly menacing shadow-shape laced with fire, but the stern, majestic figure of an armored warrior, with a diadem of stars bound across its noble brow and dark pinions sweeping from powerful shoulders to trail rainbows behind. And what its strong hands were cradling against its armored breast was not a radiator mascot but a tiny winged cherub.

"Oh," Paddy said apologetically, as Templeton gave a wondering little gasp, slack-jawed with awe. "I guess your car door's a black mirror. You weren't supposed to see that. That's the only way mortals can see us in our true form—unless, of course, they've really pissed us off. Then, you don't wanta know. Like I said, we used to be avenging angels.

"Not anymore, though. We don't get to kick ass like we did in the old days. The Boss has mellowed a lot, since the days when He was an Old Testament God. I think it started when His Son joined the Firm. The Son was human for a while, you know, so He's inclined to be a little softer on sinners."

Paddy had edged farther into the shadows as he spoke, so that the goggle-eyed Templeton could only see the little gargoyle in his talons. The old man's expression lay somewhere between mortal fear, awed fascination, and muttering affront at his visitor's apparently flip and casual remarks on a subject he clearly regarded with pious reverence.

"Hey, lighten up, Francis," Paddy said, seeing Templeton's consternation. "There's a time for everything, and if you get all sanctimonious on me, we aren't going to accomplish very much. Remember that angels were among the first of God's creation, before you humans. We've known Him a really long time."

Templeton cleared his throat awkwardly, then gave a tentative nod.

"You—uh—really *are* a gargoyle, aren't you?" he said, though the question was actually a statement of acceptance.

"Yeah." Paddy turned the little gargoyle in his claws and lifted it a little. "You know, this is even better than I expected. It's like—what it must be like to hold your own child for the first time. I never thought I'd be a father."

"A father?" Templeton said blankly.

"Well, sort of," Paddy said. "Just wait. And watch."

Concentrating, he cupped his talons tenderly around the little gargoyle, willing into it enough of his own essence to serve his purpose. After a few seconds, he gently opened his claws. The little gargoyle was glowing a dull red, and slowly blinked one tiny ruby eye.

"Better put your gloves back on before I give this back," Paddy said, at the old man's awestruck expression.

"Why? Is it alive?"

"No, it's hot. To make it alive, I'd need help from Upstairs. You know—'through Him, with Him, in Him.' Now, put on your gloves. We're wasting time. It'll burn your fingers until it cools down."

"Right, sure, whatever you say," the old man murmured, though he did as he was told. "Uh, would it be presumptuous to ask if you have a name? Doesn't seem right to call you 'Hey, gargoyle.'"

"Then call me Paddy. And don't drop Junior! Now, put him back on the car."

Chapter 3

A few minutes later, with the little gargoyle now reaffixed to the radiator, Templeton had the old Rolls Royce idling quietly before the garage doors. As he pushed them open, stepping outside to secure them so he could pull out, Paddy moved—faster than the blink of an eye—in through the open driver's door, up and over the front seats, and into the back, to hunker down on the floor and cover himself with a red tartan blanket that he pulled down from the shelf under the rear window, for it was now full daylight outside.

As the old man came back in from the alley and saw no sign of his strange companion, he glanced around the garage uncertainly.

"Uh, Paddy?" he called.

"In here."

Templeton whirled toward the source of the voice and took an involuntary step back at the sight of the tartan lump on the floor in the rear of the car.

"Get in, get in," Paddy ordered. "We haven't got all day. Or—actually, we do, but you know what I mean. Let's *please* get going."

Templeton got in. After pulling into the alley, he returned briefly to close and lock the garage doors, then resumed his seat behind the big steering wheel and put the car in gear. The tartan lump bulged a little taller behind the slit between the two front seats as the old car started moving forward, but Templeton tried to pretend it wasn't quite so close, and concentrated on his driving.

"Take us over by the quays first," Paddy said.

"Whatever you say."

The winter day was glorious, with bright sunlight glaring on streets left wet from the previous night's light snowfall, but they had to contend with heavy traffic as soon as the big car left the alley. Morning rush hour was always formidable in downtown Dublin, and in December never really let up until after the stores closed in the evening. Christmas shoppers on foot only added to the congestion, vying with vehicles at every intersection and also along the streets between. The pedestrians were not inclined to look where they were going, or to watch for cars trying to go there first.

The shiny black Rolls Royce limousine with its sweeping fenders and huge headlamps drew appreciative stares as soon as it emerged from the alley, but Templeton was used to such attention, and mostly tried to ignore it. He hoped that his tartan back-seat lump was not attracting too much attention. As he approached the very first cross street, he had to stop to let a flock of pedestrians surge across, against the traffic signals, and he glanced impatiently in either direction as he waited, starting to look for old red cars. As he shifted his gaze forward again, he thought he caught just a glimpse of the little gargoyle on the hood also turning its head to look.

He blinked and looked again, but the little gargoyle was staring straight ahead.

"Uh, Paddy?" he said over his shoulder, as he put the car in gear again and eased forward, starting to signal for a right turn down the next lane.

"What?"

"The little guy moved."

"Of course he moved," Paddy said from underneath the blanket. "What good would he be if he didn't move?"

"I thought you said he wasn't alive."

"He isn't," Paddy said. "At least not in the sense you're probably thinking. He's—sort of like an extension of me. Think of him as something like a compass needle. He's going to help us look for the bad guys."

"But—won't people notice?"

The question elicited a snort of amusement. "What's to notice? On a day like this, it's a trick of light—and they'll only catch *that* out of the corners of their eyes. Besides, they're busy shopping. Just drive."

"Right," Templeton muttered, making the turn. "Uh, can I ask you something else?"

"Yeah, what?"

"Is your name *really* Paddy?"

"No, but you probably couldn't pronounce the real one," came the slightly amused reply. "Besides, we're not supposed to tell. If you'd prefer *Pádraig,* that's fine by me. We can pick what we're called, but we tend to go by names connected with the places we guard. That's easy enough, where churches are concerned, but some of the secular buildings are a mouthful—and you wouldn't believe some of the newfangled place names the town planners think up."

Templeton chuckled despite the somewhat bizarre nature of their conversation, grunting as he cranked down his window and reached out to free up one of the lighted trafficator arms that served as turn indicators on the old car. Even some of the old place names were, to put it mildly, unusual.

"Does one of you guard the Peppercanister Church?" he said with a grin, rolling the window back up. "That'd be a mouthful, for sure."

"If that were really its name, I might agree," Paddy replied. He found himself rather liking Francis Templeton. "I don't suppose you know its proper name? Most people don't."

"You mean, its saint's name? Lemme see," Templeton said. "No, I used to know, but the old memory isn't what it once was."

"How about a hint?" Paddy said. "The Church considers him the first Christian martyr."

Templeton chuckled as he wheeled the Rolls around a corner, threading his way toward the quays. "Now, *that* I remember. It's Saint Stephen. And I notice that you didn't really say whether there's a gargoyle there—which is what I suppose I'd expect, regardless of whether this is all real or just a figment of my imagination. But that's all right," he added, glancing at the tartan lump in his rearview mirror. "I'm rather enjoying this. How about Phoenix Park? I think I've seen some carved faces up there."

"No, they're just Watchers. They can't move around, the way gargoyles can. There're some great Watchers in O'-Connell Street. The ones on the Irish Permanent building are pretty dozy, but you should talk to the sphinxes on the Gresham Hotel. Now, *they're* smart! And they don't miss much that goes on."

"Really," Templeton said, trying to take it all in. "How about the Egyptian slaves out in front of the Shelbourne?"

"The ones that hold up the lamps?"

"The very ones."

"Not those, my friend. Sorry, but sometimes a lamppost is only—well, a lamppost."

"Oh," Templeton said.

"Yeah, don't assume that every carved critter you see on a building is a Watcher, much less a gargoyle. And don't assume that, just because you can't see a gargoyle on a building, there isn't one there."

"I see," Templeton said. They were creeping eastward along the quays with the flow of traffic, approaching the great lantern dome of the Four Courts, with its guardian statues along the riverfront skyline—Moses flanked by Wisdom, Justice, Mercy, and Authority. Templeton jutted his chin in their direction.

"Those guys would have a pretty good view up and down the river," he said. "Are they Watchers?"

"A couple of them are," Paddy confirmed. "Some of them like to work in teams."

"That makes sense," Templeton said. He glanced tentatively in his rearview mirror at the tartan lump in the back seat. "And would it be fair to say that if there's a gargoyle assigned to guard the Four Courts—and I'm not asking whether there is or there isn't, mind you—he maybe hides in the dome or something?"

Paddy's throaty gargoyle chuckle must have sounded very like a low growl, for the old man cast a quick, wary glance over his shoulder and briefly cringed in his seat, making the old car swerve momentarily.

"Hey, easy!" Paddy said. "That was amusement."

"Could have fooled *me*," Templeton muttered.

"Believe me, you'd know if I was offended."

"Well, what was—"

He broke off as a garda motorcycle loomed suddenly off the car's right-rear fender and cruised alongside, its helmeted rider casting an appreciative eye along the expanse of shiny black lacquer but not even looking at the tax and insurance disks on the windscreen—both fortunately current. Grinning, the guard caught Templeton's eye and nodded before roaring off to disappear into Arran Street. Templeton relaxed visibly.

"Don't worry, you won't be stopped," Paddy said.

"Oh, not by *him*," Templeton said. "That was Tommy Moran. I drove this car for his sister's wedding."

"No, you won't be stopped," Paddy repeated. "It doesn't matter whether they know you or not. You're on official business with *me*."

Templeton started to give him a funny look in the rearview mirror, but a break in the traffic ahead gave him opportunity to accelerate through the intersection where

Capel Street met the Grattan Bridge across the Liffey—though he had to brake immediately when they had gotten through the traffic signals. Templeton glanced in his mirror again as they resumed creeping along Ormonde Quay—which seemed to have a surfeit of cars of every color except red.

"Uh, Paddy," Templeton said after a moment, "what you said about 'official business'—do the guards *know* about you?"

"Nope," came the confident answer.

"Well, can they *see* you?"

"They can see that you've got *something* in your back seat," Paddy replied. "But it wouldn't occur to them to get curious."

"Why not?"

"Remember how I told you that we gargoyles used to be avenging angels?"

"Yes."

"Well, forget about the avenging part, unless we get really ticked off, but think about what angels do. We deliver messages. Sometimes the message is not to notice us in the course of our other duties."

"Then, why am I driving you around, if you can make people not notice you? Not that I'm complaining, mind you. I haven't enjoyed myself this much in yonks."

A snort of what Templeton hoped was mirth came from underneath the tartan blanket.

"Look around you," Paddy said. "How many people do you see?"

"Er, lots," Templeton replied. Just approaching the intersection with Abbey Street, he had to jam on the brakes as the Ha'penny Bridge disgorged a lemming-like surge of holiday shoppers apparently determined to disregard the pedestrian signals.

"Make that 'Too damned many!' " he added, under his breath.

"That's right," Paddy said. "And even I can't be sure of watching all of them at once."

"I suppose not," Templeton agreed. He tried to look annoyed as pedestrians filled the crosswalk and even swarmed around the car, only belatedly accompanied by the distinctive beep-beeping sound that gave pelican crossings their name, but he found himself responding with good humor to the looks of friendly curiosity and nostalgia that greeted the old car.

"They just don't look," he said, when they were underway again. "I think somebody gets knocked down here along the quays just about every week."

"It wasn't much different in the old days," Paddy replied. "Then, it was carriages, and jaunting carts, and occasional dandies on horses. Turn up O'Connell Street next. Junior saw an old red car."

Templeton dutifully turned north into the broad, tree-studded boulevard of O'Connell Street, skittishly squeezing between a tinker's horse-drawn cart laden with sacks of peat, and a green double-decker Dublin bus belching diesel fumes; but the "red car" turned out to be a delivery van for a local merchant. Most of the other red vehicles they saw were far too new to be described as "bangers." Recent legislation requiring yearly inspection of vehicles more than ten was taking a lot of older cars off the streets.

"Paddy, you said you'd guarded Dublin for a long time,"

Templeton remarked thoughtfully. "I reckon you've seen a lot, over the years."

They were cruising past the bullet-pocked façade of the General Post Office, which everyone called the GPO—perhaps the most famous building in Dublin. It was from the GPO, with the marks of gunfire still showing on its fluted columns and Ionic portico, that the Irish patriot Patrick Pearse had read out and posted the proclamation of Irish independence, during the famous Easter Rising of 1916.

Pearse, James Connolly, and thirteen other leaders of the rebellion had later been executed by a British firing squad at Kilmainham Jail, but the seeds sown during the six days of that rebellion had borne the fruit of liberty three years later—alas, not without another three years of bickering, partition of the Ulster counties, and the punctuation of a year-long civil war. The legacies of this tumultuous beginning were still healing, and Templeton had lived through much of it. He and the Irish state were nearly of an age.

"Actually," Paddy said, "I didn't see much of what went on *here*." He peered down Henry Street distractedly as they passed. "I was guarding my cathedral. But I heard all about it from some of the other gargoyles, and I watched some of the other fighting from my bell tower. When the Four Courts got burned, a few years later, I could see the flames leaping up, across the Liffey. I only saw smoke when they torched the Custom House, but both of them burned for days. You could hear the stone cracking, when they began to cool down. It was pretty sad."

"But—if your lot're meant to guard buildings, why didn't you stop it?" Templeton asked. "When the Four

Courts burned, we lost records and archives that were irreplaceable."

"Liberty almost always has a cost," Paddy replied. "Mere buildings are the least of the price."

They were gliding past one of the city's many memorials to Charles Stewart Parnell, known as the Great Liberator, and circled slowly around the square named in his honor, still on the lookout for red bangers. The square itself compassed a jumble of baroque Georgian buildings known collectively as the Rotunda: a complex of assembly rooms, theatres, and the first purpose-built maternity hospital in the world. Along the far end of the square stretched the winter-bleak Garden of Remembrance, dedicated to all who had died in the cause of Irish freedom.

Across from that garden, gargoyles guarded openly from the heights of Findlater's Church, a Presbyterian edifice on the corner where Frederick Street met the square, but Paddy didn't point them out to Templeton—though he knew they were aware of his passage.

"It isn't my job to interfere with the greater tides of free will," Paddy went on, as they skirted the garden and turned back along O'Connell Street again, passing beneath the gaze of the sphinxes on the front of the Gresham Hotel, earlier identified as Watchers. "It *is* my job to see that, ultimately, the scales of justice always end up weighted in favor of Truth.

"That means that sometimes I have to stand by and do nothing, while the scales readjust," he said, noting several red cars pulled to the curb at Earl Street—none of which qualified as bangers. "But it also means that, occasionally, I get to kick ass—which is what I intend to do when we find the men who roughed up my verger and stole my silver!"

The old man said nothing as they passed again before the gaze of the Watchers atop the GPO—Hibernia, Mercury, and Fidelity—apparently sobered by the talk of the Troubles of the past; but as Paddy directed him to turn along the quays again, following a smart horse-drawn carriage toward the Custom House, Templeton could contain himself no longer.

"Uh, Paddy," he said tentatively. "I've been thinking about what you said back at the Four Courts, when I asked whether a gargoyle maybe hid in the dome. You said you were amused, not angry. Do you mind telling me what was so funny?"

"Well, it wasn't exactly funny—though I *was* amused. It's just that gargoyles don't 'hide.' We simply take care not to be seen, unless there's a good reason. But *if* there were a gargoyle assigned to guard the Four Courts—and I'm not saying whether there is or there isn't—that would be a fair assumption."

"Fair enough," Templeton said. "Well, if there *isn't* one, there ought to be. I can't think of a better vantage point along the river until you get to the Custom House—especially if you guys prefer old buildings." He glanced at the tartan lump in his rearview mirror. "I don't suppose you'd care to comment on the Custom House?"

Paddy chuckled again, but this time Templeton only grinned.

"I believe that the phrase used by politicians is, 'I can neither confirm nor deny.'"

"Right," said Templeton. "Then, I suppose it would be useless to ask how many of you there are—gargoyles, I mean."

"Enough," Paddy replied. "Afraid I can't be more specific than that. Like I told you, we gargoyles used to be avenging angels—and the Boss made *lots* of those. But once He got past His divine vengeance phase, He reassigned a lot of us. It was partly the stonemasons' idea, when they started building churches. Eventually, I expect we'll all get reassigned to even different duties, as man evolves spiritually. But meanwhile, we have our orders. Turn up that street, and we'll have a look over by Connolly Station."

Chapter 4

Paddy and his newly recruited associate continued to cruise the streets of Dublin all through the day, looking for some trace of the battered red car and its passengers. After a while, the little gargoyle took to nodding off, and Templeton had to keep waking him up by sounding the horn. That always turned the heads of other drivers and pedestrians alike, who would gaze nostalgically after the elderly Rolls Royce, driven by an even more elderly white-haired gentleman who seemed engaged in animated conversation with himself.

Meanwhile, Templeton listened to the tales Paddy told him of old Dublin, and some of the things he had seen over the centuries. In return, recalling their earlier conversation regarding weddings, Templeton reminisced about driving the old Rolls as a wedding car, back when both he and the car were not so old. In those days, his wife would bedeck the car's long, elegant hood with broad white ribbons festooned from the hood ornament to the front corners of the roof. Inside, in the little crystal vases on the side pillars, she would even put fresh roses she had grown in their own garden, in shades specially chosen to complement the bride's color scheme.

"It made the day that bit more special for the bridal couple," Templeton said. "And when the weather was fine, I'd crank back the sunroof so they could enjoy the sunshine and fresh air. The brides liked that, because the breeze from the open sunroof didn't mess up their hair the way an open car or even an open window would have done."

Paddy recalled gazing down at open sunroofs above other brides, from his perch above St. Patrick's, and agreed that it was a fine custom—though he kept looking for the elusive red banger.

"The best wedding, though, was our youngest daughter's," Templeton said, as they cruised past the Catholic Pro-Cathedral in Marlborough Street. "She was married right here. My godson drove the car that day. He's with the Garda Síochána—a detective of some sort. When I'm gone, he'll have the car, since I haven't any sons. That was the only time I ever rode in the back seat." He smiled in reminiscence. "I'm biased, of course, but my Aisling was probably the most beautiful bride I've ever seen—apart from her mother, of course."

"I think most fathers feel that way," Paddy said. "Do you still drive for weddings?"

"Only for friends. I only ever did it as a hobby, anyway. I was a banker, before I retired. Fairly good at it, too."

This revelation elicited a lively discussion of current banking scandals in Ireland, followed by the old man's sometimes scathing observations on local political figures. At around half past one, Templeton briefly pulled into a petrol station to refuel and grab a sandwich and cup of coffee. After that, they resumed their patrol of the city, looking for suspicious red cars.

But as teatime approached, long about four o'clock, and the evening shadows began to close in, no progress had been made on their quest. By the time the lights in the huge cast-iron street lamps began to come on, competing with the strings of colored fairy lights that decorated the city at this time of year, the old man had about decided that all they had managed to accomplish, besides spend a pleasant if odd day swapping yarns—and the Irish were good at that!— was to burn up nearly two tanks of petrol and confirm the impression in most observers' minds that dotty old men who drove around in ancient cars were wont to talk to themselves. They had ranged from Santry to Harold's Cross, and from Ringsend to Palmerston, out past Phoenix Park, and were back near their starting point, creeping through heavy traffic in one of the less salubrious parts of north Dublin.

"Listen, Paddy, this has been really good *craic,* and I've really enjoyed the outing," Templeton said, as he switched on the car's big Marschal headlamps, "but it doesn't look like we're going to find your bad guys. That car could be behind any of those garage doors we've passed. Or they could have headed right out of town."

The tartan lump that was Paddy stirred slightly behind

Templeton, suddenly aware that Junior had perked up and was really interested in something not far ahead.

"Slow down," he said. "Junior's onto something."

"He *what?*"

"He smells the silver. So do I. I told you, we get attuned to the things that belong in the buildings we guard. Go down that street! I think we're getting close."

Startled, Templeton peered out at the little gargoyle perched on his hood. It was bouncing up and down and squealing, madly flapping its left wing like one of the old car's trafficators. And at the far end of the indicated side street, a battered old red car had just nosed out of a car park, its rust-eaten front bumper pointing in their direction. Beside and slightly behind it, two rough-looking men wearing flat caps and ratty, out-at-the-elbows jackets were rolling a heavy chainlink gate back into place.

"That's them, that's them!" Paddy cried, one scaly arm emerging from under the red tartan blanket to point emphatically through the crack between the two front seats. "They must've holed up for the day! Turn left!"

"That's a one-way street," Templeton objected. "I can't go down there."

"You want 'em to get away? Turn!"

"But there's a traffic warden watching!"

"Turn now!"

"You're going to get me a ticket!"

"They're going to get away if we go around. *Turn!*"

Muttering under his breath, Templeton turned the big car ponderously into the side street. It was very narrow— an alley, really—and the old Rolls was very tall and very wide. As the big car crept almost silently closer, headlamps probing twin cones of yellowy light into the alley's deeper shadows, the little gargoyle settled down to smoldering indignation on its perch on the radiator cap, glowering from behind its shield as one of the men did a double take at the sight of the approaching Rolls.

"Hey, you, back it out!" said the man, gesturing belligerently as the big car rolled to a halt about two carlengths back from the banger's front bumper. "Can't you read? This is a fookin' one-way street."

"I doubt *he* can read," Paddy whispered from between the two front seats. "At least not the Commandment that says 'Thou shalt not steal.' Tell *him* to back out!"

"He'll kick out my headlamps," Templeton protested.

"Oh, I do hope he tries!" The gargoyle's tone held more than a hint of gleeful anticipation. "I'm just looking for an excuse! Tell him!"

Warily the old man cranked back the sunroof and levered himself to a standing position, elbows supported on the sunroof opening; the alley was too narrow to really open either of the wide doors. The second man, behind the shouter, had a pillow sack over one shoulder, bulging with something just about the right size and shape for a couple of big church offering plates.

"That's it, that's it!" Paddy whispered, as the little gargoyle began flapping its wings wildly, like an excited moth. "I can really smell it now! You've got to delay them until that traffic warden gets here! And get her to call the guards! Brazen it out!"

With a nervous swallow, Templeton shook his fist at the man.

"*You* back out, if you can!" he taunted. "I know it's a

one-way street. And I also know what you've done, you—
you *hooligan*!"

A look of guilt mingled with astonishment and panic
flashed across the face of the first man, and the second
threw his bundle into the back seat of the red car with a
snarl and pulled out a hurley stick. The expressions on the
two men's faces, coupled with the sack Templeton had
seen, were enough to convince him that they had, indeed,
found the right men.

"Get the hell out of here, old man!" the second man said
defiantly. "I don't know what you're talking about."

"I'm talking about the break-in at St. Patrick's!" Templeton said boldly, heartened to see that a delivery van had
just pulled in behind the red car, and a very beefy driver
was leaning out the window to see what the holdup was.

"Get that pile of shite out of here before I kick out one
of those fancy headlights!" the first man said.

"He'll be sorry if he tries," Paddy whispered.

"You'll be sorry if you try," Templeton repeated, though
not with quite the same conviction.

"Oh, and I suppose *you're* gonna stop him?" the second
man chimed in. "You and who else?"

As the two started forward with obvious intent, Paddy
muttered, "Get down. You don't wanta see this . . ."

Templeton collapsed back into his seat with alacrity and
ducked down behind the steering wheel, gasping as he felt
something jostle past his shoulder in a flurry of powerful
wings.

What happened in the next few seconds was never altogether clear. The first man did, indeed, launch a booted
kick at one of the big headlamps, but it never connected.

Instead, he found himself buffeted sharply backward with a forcible *whoof!* of suddenly exhaled breath, by a shadow-blur that pummelled him head over heels with repeated smacks of heavy, leathery wings.

The second attacker fared no better. He yelped as the hurley stick was invisibly wrenched from his hands in mid-swing and he, too, was jolted abruptly into the maelstrom, where both men seemed to tumble, legs and arms akimbo, in something approximating a localized tornado. Simultaneously, the horns of the Rolls, the red car, and the delivery van behind it started blaring.

Almost in the blink of an eye, it was over, with both men left dazed, bruised, and bleeding on the ground, whimpering with pain and fright as they tried to clutch at all the hurting parts of their bodies at once. Templeton had not moved, only clinging numbly to his steering wheel as the scenario unfolded, his eyes wide as saucers.

"It's days like this that I really do *love* being a gargoyle!" Paddy declared, when his shadow-form had whooshed back through the open sunroof to burrow under the tartan blanket again. "But I decided not to hurt 'em *too* much. I'm feeling mellow today. Besides, you could've had a lot of explaining to do."

Which was no more than the truth. The blaring horns were drawing attention from both ends of the alley, including that of the traffic warden. The astonished driver of the van, after pounding in vain at his stuck horn button, got out of his vehicle and came striding past the red car to see what was going on—and pulled up short at the sight of the two men moaning on the ground.

As the traffic warden squeezed past the Rolls with a

similar reaction, she glanced back queryingly at Templeton. At that moment, the Rolls's horn ceased, and the old man lifted his hands in an eloquent shrug of mystification.

"I have no idea what happened," he said, half-standing again to poke his head through the sunroof. "They just seemed to trip and fall down. Drunk, I suppose. But I suggest you call the guards. I think you may find that those are the villains who robbed St. Patrick's this morning."

With that, Templeton sank back into the driver's seat and carefully reversed the big Rolls out of the alley, doing his best to look nonchalant. The traffic warden was already punching numbers into her mobile phone, warily watching the two moaning suspects, and the driver of the van was standing over said suspects and prodding with a booted toe whenever one of them showed any sign of trying to get up. The scene was also attracting a growing crowd of curious bystanders, but none of them seemed to take particular interest in the departing Rolls Royce or its elderly driver.

When Templeton had pulled away from the mouth of the alley, leaving all the commotion behind, he reached up and adjusted the rearview mirror.

"So, where to now?" he asked, as a tartan-shrouded lump loomed slowly upright behind the two front seats. "St. Patrick's, I presume?"

"St. Patrick's will be just fine," Paddy said, before sinking back into the leather upholstery to enjoy the ride.

A quarter-hour later, mostly satisfied with the day's resolution, he had skittered into the shadows beside St. Patrick's and launched his shadow-essence back up the side of the bell tower to resume his customary post behind the crenellated battlements.

From there he watched somewhat wistfully as the stately old Rolls Royce slowly disappeared up St. Patrick's Close and new snow began to fall in the lamplight. Evensong was in progress in the cathedral below, gathering the faithful to prayer. And as the sweet treble voices of the boys from the Choir School lifted in pure praise, Paddy wondered whether his path and the old man's would ever cross again.

Chapter 5

Snow was beginning to fall in earnest as Francis Templeton eased the old Rolls around the curve at the end of St. Patrick's Close, just out of sight of the cathedral, and pulled to the curb in front of Marsh's Library. Casting a last darting glance in his rearview mirror, he set the hand brake and shifted into neutral before allowing himself a somewhat tremulous sigh, briefly leaning his forehead against the steering wheel between his two gloved hands.

His thoughts were still whirling after the events of a day that seemed less and less credible with each passing minute. The euphoria of the past several hours had already begun to give way to disbelief, but despite the outlandishness of it all, he could not remember feeling this contented in many a year.

His reverie was rudely interrupted by the splat of very wet snow against the back of his neck, coming in through the open sunroof.

"Jesus, Mary, and Joseph!"

Mouthing further mild oaths under his breath, he cranked the sunroof shut briskly and gave his collar a shake, then brushed at the snow speckling the leather seat beside him—though the fact that the sunroof had been open at all did tend to confirm that at least some of what he could sort out from the whirl of extraordinary memories had been quite real. Ordinarily, he would not have dreamed of opening the sunroof on a day like this. The snow was coming down in great, fat clumps, splatting audibly on the windscreen and almost obscuring the little dragon—or was it a gargoyle, after all?—perched on the radiator cap.

"Phyllida," he said softly, curling gloved fingers around the steering wheel, "this has been the most astonishing day. . . ."

Which hardly began to describe it. Parts of it—dashing about the city in search of evildoers, bringing them to justice—almost had the feel of the comics he had devoured so avidly as a child, growing up between the wars, full of boys' adventures and tales of derring-do and the escapades of superheroes who seemed almost tame by modern standards—at least until today! Briefly he wondered how he could have lost that sense of excitement, even as another part of him scoffed.

Gargoyles. Right!

Yet he *had* opened the sunroof at least once, even if the

rest was sheer fantasy. But did he really believe he had done it because a gargoyle told him to?

He took another look at the mascot on the car's radiator cap—surely just an ordinary chrome dragon holding an enamelled shield!—then glanced somewhat dubiously in the rearview mirror again, craning his neck this way and that to inspect the whole of the rear passenger compartment. He could see no one there now—if, indeed, there had been anyone earlier.

But then his gaze was arrested by a sight that caused him to slowly turn and stare. Though the back seat was, indeed, unoccupied, a rumpled swath of red and black tartan lay squarely in the middle of the back seat, one fringed corner spilling onto the carpeted floor.

The implication elicited a little gasp, for he always kept the tartan rug neatly folded on the shelf beneath the rear window. He certainly would never have left it in a heap in the back.

Worming around so he could reach over the back of the seat, he stretched until he caught a handful of the tartan wool and pulled it up into the front seat. With it came the scent of roses, so unmistakable that it caused him to look sharply at the little crystal vases on the side pillars, half-expecting to see some of the fragrant tea roses his wife had always placed there when he was driving for a wedding. Over the years it had become their custom for her to tuck a matching bloom into the buttonhole of his coat before he set out, in reaffirmation of their own wedding vows.

But there were no roses, and had been none for far too many years. Memory stirring nonetheless, he crushed the armful of tartan to his face and merely breathed deeply of its perfume, *her* perfume—all too quickly gone.

But even that fleeting scent had transported him back to that breath-stopping first sight of her in the local parish hall: his own bonny Maeve, like a vision from some pre-Raphaelite painting, with hair like a cloud of flame, and dancing blue eyes that crinkled at the corners, and a smile of such sweetness and honesty that even the darkest fears must yield before it. The tartan rug had been her first shy gift to him, that last Christmas before he went off to war, bought with her modest earnings from pulling pints part-time at The Brazen Head, in Bridge Street—bold work, in those days, for a girl of good family, but she was one of five, and times were hard.

After the war, they had courted in Phyllida and pic-nicked on the rug, held one another under its warmth, and later, their daughters had played on it. In time, many an-other bride had sheltered under its warmth, when the car's heater was not sufficient to stave off wintry chills. She had given him more costly gifts during the years of their long and happy marriage, but few that he treasured more.

"Ah, darlin' girl," he whispered, for his sense of loss had never diminished. But a faint smile lingered on his lips when, after a few seconds, he folded the rug somewhat clumsily and laid it on the seat beside him, letting his hand rest there as he reluctantly dragged himself back to his present contemplation of . . . gargoyles.

Shaking his head, he breathed out with a sigh, glancing again at the falling snow, at the mascot on Phyllida's radia-tor cap—had a wing just moved?—at the fat snowflakes floating through the glare of his headlamps. Then he resolutely put the old car back into gear and released the brake, and carried on to the end of the road, into Kevin Street.

But though he had intended merely to head back to the garage he rented for storing the car, instead he found himself threading his way back around to the cathedral, once again circling into Patrick's Close to draw up beside the second of the two iron gates on the south side. Pedestrians gave the shiny black car curious looks as they hurried past, heads hunched down into collars against the snow, but Templeton paid them no mind, only setting the brake again as he cautiously cast an appraising gaze over the shadow-etched angles of the old building.

He had no idea what he expected to see. Nor, given the strangeness of everything else that had happened that day, had he been quite sure what to expect when he pulled up here a few minutes earlier. He did vaguely remember cranking open the sunroof; but he had almost missed it when, without preamble, something had whooshed past him in a flurry of dark, leathery wings and disappeared, quick as a flash, like a squirt of ink against the paler shadows under the lamplight.

A gargoyle?

Right, Francis, he told himself. *Sure, and it's early Alzheimer's. Your mind is going, and you've just spent the day driving around Dublin and talking to yourself. You'll hear about this, when the word gets out!*

He heaved a sigh and craned his neck to look up at the floodlit tower that was the spire of the cathedral, wondering whether there really was a gargoyle up there. The clock in the tower began to strike the hour, and he remembered reading somewhere that the tower's other bells were quite extraordinary—not the oldest in the city, but certainly the finest. He had often heard them ringing as he drove by, but he didn't remember ever noticing any gargoyles on the building.

Not that he had ever really looked that closely, he had to confess. In fact, even though the cathedral was one of the oldest churches in Dublin, and one of the most famous, he had never even been inside. Oh, he had delivered many a bride to its doorstep, over the years. On a few occasions, when the heavens frowned and rain pummelled down on a day slated for a wedding, he had even gotten as far as the side door, holding a big black umbrella over fretting bride and anxious father.

But back when he was a boy, it hadn't been done for a Catholic even to set foot in a Protestant church. Back then, a lot of things hadn't been done.

Of course, it wasn't done, either, to hold conversations with gargoyles—but so far as he could tell, he had spent most of the day doing just that. Maybe. Either that, or he really was going barmy.

It was all too much for him to take in just now. He was hungry, he was tired, and it was getting cold, just sitting here, even with the engine running and the heater going. Time enough to think about gargoyles when he'd gotten Phyllida back to her garage—or when he'd checked in the paper tomorrow to see whether there had even been a break-in at St. Patrick's.

With a shake of his head, he released the brake and continued on through Patrick's Close again, leaving the cathedral behind as he headed north to thread his way through the heavy evening traffic. On a whim, he stopped for an evening paper before returning to the garage, and gave it a perfunctory scan after he had put Phyllida away; but he could find nothing about St. Patrick's Cathedral save a mention of the schedule of services over the weekend.

Perhaps on the news, then. In fact, remembering that no one would be home for supper anyway, he decided he would stop for a pint on the way home, and see if there was anything on RTÉ about a burglary at St. Patrick's. His daughter and son-in-law were going to an office Christmas party tonight, and both his grandsons would be out with their friends—which meant that his own supper would be something he could heat in the microwave. No doubt it would be tasty enough, because Aisling was an excellent cook, as her mother had been, but being on his own meant that there was no urgency about getting home.

Besides, he could hole up in a back booth and have another look at the paper. Maybe he had missed something, the first time through. And he always enjoyed chatting with his friends, especially at this time of year.

But his local pub was disappointingly quiet for a Friday night—probably a combination of the snow and the proximity of Christmas—and the RTÉ News at Six had only the usual reports about the peace process in the North and the latest wrangles with the European Union and how many shopping days there were left until Christmas. Watching footage of the crowds in Grafton Street and O'Connell Street—much of which he had witnessed firsthand during the day's peregrinations—he was particularly glad he had already finished his own Christmas shopping, and even had everything wrapped. Though his pension didn't allow for lavish gifts, he chose each one with care, and the recipients were always pleased—or at least they said they were.

But there was nothing on the news about the cathedral, or a break-in there, much less about gargoyles. Nor did he find anything when he went through the *Evening Herald* a second time, even fortified by a second pint of Guinness. After a third, with a couple of friends who finally showed up after the stores closed and no more shopping could be done, he reluctantly made his way home to the empty house and his solitary meal.

At least it was something he liked: leftover lasagne, with lots of cheese topping—hearty fare, for a cold winter's evening, and a far more generous portion than his doctor would have approved. Since Aisling ordinarily kept him strictly to his prescribed diet, he decided that she must have felt guilty about leaving him on his own. There was even a helping of Christmas pudding for dessert, with a side portion of custard to heat in the microwave and pour over the top. And that made *him* feel guilty, for he'd already had three pints of Guinness, when he was meant to limit himself to one.

Pleased nonetheless, he finished assembling his tray and carried it into the library with a certain sense of self-indulgence, to enjoy his treat in front of the TV. On a pensioner's income, having a second TV was also something of an indulgence, but in a household dominated by football-mad teenage boys and a son-in-law who shared his sons' passion, he had found that a separate set was the only way he could be sure of sometimes getting to watch what *he* liked. He was especially partial to old films, preferably in black and white—and as he settled into a comfy leather chair and flipped through the channels, he soon found a favorite on BBC 2. The lovely Mrs. Muir, in the guise of Gene Tierney, would be most agreeable company for enjoying a forbidden treat on a cold December night, even if he did find himself mildly envious of Rex Harrison's dashing sea-captain character.

He settled down to eat his meal, enjoying the film and likewise enjoying the ambience of the library itself, one of his favorite rooms, with its book-crammed shelves and well-waxed wooden panelling, its smell of leather bindings—all nostalgic legacies of another, more gracious era, very like the one in the film. These days, having a room set aside as a dedicated library was as much a luxury as the house itself: a somewhat eccentric Victorian confection in a no longer fashionable part of the city, most of its once extensive gardens now occupied by rather graceless terrace houses built during the thirties.

At the time, in the aftermath of the Great Depression, he had greatly resented his father's decision to sell off the surrounding land—and even that had not averted the need for a vast scaling-back of their lifestyle, though they had managed to hold onto the house. Glancing now, however, at the silver-framed photo of a handsome man in military uniform, he could well appreciate the sacrifices made by the elder Templeton to keep his family from suffering the same deprivations endured by so many others—and even then, economies had been necessary.

Yet he remembered those years between the wars as happy ones, despite economic hardships and the vague rumblings of a powerful German military machine taking shape far to the east. Business college had been *just* feasible for the young Francis Templeton, only son among three daughters; and he had still been a student when Hitler invaded Poland and triggered the Second World War.

Of course, in what was then known as Éire, the "sovereign independent and democratic state" recently constituted from the former Irish Free State, it had been called "the Emergency." The Irish government of the time had also declared official neutrality in the conflict—unable, in those first restless decades following Irish independence, to countenance any semblance of alliance with a country so recently a bitter enemy, even against so odious a common threat as Hitler.

It was a shortsightedness only recently fading away, as the Irish gradually came to accept that the islands of Ireland and Britain were natural economic partners, even if separated by the Irish Sea and somewhat differing cultural traditions. But even at the time, there had been many Irish men and women of keener vision, who recognized that, whatever the residual bitterness from centuries of British rule, the scope of German military aggression on the Continent was a threat even to "neutral" Ireland, perched on the far edge of Western Europe. Templeton's father, a veteran of the Great War, had rejoined his old regiment soon after war was declared, and Templeton himself had enlisted a year later.

Sadly, the senior Templeton was not to survive the war; but young Francis, though wounded, had returned a decorated hero, to inherit Phyllida and the old house, take up a career in merchant banking, and marry his darling Maeve. The rambling Victorian pile had been their matrimonial home, filled with laughter and the happy muddle of bringing up four bright, spirited daughters in an Ireland still finding its confidence as a newly independent state. And after her death, rather than give it up entirely, he had thought it far better to share the house with the youngest of those daughters and her family.

The decision did mean that the house was no longer really his—but neither was the responsibility, though naturally a goodly portion of his pension went toward helping with groceries and the like. He also did most of the gardening, other than cutting the grass—which wasn't a great deal, but he was insistent that no one but himself should tend Maeve's beloved roses. Upstairs, he had kept the second-best bedroom with its connecting bath, and downstairs, he could count the library as essentially his personal preserve, since the rest of the family were far too busy to have much time for books.

Those books, he realized, as he finished his dessert, were what he really had been after, when he brought his meal into the library instead of taking it in the kitchen or the family room. He hadn't been paying a bit of attention to his film. While he normally would have relished immersion in the romantic interplay between the charming Mrs. Muir and her ghostly sea captain, his gaze kept ranging along the spines of the oversized art books lined up on the library's lower shelves—and wondering whether any of them might tell him something more about gargoyles.

He decided he could put it off no longer. After depositing his tray on the floor beside his chair, he retrieved several large-format photo books on Dublin and settled back into his big leather chair.

Not that he expected he would find very much. Gargoyles, so far as he could remember, were mostly associated with Gothic buildings—and Dublin, even though settled for more than a thousand years, was mostly a Georgian city. Ireland in the eighteenth and nineteenth centuries had attracted some of Europe's finest architects, names as notable as James Gandon, Edward Pugin, Richard Castle, and the Adam brothers, but they had mostly preferred to work in a classical idiom.

Of course, a few buildings did sport gargoyles—at least the carved kind. Templeton had spotted several of them during his day spent driving around the city, and confirmed a few in his perusal of photos of Dublin.

But whether those carved shells housed entities like the one he had glimpsed in Phyllida's garage—or whether any of the day's experience had sprung from anything besides his own imagining—remained to be seen. "Paddy" had declined to confirm or deny specifics about any of the other gargoyles who allegedly guarded the city—and the existence of Paddy himself was not altogether certain. Templeton certainly *wanted* it to be true; and he had to admit that the reflection of armored angelic splendor he had glimpsed in Phyllida's door did seem unlikely to have come solely from even the most fevered imagination. It had all certainly *seemed* real. . . .

Yes, and Father Christmas seemed real, when you were a kid! he told himself sternly. *And when somebody claims to have seen the fairies . . .*

On second thought, he decided that a claim to have seen the fairies, while it *could* be drink-induced, was apt to contain at least a grain of truth. Few folk in Ireland would be so bold as to totally dismiss the possibility that the Little Folk still walked abroad in the land, especially as one got farther outside the cities. Not even the Church made pronouncements on such subjects, so *he* certainly was not willing to reject the notion.

Nor was the government. Quite recently, he could remember reading how the proposed route of a major motorway down in County Wicklow had been shifted to avoid interfering with a traditional fairy ring.

As for gargoyles, Paddy had said that they used to be avenging angels—which made sense, Templeton supposed, if one accepted that after the advent of Christ and the New Testament's teachings, the need for avenging angels had decreased. Templeton had no idea how many angels God was supposed to have created, before the Beginning. (He did recall reading that numbers in the Bible were rarely precise, and often symbolic or even notional, rather than literal.) He certainly couldn't imagine that a loving or even a merely just God would simply do away with angels that were superfluous to His needs.

Nor could he imagine redundant angels, lounging about in heaven and doing nothing except maybe praising God. The Bible did say that certain kinds of angels did just that, but again, Templeton couldn't imagine that this information was meant to be taken literally, despite what various churches had said, over the centuries, regarding a variety of subjects. Surely such angels would be reassigned to more useful occupations. Maybe even as gargoyles.

After pausing to make himself a mug of hot chocolate, he spent another hour or so browsing through some of the many books he had collected over the years, including several that featured architectural photographs of the city, but it seemed that gargoyles were, indeed, in short supply. He found some on the tower of a big Presbyterian church in Parnell Square, and a tiny one on the Unitarian Church in St. Stephen's Green, and a bigger one on the front of University Church, next to Newman House. He also spotted what looked like real, functioning gargoyles on the rainspouts above the cloister enclosure at the Dominican Priory in Dorset Street.

Then there were a few somewhat ambiguously carved figures that might or might not be gargoyles—and lots of possible Watchers. It didn't look like St. Patrick's Cathedral even had any of those, much less gargoyles.

Frustrated, he broadened his field of search. A book on Chartres Cathedral presented a wide assortment of quite striking gargoyles (though none of them looked like Paddy), but those were in France. There were also gargoyles on several English cathedrals—but none of that gave him much insight regarding the possible existence of gargoyles in his own beloved Dublin.

As to whether any of said gargoyles might be capable of independent movement—much less that they were actually angels in disguise—well, he had never, *ever* heard of such a possibility. He did seem to recall that a few years back, gargoyles had briefly captured popular imagination by means of a Disney film and a children's animated TV series—he definitely remembered action figures and lunchboxes and stuffed toys underfoot among his grandsons' boyhood clutter—but surely that didn't qualify as proof of their existence outside such fantasies.

By the time the clock in the hall began to strike midnight, with no sign of the family's return, he was starting to feel a bit of eyestrain, so he decided to call it a night and head up to bed.

Chapter 6

Templeton slept late the next morning, not rousing until his daughter came and knocked on his door.

"Da, are you awake?" she called. "It's half past nine. Will you be coming down for breakfast?"

He rolled over and looked at the clock, then sat bolt upright in bed. He had not meant to sleep so late. Phyllida desperately needed a wash, after her rather extraordinary outing of the previous day. And memories of that outing made him scramble out of bed immediately. He had even dreamed about gargoyles—and he almost never dreamed.

"I'll be right down," he called back.

Twenty minutes later, showered, shaved, and dressed, he was making his way downstairs to the family dining room. There, ranged at one end of the long table, his daughter's husband, Kevin, and both grandsons were already tucking into the hearty breakfast Aisling served up on Saturdays in the Gallagher household: a traditional Dublin fry, featuring eggs, rashers, sausage, and black pudding, along with grilled tomatoes, mushrooms, and fried bread.

Wistfully contemplating the rather more frugal fare he could expect, Templeton sat down resignedly and flapped open his napkin, settling it on his lap. In times past, he might have shared in the same tasty but cholesterol-laden repast that the others were enjoying, but his doctors had long since forbidden such culinary indulgences.

"'Morning, Da," his son-in-law said amiably, echoed by the greetings of both boys, who were young teenagers. "You're down late."

Templeton only nodded as he gulped down a handful of pills with his orange juice, glancing out at a brilliant morning.

"I was having a good sleep," he replied, reaching for a slice of brown toast. "These days, that's rare enough. Dreamed a lot, though." He was not about to mention that the dreaming had been about gargoyles.

"It looks like a fine day," he went on. "I hope tomorrow's as good. I've got a Malta 'do' in the afternoon— Christmas reception over at the Nuncio's. Marcus has offered to play chauffeur, so that the lads and I can arrive in grand style. Besides, it's impossible to drive in spurs. He said he'd come over around noon and help me give Phyllida a bath."

Both boys started to snicker, but they quickly subsided at a sharp look from their father. Marcus was Templeton's favorite godson, only child of one of his closest and oldest boyhood friends—sadly, now passed on—and as keen an old car enthusiast as Templeton himself. The fact that he was also a detective usually elicited awe mixed with excitement on the part of the two Gallagher lads, not mirth. Maybe it was the spurs. Before Templeton could inquire as to what might be so amusing, Aisling came in with his egg and a fresh pot of tea.

"'Morning, Da," she said cheerily. "Tea this morning, or coffee?"

"Tea, please, since it's fresh."

He watched her pour it, casting a resigned look at the lonely-looking rasher accompanying the single boiled egg she had put down in front of him, then began whacking the top off the egg with meticulous efficiency.

"Francis was saying that he and Marcus are going to wash the old car today," Kevin said to Aisling as she sat down at her place. "I guess it got a little muddy, with all that driving around in the slush yesterday."

Templeton glanced up sharply. All four of them were looking at him oddly.

"Da, what were you doing?" Aisling said softly. "Bridie McCutcheon said she saw you driving along O'Connell Street, talking to nobody, and Eamon Docherty saw you chattering away in Dawson Street, with not another soul in the car."

"Spying on me, were you?" Templeton said with some bite.

"No, I wasn't spying on you. But when friends who care

about you see you acting strangely, they become concerned. Maybe it's time you gave up driving. You could always—"

"I'll not give up driving."

"But Francis, you're eighty-two years old, and you've got a dicky heart," Kevin said. "And it isn't as if that old car is easy to drive."

"*That old car* is a 1929 Rolls Royce limousine—older than you are and almost older than me," Templeton retorted, "and I've been driving it all my adult life. Furthermore, my doctor thinks I'm quite fit enough to drive."

"Da, it isn't your physical fitness that worries us," Aisling said gently. "If you've started talking to yourself . . ."

Her voice trailed off suggestively, and Templeton wadded up his napkin and flung it down beside his plate, all further thought of breakfast fled.

"If you're implying that I'm going barmy, I'll thank you to put such thoughts out of your head. In fact, I had an excellent day yesterday. I was—singing, if you really must know."

"*Singing,* Grandda?" one of the boys piped up.

"Yes, singing. The last time I heard, there was no law against that, even for old age pensioners!"

"But, Grandda," said the other lad, "Phyllida doesn't have a radio."

"I bought one yesterday," Templeton said, thinking fast. "Besides, you don't have to have a radio, in order to sing along. Jesus, Mary, and Joseph, do I have to explain everything I do to the likes of you?"

"Jason, Michael, don't bully your grandfather," Aisling said quietly, motioning the two boys out of the room when they would have protested. "Darling Da, we aren't trying to gang up on you. Maybe you're getting distracted. You could have an accident. You could kill someone. You *are* getting on."

"And I've still got all my marbles," Templeton said. "*And* a clean driving record. I *like* to sing. And sometimes, I just like to drive around and look at the city. It's a marvellous old town, Dublin. I was—thinking about the old days, when your mother and I used to swan around in Phyllida." Which was true, in part. "There was a lot less traffic then, of course."

"Da . . ."

"I was remembering your wedding day, too," he went on, hoping he could restore peace. "Phyllida never carried a more beautiful bride."

"I'll not argue *that*," Kevin agreed, with an uncomfortable glance at his wife. "But we do worry about you, Francis—driving all over Dublin in that old car, burning up petrol. . . ."

"It's my petrol to burn, and it doesn't cost you a penny," Templeton pointed out mildly. "At eighty-two, driving Phyllida is one of the few pleasures I have left. I hope you're not saying that you begrudge me that?"

"No, no, of course not . . ."

"Besides, I've already told you that Marcus is driving tomorrow—not because I don't think I'm fit," the old man added. "But I have to wear spurs with my uniform, and I can't drive in spurs."

"Da, we know you love the old car," Aisling said. "Just—be careful, if you're going to do much extra driving."

"I'm always careful," Templeton muttered.

"Da . . ."

Not looking at her, he folded his rasher of bacon into a piece of toast to make a small sandwich of it, chewing off a substantial bite as he got up from the table.

"Egg's gone cold," he muttered, by way of explanation. "So's this, but that's fine, for a sandwich. I'll take it with me."

"Da, please finish your breakfast," his daughter began. "I'll make another egg."

"Don't fuss," he said. "I'll pick up something else on the way to the garage. Marcus likes sweets. I'll be back in time for dinner," he added, relenting enough to come and kiss her on the forehead before heading for the door.

Marcus already had tea made and the heater lit when Templeton got to the garage. The shipping forecast was blaring from an old radio perched on a shelf above the workbench, and Marcus himself was ensconced on a stool beside it, dark hair disheveled and the sleeves of his navy sweatshirt pushed up to the elbows, surveying the old car with a critical eye as he sipped at a mug of tea. He turned at the sound of the garage door opening, raising his mug in wordless greeting as the older man eased the door open far enough to slip inside. His pleasant, open face lit in a boyish grin as Templeton produced a plastic sack of fruit scones from one of the capacious pockets of his waxed jacket and deposited it on the workbench, also tossing his cap onto one of the pegs above.

"Oh, good, I was hoping you'd bring something to go with the tea," Marcus said, setting down his mug to help Templeton shed his jacket.

"Couldn't come empty-handed, now, could I?" Templeton said. "How long has that tea been made?"

"It's a fresh pot," Marcus replied. "Sit yourself down and I'll pour you some."

"I will, that. I had a row with Aisling and walked off without having any at home. Have we got butter for the scones?"

"No, but I brought some of Mum's strawberry jam."

"Good!"

To Templeton's relief, Marcus did not pursue the matter of the row with Aisling, busying himself with the tea—two sugars and a liberal splash of milk, the way both of them liked it—while Templeton fussed with the knot in the neck of the sack of scones. Marcus Cassidy was thirtyish—Templeton could never remember exactly how old—unmarried as yet, and shared his godfather's passion for sweets as well as vintage cars. Fortunately, his active life kept him from putting on weight. Though his late father had been an extremely successful barrister, and Marcus himself had qualified as a solicitor, the son was focusing his energies on the enforcement side of the law that had been his father's passion.

Now well into a successful career in the Garda Síochána, and currently assigned as a protection officer for government officials as lofty as the Taoiseach and the President, the lad was of that new breed of gardaí seen increasingly in Ireland in the past several decades: university-educated, multitalented, socially poised, and utterly dedicated to his chosen profession.

But he also made time to enjoy himself, with a variety seldom seen in the same individual. He played on a garda rugby team, but was also a passionate opera enthusiast. His own light tenor, had he bothered to train it, might have carried him to modest success in that field, and he could pick up a fiddle or a tin whistle and jam more than competently with professionals who made a living at it.

His attraction to the vintage car hobby had been nurtured since early childhood. His first time behind the wheel of Phyllida had been at the age of about five, sitting on a cushion on his godfather's lap and with his father in the seat alongside. Both men had proudly watched him take his driving test in the old car on the day he turned eighteen. He had passed it on the first try.

This lifelong affinity for old cars, coupled with his professional connections, had given him the cachet to be drafted as an occasional driver of the somewhat less elderly state landaulette owned by the Irish government, which was rolled out for particularly important state occasions. (Official drivers were usually drawn from the ranks of the gardaí or the army.) A mere fifty years old, the big blue and black Silver Wraith had carried presidents, princes, prime ministers, and other state visitors—and Marcus had driven not a few of them. For that matter, when more than one vintage car was required for a given state function, Templeton sometimes drove lesser dignitaries in Phyllida,

"I love just looking at this car," Marcus said, returning his gaze to the old Rolls Royce as he opened the jar of jam. "I love driving her even more. I'm looking forward to tomorrow. She does need a bath, though. It looks like you had her out and about in the snow."

"I suppose you're going to lecture me, too," Templeton said a little defensively. "Can't a fellow sing along with his radio, just because he feels good?"

He delved into another pocket of his waxed jacket and hauled out a sleek new Walkman radio trailing near-invisible ear buttons on wires, depositing the contraption almost defiantly on the workbench beside the bag of scones.

"My grandsons had the brass to point out that Phyllida doesn't have a radio," he said. He did not point out, however, that this state of affairs had only changed in the last hour, during a detour into the electronics shop beside the bakery where he bought the scones.

Marcus only raised a quizzical black eyebrow. "I take it that your venture into automotive karaoke has been seen as eccentricity," he said mildly.

Templeton snorted. "Busybodies! Aisling's spies reported back to her in a matter of hours. You can't sneeze in Dublin without somebody saying 'God bless you' in Kerry. I'll not give up driving, Marcus. I'm *not* going gaga!"

"I know that."

"You mean nobody told *you* that I was talking away to myself yesterday in the car? Everybody else in Dublin seems to think so."

"Nope, can't say I'd heard," Marcus said with a faint smile. "*Were* you?—talking to yourself?"

"No, I was singing," Templeton said stubbornly. "Naturally, I talk to Phyllida sometimes," he admitted. "All of us with old cars talk to them sometimes, usually when they're misbehaving. Not that she was misbehaving yesterday. She ran perfectly."

"Then, there's nothing to discuss," Marcus said cheerily. "You want to pass me one of those scones? I can't say that jam is quite as satisfying as butter or clotted cream, but at least if Aisling has her spies lurking hereabouts, she shouldn't be too upset. A bit of sugar's better for us than all that cholesterol!"

"True enough," Templeton agreed. "But we still won't tell her."

Somewhat mollified, he scooted his stool closer to his godson and joined in what had become a ritual on Saturdays when Marcus wasn't on duty. While they ate, Marcus told Templeton about his week.

"Oh, it was the usual madness, what with the holiday traffic—and the snow didn't help. We had a state visit, to start the week. That kept us busy. And later in the week, we had two ambassadors present credentials up at Áras. Tonight, the President has a Christmas reception for staff, but I'm not working, so I'll not worry about it."

"You must be the fair-haired boy, getting the weekend off," Templeton remarked with a grin.

"Yeah, but it doesn't happen very often," Marcus replied. "We're nearly all working New Year's, of course, what with everybody worried about the millennium bug and such, but wouldn't you know I'm also working Christmas? Not that I really mind. Give the married lads and lasses time off with their families. Some day, it'll be my turn."

"Any prospects?" Templeton asked—a routine question, to which he expected a routine answer.

Marcus grinned. "I've been meaning to tell you about that."

"Oh?" Templeton looked at him in somewhat surprised question.

"Well, there's this rather smashing doctor I met at my sister's wedding this summer. She's training as an emergency consultant. Long-distance courtships aren't my favorite thing, especially with both of us working odd hours, but she doesn't seem to mind being seen with a professional cop."

This obvious understatement brought a pleased smile to the older man's lips. "Sounds promising, Marcus. Well done! Where's she working?"

"Liverpool, of all places, finishing her qualification. But she's Irish, and she wants to come back here to practice—though there aren't many proper trauma-management facilities in this country, as yet. It's still a fairly new specialty even in the UK, though they've had emergency specialists in the States for years. She's hoping they'll open a facility down in Loughlinstown, and she can get a foot in the door there."

"That would be convenient enough," Templeton said. "She sounds like a most intriguing young woman. Does this paragon have a name?"

"Cáit," Marcus said with a grin. "Cáit O'Conor."

"Redhead?"

"Brunette. About up to my chin." He indicated her height with the flat of his hand. "Brown eyes, nice figure, long legs . . . and a wonderful wit. She's kind, and compassionate . . ." Marcus's voice trailed off with a sigh, obviously smitten. "This could be it, Francis."

"Well, for your sake, my boy, I hope it is," Templeton replied. "I look forward to meeting her." Smiling, he reached across to clasp the younger man's shoulder. "Now, let's get this car washed before the afternoon gets away from us."

Templeton carefully avoided any further mention of their earlier conversation regarding his driving fitness. Nor could he immediately figure out a casual way to ask Marcus about the break-in at St. Patrick's. Instead, while they hand-washed the old Rolls with buckets of warm water and leathered it down with a succession of soft old chamois cloths, he stuck to the safer subjects of Christmas plans and the estimable Cáit and speculations about possible millennium problems.

By the time they had finished, the car's black lacquered side panels and doors gleamed like obsidian mirrors, but reflected only the commonplace clutter of the garage. As Templeton gave the little gargoyle a somewhat gingerly polish, he found himself wondering whether he was, indeed, going off the deep end. Could he really have only imagined what he was so sure he remembered from the day before? It wasn't exactly the sort of thing you could ask a guard, even if he *was* your godson: Tell me, Marcus, have you seen any gargoyles around the city?

But maybe Marcus at least could tell him whether there really had been a break-in at St. Patrick's—or he could find out. The younger man was hidden behind the other side of the car, bent to wipe down the wheel covers, and Templeton kept his head down, too, as he carefully framed his question to sound casual.

"Marcus," he said, "I have a professional question for you. Have you heard anything about something odd going on at St. Patrick's Cathedral in the past day or so?"

"What kind of 'odd?'" Marcus replied, looking up.

"Oh, a mugging, a break-in, maybe a burglary . . ."

"No, why do you ask?"

Templeton kept his head bent over the little gargoyle he was polishing, whose ruby eyes seemed no more than red enamel in the flat glow of the fluorescent lighting overhead.

"Just wondering. I was driving past there yesterday morning, and I saw an ambulance and a garda car pulled up at the side door."

Which he hadn't, but that's what the gargoyle said had happened.

"Dunno," Marcus said. "Maybe somebody croaked at morning prayers. I can maybe find out, though, if you're really interested. What time would that have been?"

"Oh, early," Templeton said. He polished the already shiny radiator grille with his yellow duster, waffling while his mind raced ahead to concoct the plausible story line. "It was just getting light, but rush hour was already starting."

"Hmm, sort of eight-ish, then. Pretty early start."

Templeton shrugged. "I was supposed to show the car to a prospective client, but he didn't turn up. Since I already had the car out, though, I figured I'd drive around a bit. Traffic was mad, as it always is, this close to Christmas, but it was a fine day, even with the snow."

"True enough," Marcus agreed. "We had to escort some diplomats from the airport. It turned out to be the kind of day that Bord Fáilte loves to tout in the tourist brochures. This time of year, they don't come much prettier."

Templeton found himself smiling. Marcus had the public relations side of his job well in hand, always aware of the public impact of what went on around him.

"You ever been inside the cathedral?" Templeton asked.

"Oh, yes. Lots of times. In fact, I was on duty that day

when the President stirred up such a kerfuffle by taking Communion from a Church of Ireland priest."

"You think that was right?" Templeton asked. He stopped polishing to lean on one fender of the old car.

"Not for me to judge," Marcus replied, sidling over to the next wheel. "The press mostly neglected to point out that her family was with her, and they took Communion, too. It happens more often than you might think. But to hear the Hierarchy carry on, you'd think she'd committed a mortal sin."

"Well, maybe not 'mortal,'" Templeton replied, taking the orthodox line. "But Catholics aren't supposed to take Communion in a Protestant church."

"Not strictly speaking, no," Marcus agreed, "but I'm afraid I can't get all that agitated about it. We're all Christians, aren't we? Seems to me that it should be a matter of individual conscience. This island has been torn apart too long by old grudges, and people keeping the letter of the law instead of the spirit—and a lot of them don't even keep the letter of the law."

"Careful, counselor. As a member of the Garda Síochána, the Guardians of the Peace, it's your job to enforce the law."

"Well, there's civil law and there's moral law," Marcus replied. "I'll not be drawn into a debate with you about the technicalities of the Church's teachings, because you Knights of Malta are true devils when it comes to arguing the Hierarchy's side of things." He gestured toward the little gargoyle holding the Malta shield on the end of the car's long hood. "But I hope I'll never lose sight of the fact that the two may not always be one and the same. Besides,

I've taken Communion in a Protestant church myself," he admitted. "Cáit is Church of Ireland."

"Aha," Templeton murmured. "All now becomes clear."

"Now, don't you start harping on me!" Marcus said, standing up to wave his chamois at Templeton. "Mam has already given me an earful. It just doesn't make that much difference to me—or to Cáit. These days, you'd think that parents would be glad if their children have *any* faith."

Templeton had finished with the front end of the car, and moved to a perch on one of the stools for a short breather, thinking that the preceding exchange had sounded a lot like something the gargoyle might have argued, the day before.

"Well, I'll wait to see if it gets serious, before I consider flexing whatever godfatherly influence I might have," he said, though it sounded like the relationship was already more serious than Marcus had first hinted. "In the meantime, maybe I'll even have a closer look inside St. Patrick's, take a proper tour of a Protestant church. It *is* part of our national heritage, after all. That occurred to me yesterday, when I was driving past. I've stuck my head in the door lots of times, what with delivering brides over the years, but I've never actually gone all the way inside."

"Then, you *should,*" Marcus said with a chuckle, as he bent back to his wiping of the wheel covers. "I think you'll find that Protestant churches aren't so very different from ours—especially Saint Patrick's. It's been Roman, in its day, you know. In fact, I know a lot of Roman Catholic churches that seem more Protestant."

"That's what I've heard," Templeton replied. "I suppose I ought to see for myself, one of these days."

Marcus cocked him a sidelong grin. "Look out, Francis. You're mellowing in your old age."

"At least I'm not in my dotage," Templeton replied, returning the smile. "I wonder if St. Patrick's has any gargoyles," he added, in what he hoped was a casual aside. "It's Gothic, after all. A Gothic cathedral *should* have gargoyles."

Chapter 7

"How's the rest of your afternoon?" Templeton asked Marcus, when they had finished wiping down the last of the car's bright-work and were laying out the last of the sponges and chamois to dry.

"Nothing special planned. Why do you ask?"

"Thought I might just do that tour of St. Patrick's.

"What, today?"

"Well, why not? It's a nice day."

Marcus plucked at a fold of the sweatshirt he was wearing and made a face, also lifting a sneaker-clad foot at the end of a long, lean leg clad in faded blue jeans.

"Not exactly dressed for proper sightseeing, am I?" he said.

"Nonsense. Tourists dress no better. Besides," Templeton added, taking inspiration from the gargoyle's somewhat more relaxed attitude regarding churches, "maybe God would rather have people in churches—even Protestant ones—than have them worry about what they're wearing."

"Fair enough, since you put it that way," Marcus agreed. "You obviously were paying attention during our earlier discussion. You want to take my car? No sense getting Phyllida all muddy again, after we've just given her a bath."

"However, if we did take Phyllida," Templeton said, "we could park right outside the cathedral, instead of around the block. Nobody questions a vintage car pulled up outside a church. We're checking things out for a wedding."

"Yes, and if there's already a wedding there today, we create a traffic problem."

"Thus speaks my godson the cop."

"Your godson the cop can put a business card on his front dash, and nobody will bother his humble little Honda," Marcus retorted, though he was smiling. "Come on, Francis. You're just being cantankerous for the hell of it!"

"Somebody's got to keep you on your toes!"

"Quit giving me a hard time, you old scoundrel!" Marcus said with a grin, taking his godfather's bicep with one hand and grabbing his coat with the other. "You're nicked! Just come with me and get into the nice policeman's car. I'm saving you petrol, not to mention all the elbow grease I've just put into yours!"

In the end, they parked Marcus's Honda in Saint Patrick's Close, just beyond the bus stop, not far from where Templeton had stopped the night before, after delivering his strange companion back to the cathedral. Templeton had scanned the west front of the cathedral as they passed along Patrick Street, and continued to inspect the south façade as they got out of the car, gawking like any tourist. He could see no sign of gargoyles.

The entrance was at the southwest corner, down half a dozen steps into a covered porch that led through double doors into the rear of the nave. Both the porch and the cathedral floors were paved with encaustic tiles in rich shades of terra cotta and cream, olive-green and black. There seemed to be more tourists than Templeton might have expected, given the nearness of Christmas.

Behind a wooden table just inside the doors, a fresh-faced young woman in a bright red sweater was taking donations for admission to the rest of the cathedral. It was dim inside, and hushed, despite the number of people coming and going, sound echoing under the vaulting. Templeton could hear the sweet harmony of *a capella* voices in the background, men and boy choristers mixed, and wondered whether it was live or a recording. Two elderly ladies seemed to be selling tapes and CDs at a small bookstall off to the right, along with guidebooks and postcards and other souvenirs.

"I'll get this," Marcus said, reaching past Templeton to lay a five-pound note on the desk. "Two, please."

Smiling, the young woman gave him two tickets, two printed brochures about the cathedral, and a handful of change. As he and Templeton stepped past a velvet guide rope and moved toward the back of the center aisle, he handed a ticket and one of the brochures to Templeton and dropped the change into a wooden collection box for the upkeep of the cathedral.

"We can link up with one of the official guides, if you want, but like I said, I've been here before. Now, do you want the potted tour or the full Monty, as personalized by Doctor Marcus Cassidy, Esquire?"

"Oh, let's go for the full Monty, by all means, counselor," Templeton replied. "After all, it's Christmas. Lead the way."

"The full Monty it is. We'll start with the bare basics. You *are* aware, of course, that this is one of the largest churches in Ireland?"

"I think the basilica at Knock is bigger," Templeton muttered, trying not to be impressed.

"Could be," Marcus replied. "But it's a modern building."

"True enough, I suppose."

Impressed anyway, Templeton craned his neck to scan the Gothic vaulting, more than fifty feet above their heads. Still no trace of a gargoyle or even a Watcher. He wondered whether any of the funerary statues were Watchers, or if Watchers were only placed on the outsides of buildings. Yet another thing he should have asked Paddy while he had the chance. He wondered whether he would ever find the gargoyle again. Or maybe it had, indeed, been but a dream or a fantasy.

"Okay, let's start over there," Marcus said, gesturing toward a Gothic-arched door in the south wall of the nave. "The bust to the left of the door is Jonathan Swift's; the memorial on the other side is to "Stella," who might be called his muse, I suppose. They're both buried nearby— though not in the same grave, as some wags would have you believe. There's his brass," he added, pointing out a simple plaque set amid the encaustic tiles a few yards away.

It said, simply: *SWIFT. Decan. 1713. Obt 19 Oct. 1745. Aet. 78.*

"Hmmm, Dean for more than thirty years," Templeton said, translating and doing the maths.

"Aye, one of our better known Irishmen who made good. I had to read *Gulliver's Travels,* when I was at school."

"So did I," Templeton said. "And I recall a deliciously scathing essay called 'A Modest Proposal.' Something about suggesting that the Irish ought to eat their children to stay alive."

"Like I said, he wrote satire," Marcus said with an almost impish grin. "The complete title, as I recall—and let's see if I can remember the whole thing; I had to memorize it one time, to get out of detention—the full title was 'A Modest Proposal for Preventing the Children of the Poor People in Ireland from being a Burden to their Parents or Country and for Making them Beneficial to the Public.' Which is to say that he suggested the children should be eaten."

They were both chuckling as Marcus indicated that they should move on along the south aisle.

"Come on and I'll show you the Lady Chapel before we look at the choir," he said. "And there are some interesting memorials in the south transept—including a statue that's supposed to be Saint Patrick, though I have my doubts."

Templeton quirked an eyebrow somewhat dubiously. "I didn't know that the Church of Ireland was big into saints—and especially Our Lady."

"Well, they aren't big into *statues* of saints," Marcus

replied. "And other than a few carved on the pulpit, which I suppose count more as inspirational decoration, you won't see any in this cathedral. That's one of the more obvious legacies of the Reformation. You'll see niches that were *designed* for statues—this was a Roman Catholic church until Henry VIII came along—but they're all empty. There's one up there."

Templeton turned his gaze where his godson pointed, but the long, arched niche in the column above was, indeed, vacant—and no gargoyles anywhere in the vicinity.

"How is it, then, that there's a statue of Saint Patrick?" he asked. "Is that because he's our national saint?"

"Probably." Marcus led past a plaque listing previous deans. "Besides, it may not be Saint Patrick at all. It's probably made from pieces of two different statues, of different dates. But it makes a good story. Visitors like to *think* that it's Saint Patrick—and if that strengthens faith, in any way, I don't suppose one can argue."

"I suppose not," Templeton said thoughtfully. "Actually, they seem to have memorials, where we'd have statues of saints and stations of the Cross."

"Good observation," Marcus said. "But don't assume that they aren't Catholic, just because they don't acknowledge the authority of the Pope. That just makes them not *Roman* Catholic. At least that's what Cáit tells me. They pray the same Creed that we do, and acknowledge 'one holy, catholic, and apostolic church.'"

"I'm aware of that," Templeton replied. "But we *are* different, Marcus."

"Of course we are," Marcus agreed, "but maybe not as

different as a lot of folk would have us believe—and I say that not just because I'm keeping company with a Protestant. It seems to me that too many people forget about the true message of Christianity, and get all hung up in . . . in the design of the uniforms worn by the messengers who deliver it."

"Humph," said Templeton, declining to get into a theological debate—though he found himself wondering how Paddy would respond to such a notion. Actually, it sounded like something he would have said. Paddy, too, had talked about messengers—which made sense if he was, as he said, formerly an avenging angel. Nor had he seemed particularly concerned about denominational distinctions—which was somewhat disquieting, if he really was God's messenger. Templeton wasn't sure he wanted to believe that the differences really didn't matter.

Of course, none of it might be real. . . .

Determined to keep his eyes open for gargoyles, Templeton followed along dutifully as Marcus led him past a succession of brasses and marble plaques and other memorials lining the south aisle, pointing out an occasional familiar name. Just before they reached the transept, they briefly had to stand aside so a double file of fresh-faced boy choristers could pass, wearing choir cassocks of an unusual shade of soft, greyed blue.

"Apparently that was live music, when we came in," Marcus said, noticing his godfather's scrutiny of the blue cassocks. "They must be practicing for Christmas. Are you wondering about the color?

"It's called Patrick's blue, from the Order of Saint Patrick," he went on, at Templeton's nod. "We'll see the banners of the last knights hanging above the stalls in the choir. If you see a clergyman with a bit of that color piping at his collar, he'd be a canon of the cathedral. And the dean gets to wear the cathedral seal at his throat on ceremonial occasions, suspended from a watered-silk ribbon of Patrick's blue. It makes a nice connection with the cathedral's history."

"True enough," Templeton agreed, as they continued into the south transept. "What, exactly, is a dean, anyway? I've always wondered."

"Hmm, near as I can figure out, in very simple terms, he's the chap who's actually in charge of a cathedral—sort of *in loco episcopus,* if that's the correct Latin. It goes back to monastic days, and chapters of monks and such. Sometimes I'm not sure if even Anglicans fully understand how it all works."

Templeton snorted, idly wondering whether Paddy understood it. "Did you pick all that up from Cáit?"

"Some of it. Come on and I'll show you that statue of Saint Patrick."

They inspected the statue and several memorials in the south transept, then reentered the south aisle and continued to its end, where a chest-high screen and gate of iron and brass closed off a small side chapel and a much larger one off to the left. The frontal on the side altar bore a green eight-pointed cross, indicating its dedication to the Order of Saint Lazarus, a chivalric order similar to Templeton's own Knights of Malta.

"That's the Lady Chapel, over there," Marcus said, indicating the large, bright chapel area behind the high altar. "It looks like you have to enter it from around the other side. And *that*," he said, pointing to a large, thronelike chair set just inside velvet ropes, "is the chair in which William III is said to have parked his royal backside when he visited the cathedral, shortly after the Battle of the Boyne."

"I suppose even King Billy had to sit somewhere," Templeton remarked. "Looks comfortable enough."

"Only if you don't mind being bit in the butt by horsehair poking through the upholstery!" Marcus said playfully, turning to gesture Templeton back the way they had come. "Come on, and we'll have a look at the choir now. I've saved the best until last."

Though Templeton thought to himself that "the best" would have been a gargoyle or two, he listened dutifully to Marcus's thumbnail description of the Order of Saint Patrick.

"It was equivalent to the Order of the Bath in England or the Order of the Thistle in Scotland," Marcus told him, as they passed under a lectern in the form of a great brass eagle, just beside the entrance to the choir, whose wings supported the desk from which the scriptures were read. "Not nearly as old, of course, and defunct now, but the banners are still here."

His gesture swept upward as they came before the iron and brass gates leading into the choir. The lofty space beyond was a serene and harmonious melding of light and dappled shadow, color and curve, its sweep drawing the eye upward from the rich, variegated tones of tiled floor and mellow oaken stalls, past the carved canopies of the knights' stalls to the arched colonnades and the open, airy grace of the Gothic vaulting above. The whole afforded a fitting frame for the high altar and the arched vista into the Lady Chapel behind it.

Utterly enchanted, Templeton cast his gaze more lingeringly over the carved oak of the choir stalls, each end finished with Gothic tracery and capped with a finial in the shape of an intricate fleur-de-lis. Brass candlesticks shaded with glass marched along the slanted desks of the first two rows, to light the choristers' music. The back row on each side comprised the former stalls of the Knights of Saint Patrick, each Gothic canopy adorned with a crested helm and sword—and above, the banners of the last knights, the rich colors hardly dimmed by dust or the passage of time.

"If you come for Evensong," Marcus said with a sly grin, "they usually let you sit behind the choristers, up in the stalls. It's a shame that sung offices are a tradition we've mostly lost in the Roman Church, other than in monastic settings."

Templeton nodded distractedly, turning his gaze toward a quest for silver on or around the high altar, which was dressed for Advent with a handsome frontal of purple brocade, banded with dark blue velvet. There were two sizable silver candlesticks and a simple, rather modern-looking gilt cross on a ledge behind the altar—actually, on the top of the wall dividing the chancel from the Lady Chapel farther east—but no other silver that he could see. He wondered if that was because of the recent burglary or because it wasn't ordinarily kept out, other than during services. Beyond, the stained glass of the Lady Chapel windows was aglow in the afternoon sun.

"You're right about this looking a lot like a Catholic

church," he said to Marcus in a low voice, though the brass altar rail, with its Gothic arches, was a feature rarely seen in a Catholic church in recent years. Yet another of the casualties of Vatican II, along with Latin and Friday fish and ladies' hats, so lamented the day before by Paddy the gargoyle, not to mention Saint Christopher and a slew of other "defrocked" saints.

Reminded again of gargoyles, Templeton cast his gaze upward once more—and let it pass along what appeared to be a shadowy gallery corridor screened behind a row of double Gothic arches, just above the great arch that looked into the Lady Chapel. And above it ran a second, narrower passage, at the level of the five graceful stained glass windows lighting the east end of the choir.

Now, *those* were interesting. If the cathedral did have a gargoyle, and it wanted to prowl inside the building that it guarded, Templeton reckoned that such passageways might be the way to do it.

If a gargoyle could fit through them. The lower gallery appeared reasonably accommodating, but he wasn't sure about the upper one. However, they did seem to run along the sides of the choir as well, and back into the nave, he noted, as he turned to scan.

"The organ is up there," Marcus said, seeing the direction of his gaze, and gesturing toward the north side of the choir. "And let me show you the spiral stair that gives access to the organ-loft. Have you seen enough here?"

Templeton nodded and let Marcus conduct him toward the north transept, still casting surreptitious glances up at the intramural passages. This part of the cathedral had a military focus, with tattered regimental colors displayed just below the galleries on all three walls, in tribute to the war dead of many an old Irish regiment—like the Knights' banners, yet another legacy of Ireland's colonial past. Quite possibly, there were colors from Templeton's old regiment, the 8th Hussars, but that wasn't why he had come here. Noble pairs of carved hounds slept at the foot of two cenotaphs set against the north wall, flanking a large Celtic memorial cross—more Watchers, perhaps?—but again, Templeton didn't know whether Watchers were placed inside buildings.

Profoundly unsatisfied, Templeton found himself continuing to search the upper reaches of the cathedral as he and Marcus moved back along the north aisle and headed toward the rear of the building, scanning more of the narrow gallery walkways running the length of the nave, just above the taller arches that supported the vaulting and divided the nave from the two side aisles—clerestory arches, he thought they were called.

And truly excellent vantage points for a guardian gargoyle.

But how to get up there to look?

Templeton was pondering this imponderable when he nearly wandered into a group of tourists clumped around a young man in a verger's purple cassock, who was telling them about an ornate memorial far at the back of the cathedral, erected to a seventeenth-century Earl of Cork. Templeton murmured an apology, and was about to ease on past, when he realized that the man had a beauty of a black eye and one hand bandaged.

Good Lord, could this be the very verger whom Paddy had mentioned, roughed up by the two who had stolen the alms basins? Did he know yet that the items had been recovered? (*Had* the items been recovered? Had they even been stolen?)

The man's presence here in the cathedral was Templeton's first real evidence that he had not just imagined the events of the previous day. *He,* at least, was real.

But how much of yesterday was fact, and how much fanciful embellishment? How much did the man know? Did Templeton even dare to speak to him, especially with Marcus present? He mustn't mention gargoyles, of course, but perhaps he *could* at least find out whether the part about the burglary was true.

Chapter 8

"Marcus, I think that's the man I saw outside the cathedral yesterday," Templeton whispered, catching his godson's sleeve and repeating the half-lie he had concocted earlier.

"Looks like he got mugged," Marcus whispered back.

"I wonder if we could speak to him," Templeton said. "I'm dying to find out what happened."

"Suit yourself," Marcus replied. "But don't you think we should let him finish his tour first?"

"Let's tag along, then. We can listen to the rest of his spiel, and then buttonhole him."

Nodding good-naturedly, Marcus let himself be drawn into the back of the group of tourists, who were meandering toward the baptistery, right beside the exit. Beyond the tourists, Templeton could see a Christmas creche with knee-high figures.

"Now, I mentioned earlier that St. Patrick's has no undercroft or crypts," the young verger was saying. "That's because, in medieval times, the River Poddle ran right by the front of the cathedral, out where Patrick Street is now. I also told you that, in other churches, undercrofts and crypts tend to be among the oldest parts, since successive new churches were usually built on older foundations, and often incorporated older parts of the building. That's certainly the case at the other very old churches here in Dublin: Christ Church Cathedral, St. Werburgh's, St. Michan's. At St. Patrick's, however, the water table is too high. Any undercroft or crypt would have been flooded—so we have none, and never have had.

"That being said, this is the oldest remaining part of the original cathedral that Archbishop Comyn built in 1191," he continued. "It was probably the entrance, and it may have been built on the site traditionally associated with Saint Patrick and his well, where he baptized his first converts in this area. You can see him depicted in the center of the three lancet windows there in the west wall. This association with Patrick makes it entirely appropriate that this area should eventually become the baptistery for the cathedral erected here. And at this time of year, as you can see, it also houses our Christmas creche, which is set up each year by the children of the choir school across the road.

"The stone font is medieval, but I'm afraid we don't know much else about it. The floor tiles, however, are believed to be the oldest in the cathedral. They were found under some later flooring in a part of the south transept, during restoration work done in the 1800's, and reset here. The encaustic tiles in the rest of the cathedral are reproductions laid in 1882. The designs are based on other medieval tiles also found in the south transept." He glanced around his audience. "Does anyone have any questions?"

There were a few. Templeton waited in the background with Marcus until the tourists had finished and begun to disperse. As the last one drifted off and the young verger glanced at him in inquiry, Templeton moved in closer.

"Sorry I only caught the tail end of your tour," he said apologetically. "This is my first visit." He nodded toward the black eye and bandaged hand. "Hard duty, guarding a cathedral?"

The young man gave him a sour grin. "Harder than you might imagine. We had a break-in here, early yesterday morning. I had the bad luck to tangle with a couple of the culprits. Got a few stitches for my trouble, too," he added, lifting his bandaged hand.

"Hmm, battle wounds in the service of the King of Kings," Templeton said with a faint smile. And then, in explanation, "Sorry, I'm a Knight of Malta, so I tend to think in images of chivalry. Did they get away with much?"

"Yeah, two of the big Georgian silver alms basins that we put out on the altar for major feast days. Amazing thing is, the guards got them back before the end of the day. The dean announced it this morning, right after Matins."

"I guess we're more efficient than I sometimes think," Marcus murmured, shrugging as the man glanced at him questioningly. "I'm with the gardaí. We aren't usually that lucky. This is my godfather. Apparently he was driving past when the ambulance guys were taking care of you, and asked me this morning whether I knew anything about it."

"Were you, now?" The verger glanced from Marcus to Templeton. "Well, I'm honor-bound to tell you that, technically speaking, it wasn't the guards who recovered them. A lorry driver collared the culprits, and a parking enforcement lady called the guards. There was a bit of confusion, as you can imagine. But at least they got the silver back. And well done, *whoever* was responsible."

Templeton agreed that the recovery was, indeed, a good and amazing thing, greatly relieved that no monstrous black Rolls Royce car had been mentioned, and asked whether the silver was back in the cathedral yet.

"No, but we've been promised it will be returned in time for services in the morning," the verger said, as the clock in the tower began striking the hour. "Tomorrow is our big carol service for the last Sunday of Advent. We like to bring out a lot of the good silver, since it's sort of a preview for the traditional Christmas Eve service. Helps set the festive mood. We've had to institute a ticket system for Christmas Eve itself, because so many people want to attend, and those who can't get tickets tend to come tomorrow, so they can still hear the music."

The clock finished striking as he spoke. After a few seconds' pause, the other bells started ringing rounds, their tuned voices tumbling down the scale in halting but exuberant succession.

"That's bell practice starting," the verger said, noting that both his listeners had cocked their ears to the sound. "They practice ringing most Saturday afternoons. We have fourteen bells, though they aren't all rung anymore. Some of them are very old. If you want to know more than that, I'm afraid you'd have to talk to one of the bell-ringers."

"Could I do that?" Templeton asked, on impulse, for it had occurred to him that if a gargoyle lived in the bell tower, this was a good excuse to get closer. Besides, the bell-ringers might know if there was a gargoyle somewhere on the roof.

Marcus raised an eyebrow, but the verger looked nonplused.

"Sure. I'll see if you can go up," he said. "They usually don't mind a visitor or two. I'm sure someone would be glad to tell you more about things."

"Please," Templeton said. "I'd like that."

When the verger had disappeared through a nearby doorway, gathering the skirts of his purple robe to head up a narrow spiral stair, Marcus glanced at his godfather.

"Are you sure you want to go up there?" he asked. "It'll be a stiff climb."

"I'll take it easy," Templeton said, considering explanations that would sound plausible to Marcus. "It's something I've always wanted to do. I've never been in a bell tower before."

"Actually, neither have I."

The verger poked his head out the arched doorway a few minutes later and summoned them with a nod.

"Good news. I can take you up. Watch out, though, or they'll try to sign you up. It's a pretty esoteric occupation, ringing. They're always looking for new recruits.

"Oh, I'm afraid I'm past that, son," Templeton replied, falling in behind the young man and starting to climb. "I'm eighty-two years old."

"Don't let *that* stop you!" the verger said over his shoulder. "The bells are pretty heavy, but ringing doesn't require much physical strength. Kids as young as ten or twelve do it, girls as well as boys. The hardest part is getting up there. The tricky bit is memorizing the sequences of changes. You happen to remember a Dorothy Sayers mystery written in the thirties, called *The Nine Tailors*."

"I've heard of it."

"I've read it," Marcus chimed in, from behind Templeton.

"Well, then, you'll know that the story's premise pivots on change-ringing. That's where a lot of people first hear about it, unless they've lived near where bells are rung—and even then, they rarely bother finding out more about it. Most people assume that it's all electronic, these days. But the ringers will tell you all about that, if you ask them. They ring from a special ringing room, and the bells themselves are in a separate chamber above that."

Templeton said nothing, saving his breath so he could concentrate on climbing. The stairs seemed steeper with every step. Maybe it hadn't been such a good idea to attempt this long climb—but he was determined to find out if there were any gargoyles on the tower.

The turnpike stair ascended in a tight clockwise spiral encased in one corner of the bell tower, and was quite steep, the steps uneven from centuries of use. Templeton kept one hand on the central newel post and the other on the outer wall of the stairwell as they climbed, increasingly forced to use those as handholds to pull himself up. Marcus followed right behind, watching him somewhat anxiously. Several times, they passed arched doorways heading off into the fabric of the building, perhaps giving access to the intramural walkways Templeton had noticed from the cathedral floor.

He had to pause for breath about two-thirds of the way up, casting a reassuring glance back at Marcus. Right after he started climbing again, the bells began to fall silent, one by one, until only a single bell continued two or three more times on its own before likewise going mute.

"They're just taking a break," the verger called down to them. "They'll start again in a minute or two. There are always some fairly new ringers at practice sessions, so they ring short sequences when they're first learning."

Templeton only nodded and kept climbing, relieved to see the verger disappear at last into another of the arched doorways. When he reached it himself, his chest was a little tight and he was still breathing hard—he could even hear Marcus puffing behind him—but the young verger was waiting to offer him a hand into the large, square chamber beyond.

"You all right?" he asked.

"Yeah, I'll be fine," Templeton said.

Beyond, there were six or eight people standing in an irregular semicircle under as many long ropes snaking down from small, neat holes in the room's ceiling. A few more ropes were swagged to the side, out of the way. The dangling ropes all had thick, fuzzy handgrips of red, white, and blue, about a yard long, on the parts above the ringers' heads. "Tails" of plain rope continued below. Several of the ringers were testing the height of the handgrips, some of them adjusting shallow, carpet-covered boxes beneath their assigned bell ropes. A few were already standing on such boxes.

"You can watch from over here," the verger said as he ushered Templeton and Marcus to some straight-backed chairs under one of the chamber's narrow lancet windows. "Enjoy yourselves."

As the newcomers sat down, the movement underneath the bell ropes gradually ceased, the ringers settling with both hands on the fuzzy handholds above their heads and the tails of rope looped up with their left hands.

"Look to," said a middle-aged man to the far left of the lineup—which apparently was a signal that they were about to begin, for all eyes flicked in his direction. "Treble's ready," the man said then, starting to pull gently on his rope. "Treble's going . . . she's gone."

As he said it, all the others followed suit in clockwise order, according to some arcane protocol probably best understood only by other bell-ringers. Templeton couldn't tell whether the leader's bell had been the first to sound, but he did quickly notice that each sequence of ringing started with the lightest bell and descended down the scale.

"If I remember my Dorothy Sayers," Marcus said beside him, "I think this is called 'rounds'—when they simply ring in descending order, treble to tenor, and keep repeating. If they intend to progress to changes, then pretty soon—and I have no idea how they know when to start, or how they do it—they should begin changing places in the ringing order, two bells at a time—whence comes the term 'change-ringing.' The ringing sequence for each individual bell is a mathematical progression—and *that,* I'm afraid, is just about the extent of my knowledge on the subject."

Templeton managed a nod and a tight smile and rubbed distractedly at his left arm, listening closely for variations.

Soon he caught a subtle shift in the order of ringing. The bells weren't as loud as he'd expected, muffled by the ceiling of the ringing chamber between them and the belfry above, but they certainly discouraged idle conversation. Besides, there was a sign tacked to one section of the room's old linenfold wainscoting that said Silence During Ringing.

Arched wooden plaques elsewhere on the walls told of famous peals rung from the tower in the last several centuries, with incomprehensible names like Treble Bob Majors, Grandsire Triples, and Caters. A "peal" apparently consisted of something in excess of five thousand separate changes of sequence, and could take three hours or more. One that particularly caught Templeton's fancy told of a muffled peal of Grandsire Caters rung on nine bells plus the tenor, on January 26, 1901, as a last token of respect for Queen Victoria. The feat had taken more than four hours.

Another sign gave statistics on each of the bells. Their very names sounded like a litany of prayer: Latin phrases like *Venite Adoremus*—Come let us worship—and *Te Laudamus*—We praise Thee—and *Te Glorificamus*—We glorify Thee. The Treble, which always started the peals, was called *Sursum Corda*—Lift up your hearts—a fitting name, Templeton decided, for the leader of bells dedicated to calling the faithful to worship and singing the glory of God.

Which was all quite interesting, if somewhat outside Templeton's previous experience, but it had nothing directly to do with gargoyles. Nor dared he *be* direct. But at least he was up here.

Now he simply had to find a way to inquire about gargoyles without anybody thinking it was odd. Because if the cathedral really did have gargoyles—or *a* gargoyle—he or they were apt to be up here somewhere. He certainly hadn't seen any down in the nave.

As the bells continued to ring, he found himself considering whether he might even be able to gain access to them by way of one of the passageways he suspected lay through some of those doorways he had noticed on the way up.

Chapter 9

Exploration of those passageways might, indeed, have yielded further enlightenment on the subject of gargoyles, for the clerestory level was Paddy's favorite haunt when not on duty outside, behind his tower parapet. So long as they took care not to be seen, gargoyles were quite free to prowl the precincts of the buildings they guarded, no matter the phase of the moon. The narrow gallery passages circling the upper nave and transept afforded numerous discreet vantage points from which he could observe.

Paddy counted himself particularly fortunate to be guarding a great cathedral, especially one with as long and distinguished a history as St. Patrick's. He never tired of watching the cathedral at work—and the Advent season was perhaps his favorite time of year.

The liturgical cycle had two great seasons of preparation, when the Church paused to anticipate its greatest feasts. Neither had full meaning without the other. The observances of Lent, leading up to Easter, were more solemn and penitential, intended to focus man's meditations on sacrifice and redemption and the astonishing Mystery of the Resurrection; but the parallel season of Advent was a time of anticipation and promise, awaiting the wonder of the Incarnation, the Word made Flesh, a celebration second only to Easter in the Church's yearly cycle of prayer and praise.

On this eve of the Fourth Sunday of Advent, the last before Christmas, Paddy's cathedral was preparing to welcome the Child foretold by the prophet Isaiah: "Behold, a virgin shall conceive, and shall bring forth a son, and they shall call His name Emanuel, which means 'God is with us.'" The morrow would see that ancient prophecy moving toward fulfillment. The words of Saint Luke's Gospel also recalled the role of one of Paddy's angelic colleagues.

In the sixth month the angel Gabriel was sent from God unto a city of Galilee, named Nazareth, to a virgin espoused to a man whose name was Joseph, of the house of David; and the virgin's name was Mary. . . .

On each of the three preceding Sundays, counting off the weeks until the Child should be reborn, an additional candle had been lit on the Advent wreath—purple, to mark the time of reflection, but tomorrow's candle would be pink, in anticipation of the joy to come. A few days ago, Paddy had watched the children from the Choir School set up the Christmas creche in the baptistery: the empty stable with its empty manger, which would become the throne of God made Man. It was an old, old story being remembered here: of a little human family journeying toward a destiny in Bethlehem, two millennia ago, touched by a Divine Grace that transcended even the more general miracle surrounding the conception of any new life.

The season itself, of course, was even older than the story being retold within these walls. Long before the coming of the Son, humankind had awaited and welcomed the rebirth of the Sun, one of the earliest of the symbols on which humankind had seized, as a physical embodiment of the One Who had brought it and all creation into being. This season of the winter solstice marked the pivot-point on the wheel of the year, the reversal of lengthening nights and ever shorter days, affirming the promise of reborn Light and the eventual coming of spring. Even the babes in arms seemed somehow caught up in the awe of this ever-magical time of year.

The preparations of the coming week, in the final run up to Christmas itself, would bring their own unique magic, heralded by the morrow's special observances. Still to come were the decorations to be set in place by the ladies from the Altar Guild: the fragrant swags of evergreen, and flowering poinsettia plants, and wreaths of fir and holly on all the pillars. Christmas Eve would see the cathedral drenched with candlelight, and aglitter with the twinkling fairy lights on the big Christmas tree to be erected behind the altar, in the Lady Chapel.

And above the creche, with its figures of the Holy Family and shepherds and wise men—though not yet with the Holy Child in the manger—a *papier mâché* representation of a herald angel suspended by wires above the stable roof. That was one of Paddy's favorite parts.

Of course, the figure looked very little like holy Gabriel, who probably had made more recorded appearances before humans than any other angel of the Heavenly Host. But Paddy knew that the artists had done their best, with only frail human imagination to supply the details they could not see through the heavenly glory. Paddy himself had been present at that first Christmas, along with every other angel under heaven, to sing the miracle of the birth of the Prince of Peace, at that midnight hour when, for a hushed eternity of suspension outside time and space, there had been no need for avenging angels or even guardian gargoyles.

The clock in the old tower began to strike the hour, jarring Paddy from his fond remembrance of that long ago night. Crouched in one of the galleries of the south transept, he had been gazing back idly in the direction of the baptistery, with its creche and *papier mâché* figures; but as the clock finished striking three and gave way to bell-practice, he suddenly realized that one of the men walking across the far end of the nave with young Philip Kelly was none other than his friend of the previous day, Francis Templeton.

Good Lord, how had that happened? How had Templeton gotten here without Paddy seeing him? The approach of the old Rolls Royce should have raised instant alarms, for Paddy purposely had not neutralized the little gargoyle mascot on the car's radiator cap, on the chance that circumstances might permit future partnerships. The only answer had to be that Templeton had not come here in the old Rolls Royce.

An even more important question was *why* Templeton had come. Furthermore, he seemed to have someone else with him: a tall, good-looking young man who carried himself like a soldier or a policeman.

As Paddy watched in astonishment, young Kelly left the pair and disappeared through the door leading up to the bell tower. Not only did Templeton and his friend show no sign of leaving, or even continuing to wander the cathedral—for Templeton had mentioned the day before that he had never been inside—but they drifted purposefully in the direction where Kelly had disappeared, deep in conversation.

Did they mean to go up into the bell tower? Worse, had Templeton told his companion about his experience of the day before?

It took Paddy several anxious minutes to thread his way back through the maze of intramural passages until he reached the one that led to the tower. By then, Templeton and his companion were climbing the tower stair behind young Kelly. Paddy was working his way closer to the level of the ringing room, which was certainly the destination of the three, when he very nearly blundered into an old acquaintance who rarely made an appearance right here in the cathedral.

He did a double take at the form his angelic colleague had taken today, kitted out in a fine three-piece suit, looking for all the world like a prosperous banker or solicitor. Those assigned as Death's Deputies never used their own names or forms, but Paddy knew this one from time immemorial.

"What are you doing here?" Paddy blurted, though he had a sinking feeling that he already knew the answer.

The other inclined a graceful countenance that resembled several matinee idols currently enjoying popularity in mortal circles.

"I was sent for Templeton," Death said. "I would have taken him on the stairs, but then I realized that you were nearby. I prefer to be mannerly, when intruding on a colleague's territory."

"Oh, please don't take him yet!" Paddy protested. "He's a nice old man."

"'Old' being the operative word," Death replied. "'Nice' has nothing to do with it. Besides, you know the rules. He saw your true form."

"That was an accident!"

"Accident or no, he saw you."

"He wouldn't tell."

"Maybe not. But maybe he has already. Besides, he was already booked for Transition. His wife asked to have him Home for Christmas. He's known for quite a while that his time was growing short."

"Well—Christmas is still nearly a week away. He was really helpful yesterday. Does he have to go right away?"

"He certainly should," Death replied. "I have a busy schedule for the holidays. I hadn't planned on an extra trip.

It's easier for all of us if I just take him when he goes back down the stairs."

"But—he was supposed to have at least a bit more time," Paddy pleaded. "Please reconsider. It's my fault. It isn't fair that he should be penalized. If you don't want to make a second trip, let *me* handle it."

"Are you sure you could manage it?" Death said doubtfully.

"I've taken people before."

"Yeah, Vikings and other bad guys. That doesn't take much finesse. I thought you liked this Templeton."

"I do."

"And you can be subtle?" Death asked. "I was going to be quick about it. You know he has a bad heart."

"I can think of something," Paddy said. "I'd just like to not be responsible for cutting his time any more than it has to be. I know you have your orders—but we have flexibility as well."

Death frowned, glancing impatiently at the stairwell beyond, and then back at Paddy.

"How long was he with you yesterday?"

"All day—six or seven hours, probably."

"All right. You know that, in such cases, we usually take people within twenty-four hours, but the rules do allow us some leeway. I can give him a day for every hour he spent in your company. Will that make you happier?"

Paddy managed a grim gargoyle smile.

"It's the best I—or he—could hope for. I won't let you down."

"Just be certain you don't let Him down," Death replied,

glancing upward. "If everybody lived beyond their allotted span, the overcrowding on Earth would be even worse than it already is. I want him before the New Year, understand?"

"I understand," Paddy agreed.

Chapter 10

While Paddy and Death's Deputy were discussing Templeton's fate, Templeton himself had found an opportunity to inquire obliquely about gargoyles.

"I don't suppose there are any gargoyles on this cathedral, are there?" he asked, after one of the girl bell-ringers had given him and Marcus a quick tour of the ringing room, during a break between "touches," as the short sequences of ringing were called.

"Not that I know of," she said, "though you'd think a Gothic cathedral would have them, wouldn't you? I wish there were. I'd draw them, if I found any."

It emerged that the girl was studying architecture at

University College Dublin, and liked sketching details of medieval and Georgian buildings.

"There's a little one on the front of the Unitarian Church in Stephen's Green," she said. "I did quite a nice sketch of him. And there are some gargoyle heads on a church over in Sandymount—actually, on the chimney of the vestry. There's a dragon, too. But I think they're all technically what are called 'grotesques.' Strictly speaking, a gargoyle has to be a functional drain spout."

Templeton nodded, thinking that Paddy had not looked at all like a drain spout of any variety, though he had certainly been functional enough when he roughed up the two thieves.

"No, I don't suppose there are many of those," he allowed.

"No, I can only think of two here in Dublin—and they're modern."

"Modern gargoyles? Really?" Marcus said.

"Yeah, they're on a block of flats not far from here—faces of the North and South Winds, with their cheeks puffed out to blow—a nice touch of humor. The man who did them is also a former Dublin City Architect."

"I think I might have met him once," Templeton said. "Did he design the Garden of Remembrance?"

"That's the man." She grinned. "Did you know he's got all the bits in his garden from the original entrance portico to the old Abbey Theatre?"

"You mean, that was saved?" Marcus said, incredulous. "I *loved* the old Abbey! I know they needed a bigger theatre, but I was really sorry to see it knocked down."

"Well, he has every piece, all numbered," she replied. "Most of the rubble went for landfill, as so often happens, but he persuaded them to number the portico stones and dump them in his garden instead. Rescued some playbills and posters from the lobby, too. His dream is to see the portico reconstructed as part of the museum complex that's going in at the old Collins Barracks. He'd like it to be part of a display on Ireland's theatre heritage—once everybody can agree on exactly where to put it. But thank God for people like him, or most of the city would soon be torn down and replaced with modern monstrosities—'carbuncles,' as the Prince of Wales once referred to them. Look what happened at Wood Quay."

Templeton only rolled his eyes. Excavations at Wood Quay had revealed remains of the oldest and most extensive Viking settlement yet discovered in the Dublin area, but all of it was now buried under two hideously modern office blocks between Christ Church Cathedral and the Liffey. A local priest who had led the campaign to save Wood Quay had ended up bankrupt and in jail over the affair.

He would have liked to continue the discussion—especially the talk about gargoyles—but the ringers were beginning to organize themselves for another touch, and their informant was being summoned to one of the bells.

"Well, thank you for taking the time to show us around," he said. "I suppose we ought to go back downstairs, and let you folk ring in peace."

"If you can call it that, when these bells get going," the girl said with a grin, taking up position. "You're welcome to stay if you like."

"Thanks, but we'd better be going."

"Look to," said the man on the treble bell, starting his pull. "Treble's going . . . she's gone!"

Again the bells far above began to ring in rounds, their sound becoming muffled as Marcus ducked first into the stairwell and Templeton followed after, closing the door behind him. It was easier going down, though they had to tread carefully on the worn stone steps, keeping their balance with a hand on the center newel and outer wall. When they reached the bottom, Marcus stood aside and waited for Templeton to emerge, giving him a curious look.

"*Gargoyles*?" he asked, raising an eyebrow.

"It was just a thought," Templeton replied a little testily. "A Gothic cathedral should have gargoyles."

"And here I thought you wanted to find out about bells," Marcus said. "But you weren't interested in bells at all, were you?"

"I told you I wanted to go up in a bell tower," Templeton said, "and I did! Now, will you let it drop?"

"Suit yourself," Marcus replied.

They spoke of other things as they made their way out of the cathedral, but Templeton's garda godson was not altogether happy with the exchange, and wondered what was really going on.

Paddy, meanwhile, had sped to the bell tower stair after bidding adieu to Death's Deputy. He thought it unlikely that more humans would be climbing up to the belfry during ringing practice, so he hid himself just beyond the curve of the spiral stair, where it continued on past the ringing room to the bell chamber, and waited for Templeton to leave. He wondered who the younger man was who had accompanied him—and wondered what on earth had brought him to the cathedral.

It could not be mere chance—not after their adventure of the day before. By Templeton's own admission, he had never been in the cathedral before. While it was just possible that the old man had been drawn to the cathedral by Death—for climbing the bell tower stair would have been an apt way to trigger the heart attack that was likely to cause his demise—Paddy had to wonder whether, by some quirk of fate, Templeton had been seeking Paddy himself.

He watched as the younger man and then Templeton started carefully down the worn stairs, following silently, ready to duck into one of the intervening doorways if he detected sounds of someone else coming down—though that was not likely during bell-ringing practice. He had checked from above, in the space between the ceiling of the ringing room and the floor of the belfry itself, and everyone still in the room was ringing a bell. Nor could anyone else come up the stair until Templeton and his companion had reached the bottom.

But though he listened carefully, the pair said little as they descended—and he dared not follow them back into the cathedral, though he zipped back up to the first-level gallery and watched them heading toward the exit. They were talking then, and Templeton seemed somewhat agitated about whatever they were discussing, but even Paddy's keen gargoyle hearing could not pick out their words. He streaked back up to the parapet that was his usual outdoor guard post in time to see them getting into a little red car, not the big Rolls Royce of the day before.

He spent the rest of the day brooding, wondering what had provoked the visit—and regretting that, by his own moment of impetuous intervention, he now was bound to be the death of the old man.

The cathedral's day wound down. There was no sung Evensong on Saturdays—the one day off for the boy choristers from the choir school across the street—but because it was close to Christmas, even said Evensong was well attended. Thoughtful tourists, wishing to experience the cathedral at work, mingled with folk ending their day of shopping with half an hour of serenity before plunging back into the mad dash of preparations for Christmas. Many of them, Paddy knew, actually took the time to think about what Christmas really meant.

He watched and listened, as he usually did, from one of the narrow galleries running the length of the nave. It was too risky to watch from above the choir, because the choir stalls faced inward. Sundays were all right, because only the choristers and clergy were seated in the stalls, and they were always intent on their music or their readings, or else focused on what was happening at the altar; but during the week, other worshippers seated behind the choir often turned their gaze upward, especially visiting tourists, letting their eyes feast on the beauty of the cathedral while their ears partook of the beauty of the voices raised in praise of God. On Saturdays, with no choir to hold their attention, the eyes of secular worshippers were even more inclined to wander upward; and one of the first instructions to any gargoyle, on taking up his post, was not to let himself be seen without good reason.

Accordingly, Paddy lurked in the gallery on the north side of the nave, glad to see young Philip Kelly at his verger's post, taking particular comfort from the collect that the priest offered just before the final blessing.

"O God, from whom all holy desires, all good judgments, and all just works proceed: Give to Your servants that peace which the world cannot give, that our hearts may be set to obey Your commandments, and that we, being defended from the fear of our enemies, may pass our time in rest and quietness; through Christ Jesus Your Son our Lord."

They were words conceived by humans to acknowledge what was essentially Inconceivable, at least within the limitations of human experience, but the prayer was one of the more heartfelt of those offered daily by beings ever stretching to understand and be in harmony with their place in God's plan for the universe. As a servant of that God in Whose honor this cathedral had been built, Paddy's understanding was at once more profound and more basic than that of the humans among whom he was charged to move, for angels were of a different magnitude of Creation than mortals.

Nonetheless, he found in the human words a measure of the peace being besought, and felt the benison of grace enfolding all present—for God always heard the prayers of His own. As Evensong ended and the clergy filed out of the choir, worshippers following in ragged groups, some lingering in the stillness, Paddy watched the ladies of the Altar Guild going about their business, preparing the altar for Sunday services the next morning. While they were working, a pair of gardaí came into the cathedral and returned the silver alms basins, which young Philip Kelly put out of sight in the aumbry cupboard to the right of the high altar, ready for use in the morning. By the time the tower clock struck eight o'clock, everyone else had left, the lights were out, and Kelly was locking up the last of the doors, up in the south choir aisle.

Heaving a heavy gargoyle sigh, Paddy descended to the cathedral floor, checked all the doors, then went up to his usual watching post behind the tower's parapet. Snow was falling again, muffling the city in a blanket of white, so he guessed that it probably would be a quiet night.

But he found his thoughts returning to Templeton as his gaze roved the slated rooftops and chimneys, watching the city wind down for the night. He had promised Death's Deputy that he would bring Templeton Home before the new year. Aside from having to decide how best to do it—for he was determined not to cause the old man undue distress—he didn't even know where Templeton lived, though he knew he could find out.

It couldn't be very far from the garage where Templeton kept the big black car, for he knew that the old man walked to get there. One of the Watchers in the area would probably know. And Paddy's secondment for duties outside his usual job description, as a deputy to Death's Deputy, meant that he was permitted to leave his post outside the normal times when gargoyles came together in conclave. He just had to make certain that he wasn't seen, especially in his true form. He didn't want anyone else being called Home prematurely, because they had seen what they oughtn't.

He was contemplating the various things Templeton had told him, about the things and people he had loved in his life and the things he enjoyed, when he sensed a benign intruder coming up the stair. Curious, he *whooshed* down to the door that led back into the bell chamber, and was surprised to see the wizened form of one of the monkeys from the old Kildare Street Club ascending the spiral stair. The monkeys served as messengers for the gargoyles, and had unrestricted mobility whenever it was needed for the performance of their duties.

"C.C. asks you meet him in crypt at Christ Church," the monkey said succinctly. "I watch here while you go."

Paddy furrowed his gargoyle brow. The monkeys were very junior in the gargoyle hierarchy, but a summons from the Christ Church gargoyle must be taken seriously.

"Do you know what he wants?" Paddy asked.

"He not say," the monkey replied. Monkeys did not waste their words. "City sleep. I watch."

Nodding agreement, Paddy went back up on the parapet, the monkey following, and scanned all around the cathedral. The city, indeed, was asleep, with few cars on the streets and virtually no pedestrians out in the snow. From their perch more than a hundred feet above the ground, Paddy could see the somewhat stubbier tower and steeple of Christ Church Cathedral a little over a quarter mile to the north, with the similar but smaller tower of St. Audoen's a little to the left. (All three churches had the stepped battlements peculiar to Irish architecture, and all three had notable peals of bells, though Paddy's were the finest.)

"I'll be back as soon as I can," Paddy said, comfortable enough to leave the monkey in charge. Monkeys couldn't actually do much if there was trouble, but they could certainly raise the alarm.

With that, his essence already outside the stone shell from which he usually watched, Paddy threw himself over the parapet, plunging earthward in a rush of velvet shadow, wings spreading just in time to make a gentle landing.

He had come down on the north side of the tower, so it was an easy matter to slip through the wrought-iron railings that divided churchyard from adjacent park and gain the shelter of St. Patrick's Well, where he landed lightly amid the rubble and trash at the bottom and squeezed through a drain, quickly gaining access to the ancient passageway connecting St. Patrick's to Christ Church. He needed no light to see, but the tips of his wings again struck sparks from the low ceiling as he raced along the passage.

In due course, he emerged in the southernmost part of the vast crypt beneath Christ Church Cathedral, where C.C. was waiting with the gargoyle of St. Audoen's, known as Audie. These two together with Paddy constituted the three senior-most gargoyles of the Dublin Watch.

"This looks serious," Paddy said, nodding to his two colleagues. "What's up?"

"Maybe trouble," C.C. said sourly. "You remember the news we heard about the break-in at St. Michan's, night before last?"

"Yes, of course."

"Well, we've had a query from Headquarters. They want to know if any heads were stolen."

"Heads?" Paddy said.

"Yeah, heads."

Paddy looked at the St. Audoen's gargoyle, but Audie just shrugged his heavy gargoyle shoulders.

"Well—do we *know*?" Paddy asked, turning back to the Christ Church gargoyle.

"No, we don't. But we'd jolly well better find out by to-morrow night, because Headquarters is sending someone Very Senior to hear all about it. An Extraordinary Conclave has been called. If we mess up, we could end up guard-ing—well, you don't wanta know."

Indeed, Paddy did not want to know anything about it. To lose his custodianship of St. Patrick's was unthinkable.

"All right," he said. "It sounds like we go over to St. Michan's and check things out."

Chapter 11

At least getting *to* St. Michan's did not present any difficulty. Though not used as often as the passageway Paddy had just travelled, there was a very ancient tunnel that ran all the way under the River Liffey from Christ Church, to emerge in one of the vaults beneath the more modest St. Michan's.

Cut-stone steps thick with the dust of centuries descended toward the river from the higher level of the cathedral undercroft. Brick-lined walls gave way to stone, and dust and cobwebs gave way to damp as the three gargoyles passed below the level of the riverbed.

They covered the fifty yards directly beneath the river with some alacrity, for none of them much liked being this far underground, and with the weight of a mighty river above their heads. Though unaffected by merely physical conditions of the material world—they were, after all, angels—their long exposure to human notions of corporeal discomfort lent haste to their passage.

Crouching low, wingtips scraping against the dripping ceiling of the tunnel, the three splashed their way through stagnant puddles that sometimes sloshed over taloned feet. Startled rats scurried before them at first, for intrusion was rare save by their own kind; but coming to no harm, the creatures soon paused to watch in fascination, instinctively sensing the angelic nature of these intruders into their subterranean realm.

Very quickly the three gargoyles reached the other side and sped up another steep, narrow stairway lined with stone. This led, in turn, into a more crudely executed passageway hewn from the rough limestone, running more or less on the level and ending, at last, in a small, vaulted chamber whose dirt floor was dry as death, and undisturbed for at least decades. Several sections of discarded wooden panelling leaning against the back wall of the chamber obscured the tunnel opening, and the other end was closed by a barred gate of iron.

Cautiously the three emerged from behind the panelling. Along both side walls, ancient coffins were stacked three- and four-deep, festooned with dust-heavy cobwebs, some of them still adorned with shreds of rotted velvet coverings or showing the remnants of painted decorations. A few had partially collapsed under the weight of the coffins above, leaving gaps through which bones and mummified remains could be seen, but there were no signs of damage other than from the passage of time.

"Well, just offhand, I'd say that this isn't the vault where the vandals worked their mischief," C.C. said, shuffling up to the barred gate and passing through it like butter through a sieve. "Doesn't look like there's been anybody down here in years."

"Well, there are five other vaults," Paddy said, following him into the corridor, which was studded with a full dozen barred gates, set in facing pairs. "I guess we'll have to check all of them, until we find out which one it was."

"Terrific," Audie grumbled, as they quickly began checking each of the remaining crypts in that vault. "A wonderful lead-up to Christmas. We get to go poking around where dead bodies should be left to sleep in peace—and just because a few lager louts got to feeling frisky. I liked it better in the old days, when we used to give the Vikings what-for. At least they did honest pillaging. Vandals these days just break things up for the fun of it, because they haven't got anything better to do."

"*I'll* give 'em something better to do, if I find out who did it," C.C. muttered.

With Audie uttering a deep gargoyle chortle of anticipatory delight, the three made their way to the steep stone stair that led out of the vault. Paddy went up first, pausing to peer out through the slit between the two heavy iron doors that closed the entrance from the outside, like a hatch. It was the most exposed of the five entrances that most people knew about, opening at the southernmost portion of the church's east face, which fronted onto Church Street, but at this hour, and with snow still falling, there was no one about. (Unlike most churches, St. Michan's was built on a T-plan rather than a cross, with the top of the T across the east end of the nave.)

"Okay, looks clear," Paddy said. "As I recall, the next vault is just around the corner of the building, but it's still a bit out in the open, so let's leave that one until last. With luck, we won't have to bother with it."

"Go," said C.C.

In a blink, Paddy had oozed through the crack like a sliver of shadow and whisked around to shelter in an angle of the building which could only be seen from the silent, snow-shrouded churchyard. Audie and C.C. arrowed after him. The entrances to two more of the vaults were nestled in the angle, close against the sides of the church and almost flush with the ground, the double iron doors of each piled with several inches of snow and secured both with internal locks and with padlocked chains through the handles. Neither, of course, was any deterrent to gargoyles.

"Either of you have a preference for which one to look at next?" Paddy asked softly.

"I'd look in the one on the left," said a small voice from behind them.

Being angels and therefore unaffected by physical danger, the reaction of the three gargoyles could not be described precisely as alarm, but they whirled quickly, nonetheless, to see—no one.

"I'm down here," said the voice, from close beside one of the ornate Victorian tombstones.

There, blending with the dappled shadows cast by a faraway streetlight, sat a small, very self-possessed grey and tan tabby cat with a white bib front, thick grey-and-black banded tail curled demurely around pristine white forepaws. A thin drizzle of white across one side of her muzzle gave the appearance of a permanent milk-splash. It looked to be quite a young cat.

"Ah," said Paddy, with a glance at his two colleagues. For cats, being accustomed to look at kings and princes and anything else they fancied, were little more impressed with angels, even in the guise of gargoyles. The grass-green gaze turned upward at the three of them was curious but not at all diffident, quite unfazed by their celestial origins.

Hunkering down beside the little animal, Paddy bent his great gargoyle head closer, well aware that cats, like most animals, needed no black mirror to see a gargoyle's true form.

"So, little one," he said softly, "why is it you think we should look in the one on the left?"

"Well, you're obviously here about that break-in a few nights ago," the cat replied.

"That's true," Paddy admitted. "I take it that you saw what went on?"

"Of course," said the cat. "I live in the next street, but this is where I hunt at night. And in the summertime, sometimes I go down into the vaults when the guides aren't looking. Occasionally, I do get locked in overnight," she conceded.

Flicking a furry ear, she paused to give a nonchalant lick to one paw and briefly groom the whiskers on that side. Paddy heard C.C. and Audie shifting impatiently behind him, but he knew better than to try to hurry a cat.

"There were three of them," the cat finally went on, after

finishing her whiskers. "Nasty little men they were, with big, clumpy boots and lots of stinky beer and cigarettes, but they didn't try to bother me. I don't think they saw me. It was really cold that night, and they were really drunk."

"I don't suppose you happened to go down there?" Audie said.

The cat looked at him somewhat disdainfully for presuming to interrupt her narrative, then pointedly returned her gaze to Paddy.

"It wouldn't have been very bright to do that while they were still there," she said somewhat haughtily. "I don't like smoke, and I didn't like the look of their boots. But naturally, I checked the place out after they'd gone. We cats have to know what's going on in our territory. They left a big mess. It was hours before anyone else came, after it got light. By then, it was time to go home for my breakfast."

C.C. snorted, and Audie only just contained a growl of gargoyle frustration, but Paddy controlled a gargoyle smile, signalling the others to let him handle this, and scrunched down closer to the cat's eye level. In the grand scheme of things, cats were very good at keeping their priorities straight; and as observers went, they were almost as good as Watchers, with the added advantage that they could move around.

"Probably a very wise decision," he agreed. "Good cat, we would be very grateful to have your services as guide down below, if you would be so kind as to assist us."

"I thought you'd never ask," the cat said happily, trotting over to the padlocked iron doors, tail like a question mark, where she swivelled her head around to glance expectantly among the three of them, mostly from upside down. "Are you going to make the chains fall away, like they talk about in the Big Book?" she asked eagerly.

"Why, how do you know about *that*, little one?" Paddy said in some surprise.

"Oh, I heard my human reading about it one time," the cat replied, as the three gargoyles moved closer to the pad-locked doors. "After supper, she likes me to sit on her lap while she reads aloud from this great Big Book. In the mornings, sometimes I sleep on it in the sun.

"Anyway, there was this fellow named Peter, I think she said it was, a long time ago, and one of your kind came and made his chains fall away." The cat cocked her head thoughtfully at Paddy. "Of course, I suppose you *could* just slip through the crack between the doors. But you should remember that I can't. Cats can't *really* walk through walls the way humans sometimes think we can."

"Indeed, not," said Paddy, "but you can be carried through." He leaned down and made a cradle of his huge gargoyle talons in invitation. "May I?"

With a little chirrup of delight, the cat bounded into his arms to snuggle happily against the great gargoyle chest, totally unafraid, her little body vibrating in an audible purr; for bliss lies within the compass of an angel's embrace. When Audie and C.C. had squeezed through the crack be-tween the two iron doors, Paddy followed them with his purring passenger, dropping lightly to the foot of the steep stair inside.

"It's really dark in here," the cat observed.

At the will of the gargoyles—for their small feline

friend could not see in total darkness the way they could—soft light flooded the vaulted chamber, emanating from the gargoyles themselves. This second vault was much shorter than the first one they had inspected, with only six arched crypts opening off it, three to either side. Five of these had barred screens with iron gates, but the sixth, the last on the left, was closed by only a flimsy grillwork of heavy wire.

"That's the one where they broke in," the cat said, jumping down from Paddy's embrace and trotting to the far end of the corridor. "They built a fire out here in the passageway, and littered the place with empty cans." She paused outside the wire grillwork and wrinkled her nose. "And they pawed at the dead humans in here. They bothered some of the others, too," she added, indicating the other crypts.

Scowling ferocious gargoyle scowls, the three gargoyles crowded to the far end of the corridor to look inside the crypt barred by wire. Unlike the ones they had already inspected, the coffins in this crypt were not stacked. Paddy recalled that this was the one where tourists were allowed to view a few of the famous "mummies of St. Michan's." Though several relatively intact coffins were pushed against the wall to either side, their lids adorned with a few skulls and other assorted bones, there were three open coffins in the middle of the chamber, their heads pointed away from the doorway, and another open one beyond, set parallel to the back wall.

"I wish they'd let these people rest in peace," Audie grumbled. "Why do humans want to gawk at things like this?"

"Because they're both fascinated and frightened by death, I think," C.C. replied. "It's the greatest of human unknowns, and every living creature has to make that last journey alone, past physical death. They have a hard time conceiving of existence that transcends the physical."

"Well, they know that their bodies go back to dust, back to the elements," Audie pointed out.

"Yeah, but a lot of them think they're going to get back a renewed physical body, come Judgment Day," Paddy chimed in, "and they get hung up on the idea. They lose sight of the fact that it's their immortal souls that count. Truth is, they won't need or want physical bodies by then. It will be a whole new order of existence for them."

"Yeah, but earth's order of existence right now is that bodies should go back to dust," Audie said, gesturing toward the coffins, whose occupants, though dust-shrouded, had been mummified by the dry air of the limestone crypt, their flesh shrunken away beneath brown, leathery skin, still festooned in crumbling remnants of clothing. "This is an anomaly. What is He thinking, when He lets this kind of thing happen?"

Paddy chuckled. "You trying to second-guess the Boss?' he asked. "Actually, I think it might have something to do with reminding people how well designed their bodies are. And of course, people are usually interested in how other people lived, years before. It isn't as if the former owners of these bodies are hanging around here."

While they debated, the cat had squeezed through the wide mesh of the wire grille and jumped up onto the end of the center coffin, balancing gracefully on the corner edges at one side as she surveyed the bodies, left and right. The body in the coffin farthest to the right was mostly skeletal, but the one in the leftmost coffin still could be identified as a woman, said to have been a nun. The man in the middle was missing his right hand and both feet.

"Where are his feet?" the cat asked. "For that matter, where is his hand? Did those messy humans take them?"

"No, they've been gone a long time, little one," Paddy replied, "though I think that other 'messy humans' did, indeed, take them a long, long time ago."

In fact, popular tradition suggested that the man had been a criminal, executed in a nearby prison, but Paddy remembered the man's burial, some four centuries ago, and knew he had merely been the victim of vandalism in the intervening years. Besides that, an executed criminal would not have been buried under once-fashionable St. Michan's. (It was true that the famous Sheares brothers were buried in one of the other vaults—hanged, drawn, and quartered as traitors by their English captors, after the ill-fated Irish Rebellion of 1798—but the pair had been political martyrs, not common criminals.)

"That's the crusader in the back, isn't it?" C.C. asked.

"Yeah," said Paddy.

"He's still got his head," Audie pointed out.

"Yeah," Paddy said again. "I wonder what all this head business is about?"

"What about heads?" the cat asked, looking up.

"We were told that his head might be missing," Paddy said, before either of the others could answer.

"Oh, not *his*," said the cat.

"Then, is some other head missing?" C.C. demanded.

"No, but those nasty men took one of the coffins outside," the cat replied, "and one of them was playing kick-ball with a head. It was only a little one, though, and other men came in the morning and put everything back."

The three gargoyles exchanged perplexed glances, and Audie rumbled, "I'd sure like to know what's going on."

"I guess we'll find out tomorrow night," C.C. retorted. "We need to see anything else?" he said to Paddy.

"I'll just have a closer look before we go," Paddy said.

Accompanied by the cat, who walked delicately along the edge of the center coffin, Paddy oozed through the wire grille and shuffled back to the crusader's coffin. So far as he could tell, and judging from what he remembered of the body's condition on previous visits, the reports they had heard of damage to this particular body seemed to have been exaggerated. (Not that Paddy spent a great deal of time inspecting long-dead bodies, but one did tend to make periodic rounds of unusual sites, during a gargoyle career spanning nearly two millennia.) The skeletal right hand, its mummified skin stretched taut over the bones, was dark brown and shiny from being touched for luck by thousands of tourists over the past several centuries—which, perhaps, was what had saved the old crusader from serious vandal-ism by the lager louts of earlier in the week. The supersti-tious might think that abuse of such a good luck charm might result in *bad* luck.

"What do you think?" he asked the cat, who had jumped down on the floor to stand on her hind legs beside Paddy and peer into the coffin beside him.

"He's pretty old, isn't he?" said the cat.

"Yes, one of the oldest ones here," Paddy replied. "Maybe as old as eight hundred years. The church above us is much newer, but the crypts and some of the foundations probably date back to Viking days. I don't suppose you know about Vikings."

"No, and she doesn't *want* to know about Vikings," Audie said irritably. "They were terrible people."

"They were people," Paddy said, reaching down to pick up the cat again. "Come on, little one. We'll take you out of here. You'll be much better off going home to your human than poking around anymore down here. Besides, it will be dark, once we leave."

"There might be mice," the cat said hopefully.

"Maybe," Paddy replied. "But the vaults might not be opened again until after Christmas, and then where would you be? Besides, I think it's quite likely that your human will indulge you with a few bits of Christmas turkey—but only if you're around to eat it. Does that sound nice?"

Licking her chops in anticipation, the cat rubbed her head against Paddy's scaly gargoyle chest, purring blissfully, and snuggled down to let herself be carried back to the steep stair that led out of the crypt.

Chapter 12

It was nearing dawn by the time Paddy got back to his post in the tower at St. Patrick's. The outing to St. Michan's, while agreeable enough a diversion from normal routine, had hardly been enlightening, so far as explaining any reason for the special conclave called for the next evening. At times like this, Paddy found it both puzzling and even mildly amusing that relatively minor functionaries like himself were regularly dispatched to investigate earthly goings-on, when an omniscient Boss was perfectly capable of Knowing what He needed to know—though Paddy always welcomed the opportunity to delve beyond his usual job description.

Not that boredom was any part of a gargoyle's lexicon.

How could one possibly be bored, when possessed of the supreme contentment that came of working in absolute harmony with God's Master Plan? However, the occasional departure from routine did enable even angels to share more directly in God's infinite variety.

What caused the occasional blip in that Plan was free will. The angels were possessed of it, of course. Himself numbered with all the other angels among the first of God's creation, Paddy well knew what a particular mark of Divine favor it was for God to have granted free will to His later human creations—but free will did have its complications and perils.

That was why Paddy's original assignment had been as an avenging angel; for free will meant that humans could and often did insist on making the most appalling choices, and *someone* had to deal with the consequences and clean up the mess. (The Boss was very big on delegating authority—and small wonder, given the size of the universe He had to oversee.) At times, humanity seemed alarmingly prone to screwing up in a big way. Paddy liked to think that the New Testament really had made a difference in the way humans treated one another—and he chose not to waste his time worrying whether any other holy books had been any more successful in getting God's point across—but sometimes he wondered whether quite so many avenging angels should have been reassigned.

In that regard, Paddy sometimes missed his former duties as an avenging angel—though circumstances did change on earth, even if God Himself was changeless, being All Perfection and, therefore, having no need of change. His Master Plan had been laid down at the moment of Creation, but only God had a broad enough perspective to see and understand it all.

Trouble came when humans misunderstood that plan, or understood only a part of it—or discarded it altogether. Mistakes and, worse, flagrant disregard, always had their consequences, either from the action itself or from Higher Up—which was where avenging angels came in. Paddy had to admit that smiting evildoers and acting as the implacable scourge of God's Righteous Anger could be extremely satisfying, in its place—and he had smitten and scourged with the best of them, in his avenging angel days. But gargoyle duty did have its own rewards. Gargoyles were, after all, still angels.

In general, a gargoyle had more broadly discretionary authority than an avenging angel, given leave to deal semi-autonomously with a wider range of lesser infractions and just downright mistakes than those attracting specific heavenly wrath. Being earthbound, gargoyles were even permitted to engage the occasional assistance of earth's creatures, many of whom were quite capable of discerning a gargoyle's true nature—like the little cat at St. Michan's. Cats and dogs were particularly good at seeing into the invisible world.

Humans were in a different category, being at once the most perfected and most worrisome of God's creations. Having been made in God's image, and imbued with a spark of the Divine, they had the capacity for many God-like qualities—but they could also come near to rivaling Satan himself, when it came to making really big mistakes.

Free will again. Sometimes Paddy wasn't sure whether that was any better an idea than reassigning so many avenging angels. Fortunately, free will also meant that most humans did get it right eventually, for in the Beginning, God had looked upon His creation and seen that it was good.

It was when the goodness wore a little thin and individual humans got off on the wrong track that Paddy and others of his kind were called into the fray. Fortunately, other individual humans could sometimes be enlisted to assist; unfortunately, they were also subject to certain rules that even an angel could not countervene.

The case of Francis Templeton particularly bothered Paddy. The visit to the vaults at St. Michan's had reminded him again of human mortality, at least on the physical plane, and he very much regretted that his own carelessness was going to be the cause of Templeton's premature passing. Without the old man's assistance, it might have been necessary to take far more extreme measures against the two thieves they eventually cornered—and Corporate Policy was to use minimal force whenever possible.

Unfortunately, assistance like Templeton's, however well-intentioned, was not without its possibly adverse consequences, at least in the short term. It was one of the Unwritten Rules that humans were not supposed to find out about the true nature of supernatural entities like angels and gargoyles while still inhabiting physical bodies. The only exceptions were saints. Guessing was one thing; actually seeing physical evidence was quite another matter. It had to do with not making things too easy in the faith department. There was also the danger that they would tell others about their experiences—though Paddy didn't think that Templeton would spill the beans.

That was why, if they did find out prematurely—especially if they saw a gargoyle's true form—death must shortly follow. Like Paddy, Death's Deputies had a certain amount of discretion regarding when they took someone, but extended reprieves could only be granted by Executive Decree from Upstairs. That was not likely to happen just because Paddy had overlooked the fact that the polished door of Templeton's old Rolls Royce was as good as a black mirror.

Rank carelessness! The sort of mistake that even a very green gargoyle should not have made—and Paddy was supposed to be about as seasoned as they came. Maybe he'd been at this assignment too long.

It was all far more dismal than he wished to contemplate. He was not looking forward to telling his friend, but he also didn't want anyone else to do it. Certainly, he didn't want Death to just show up unannounced and take the old man.

Maybe he could work something out, find some way to get Templeton a longer reprieve. It wasn't that being dead was such a terrible thing, especially for someone who had led a reasonably righteous life. After all, it meant that Templeton would be going Home. But Paddy *had* rather enjoyed the old man's company. He'd had a number of human friends, over the centuries, and had even watched over some of them as they crossed to the Other Side.

Any friendship with humans came with the knowledge

that their mortal span was limited, but it was frustrating when a friendship got nipped in the bud before it even got off the ground. Paddy loved being a gargoyle, and accepted the solitude of his lofty guard post as a given, but occasional interaction with others was also a welcome diversion. He always looked forward to the monthly gargoyle conclaves. Extra ones, like the one called for tonight, could be a mixed blessing, but he wasn't now expecting that to yield much out of the ordinary. After all, he and C.C. and Audie had already determined that the head of the crusader mummy had not been stolen—which, presumably, was the whole reason for calling an extra conclave in the first place.

That made him wonder what was going on—or, what *would* have been going on, if the head *had* been stolen. He spent most of the rest of the day speculating about that mystery, in between watching Sunday morning services from the clerestory galleries and patrolling from the bell tower in between.

By late afternoon, as the cathedral prepared for the carol service and Paddy himself prepared for the arrival of other gargoyles and their inevitable barrage of questions about the situation at St. Michan's, he still had reached no satisfactory conclusion. On Sundays and feast days, and especially the eves of the three great feasts of Christmas, Easter, and Pentecost, gargoyles had leave to wander the city at will, just as they did when the moon was dark—additional gargoyle vigilance, lest any evil disrupt these important celebrations—but over the centuries, it had become the custom for the gargoyles stationed in sacred buildings to play host to those of their kind assigned to secular buildings, or whose churches no longer served a sacred purpose. (Gargoyles, of course, being a species of angel, had no *need* to make communal affirmations regarding their Creator and His Goodness, since they possessed firsthand and intimate experience of the Divine Presence; but it gave them pleasure to attend as their human charges sought closer understanding of and communion with the One Who had created all of them, and to bask in the glow of faith that powered human prayer.)

The gargoyles' favored venues were St. Patrick's and Christ Church Cathedrals, because both churches contained vast warrens of shadowed galleries from which to watch unobserved. While Paddy's cathedral had the better vantage points, most of his colleagues preferred Christ Church, especially for daytime services, since it could be accessed directly via the network of underground tunnels, with little risk that a gargoyle might be seen coming or going. In winter, however, at least for the vigils of feasts and for services held in the late afternoon or evening, the shortened daylight hours permitted safe enough access to St. Patrick's, for that final dash from Patrick's Well to the shelter of the cathedral tower. This close to the winter solstice, the dusk normally started to close in by four o'clock—and was descending even earlier today, as a glowering sky threatened snow in the next hours.

Nonetheless, only three other gargoyles made their way to Paddy's bell tower as the bells pealed forth their call to worship and people filtered into the cathedral far below. Paddy decided that the others must be going to Christ Church instead, because of the conclave scheduled later in the evening. The gargoyle from St. Andrew's, Anders by name, whose church was now a tourist information center, almost always came to St. Patrick's for high state and festival occasions, as did Phoenix, the solitary gargoyle charged with guarding Phoenix Park. (The latter was a very important secular assignment, because the President made her home in the park, at Áras an Uachtaráin, the former Viceregal Lodge.) The other regular attendee was Gandon, the eager and relatively new gargoyle assigned to guard the Custom House, who regarded Paddy as something of a mentor, and enjoyed hanging out with him when duties permitted.

The three of them arrived only minutes before the service was to begin. They had been coming for years, so they knew the best vantage points; but in light of his recent blunder concerning Templeton, Paddy took care to remind each new arrival that some sections of the clerestory galleries were temporarily off limits. Though only electricians—and gargoyles—normally had access to the narrow passages, the choir master was fond of stationing his soloists at various points all over the galleries for these special services attendant upon the Christmas season, so that their voices came from various parts of the cathedral; and the younger boys, especially, were sharp-eyed and mightily curious, and could not be counted upon to stay strictly where they were meant to be. Nonetheless, Paddy had sussed out their locations, and was able to alert his colleagues.

The bells had been ringing some simple changes as four o'clock approached, but now dropped out, one by one, leaving the tenor to toll solo a few times before it, too, fell silent. Inside, an expectant hush slowly settled over the large congregation seated in the nearly darkened nave, the gathering gloom illuminated by candlelight in choir and chancel and a few holly-bedecked candelabra set at strategic locations along the long nave aisle.

The clock in the bell tower began to strike four—somewhat muffled inside the cathedral. The choir and clergy had moved into position at the rear of the nave and back along the north choir aisle, ready to process in, the choristers in white surplices over their cassocks of Patrick's blue, white frills at their throats and music clasped to their breasts, youngsters preceding the adult choristers. The clergy wore the varied hoods of their academic achievements over surplices and more sober robes.

A crucifer and a pair of acolytes with tall brass torches waited to lead the procession in, with several purple-gowned vergers spaced amid choir and clergy to shepherd with their wands of office. Bringing up the rear, the very last in the column, was the dean, a cope of shimmering gold and blue brocade upon his shoulders, the golden seal of the cathedral pendant from a ribbon of Patrick's blue at his throat. As the fourth stroke of the hour faded into stillness, the voice of the dean's vicar read out the words of a traditional call to worship, from far in the rear of the nave.

"Beloved in Christ, at this Christmastide let it be our care and delight to hear again the message of the Angels, and in heart and mind to go even unto Bethlehem and see this thing which is come to pass, and the Babe lying in a manger. . . ."

It was one of Paddy's favorite bidding prayers, because it declared part of the role of God's angelic messengers in the story of the Incarnation. Other angelic participation would be declared in the course of the lessons read as the service progressed.

Paddy also liked the choir's solemn entry, heralded by a carol whose tradition went back for centuries, the first verse sung *a capella* from high in the rear of the cathedral by a solo boy soprano:

> *Once, in royal David's city, in a lowly cattle shed,*
> *Where a mother laid her baby in a manger for his*
>   *bed.*
> *Mary was that mother mild,*
> *Jesus Christ, her little child. . . .*

Organ and choristers joined their voices for subsequent verses and the candlelit entrance procession which made its way slowly eastward, light from the torches accompanying the processional cross. Candlelight brightened the music desks in the choir stalls as well, and shone from the ledge behind the altar, gilding the white linens on the altar, burnishing the faces of the choristers and then the readers who came forth, escorted by vergers, to proclaim the nine lessons prophesying the miraculous event commemorated yearly in the Church's calendar. The youngest boy chorister read the first lesson, from behind the great brass eagle whose wings formed the lectern on the Epistle side, just inside the choir, with successively senior lay readers and clergy reading in turn. The dean would read the final lesson. Interspersed with the lessons were the carols and anthems of Christmas, underlining the story being told.

The melding of readings, music, and candlelight wove

its special magic, as it always did, repeatedly recounting the role of angels. Particularly pleasing to the gargoyles was a reading about seraphim, from the sixth book of the prophet Isaiah:

> *I saw also the Lord sitting upon a throne, high and lifted up, and His train filled the temple. Above it stood the seraphim: each one had six wings; with twain he covered his face, and with twain he covered his feet, and with twain he did fly. And one cried unto another, and said, Holy, holy, holy, is the Lord of hosts: the whole earth is full of his glory. . . .*

In such manner did the service unfold. Outside, snow began to fall and winter reigned, but inside, the anticipation of that first Christmas was revealed and re-created through word and song. The boys from the cathedral's choir school sang like angels, as they always did, but what Paddy liked most was afterward, when choir and clergy had retired and people began streaming out of the cathedral, past the creche: the looks of wonder and anticipation on the faces of the children, from the wobbliest toddlers, who were barely able to walk, right up to the ones who fancied themselves far too grownup to get too excited by Christmas.

True it was that most of this excitement came of wishful optimism regarding the presents the children hoped to receive from Father Christmas; but in the case of these little ones, Paddy thought that this did not much detract from the reason behind the custom of gift-giving. While few of the young ones would comprehend, just yet, the true significance of the gifts brought by the Wise Men from the East, who had followed a star to find the Child foretold, most of them knew what the Three Kings had brought, if only from the Christmas carol named for them, gifts of gold, frankincense, and myrrh. A few of the older ones might even be able to tell how these gifts foreshadowed the Child's future role as King, God, and Sacrifice.

But that story was mostly for the future. Children, most of whom had baby brothers and sisters of their own, could identify fairly easily with the Christmas story, and the Baby Jesus, whose adoring mother had held her precious infant in her arms the way their own mothers held their babies. The miraculous birth was far more comprehensible to these little ones than the darker Mystery of Easter's Death and Resurrection.

When the choristers in the galleries had come down, and while the congregation dispersed and the bells rang a special touch in celebration of the season, Paddy and his guests made their way back up to his watch post behind the parapet. Until now, the three had refrained from indulging their curiosity about Paddy's mission of the night before, but all of them knew that he, C.C., and Audie had been sent to investigate the state of the crusader mummy at St. Michan's.

"If you're hoping I can tell you about tonight's meeting, I'm afraid I have to disappoint you," Paddy said, as they gazed out over the city. "I don't suppose any of you have heard what this is all about?"

It was snowing rather heavily, a biting wind gusting and

eddying around the spire of the old bell tower, and they could all smell the reek of power that had summoned a heavy snowfall when only flurries had been forecast. On a Sunday night, with the snow encouraging most humans to stay indoors, even gargoyles would be able to move with relative ease. It made Paddy wonder whether there might be more to the night's coming meeting than any of them were expecting.

Anders snorted, his gargoyle breath puffing a new gust of snow up the cathedral spire. "We were hoping *you* could tell *us* what's going on."

"That's right," Phoenix agreed. "Out in the Park, I never hear any of the good stuff. What do you suppose is so important that they'd call a special conclave? Why should it matter whether a mummy's head was taken? *He* doesn't need it anymore."

"I couldn't begin to guess," Paddy replied. "It looked like an ordinary head to me."

"It just doesn't make sense," Anders said.

They continued to speculate for the next several hours, until it was time to make their way to the conclave. The clock was striking eleven as they streaked down the shadowed sides of the bell tower and into St. Patrick's Well, then down through the series of underground passages that led to the chamber underneath Dublin Castle. In the next little while, every gargoyle in Dublin arrived, all of them milling and grumbling, but amid an air of growing anticipation, for no one knew who might be sent from Upstairs.

After a few minutes, C.C. called them to order, gesturing with a taloned claw for all of them to take their places

on the tiered ledges. A certain amount of muttering continued until, very shortly, a rippling flare of rainbow radiance
momentarily blinded even gargoyle vision, heralding a
new arrival.

Chapter 13

A collective gasp whispered among the gargoyles—quickly stifled—as the rainbow glare died down and they could see again. No one had been expecting an archangel or, indeed, any other angel of great seniority—at most, some middle-ranking angelic messenger delegated to follow up on the rather puzzling inquiry of the previous night.

Before them, however, arrayed in all its glory, was one of the fiery, six-winged seraphim described in the Scripture reading most of them had heard only a few hours before, who normally passed their time attending close by the Throne of Heaven. Many-eyed and four-faced, the highest-ranking of all the angelic host, they were said to number only four in all Creation, and almost never came down to earth.

Accompanying the seraph was quite a ferocious-looking gargoyle no one had ever seen before, with an elegant dragon head, magnificent curling horns, and swooping bat wings. The arrival of so august a pair caused quite a stir among the relatively provincial gargoyles of Dublin, but Paddy decided he was not going to be all *that* impressed.

"My companion is the senior gargoyle from Notre Dame de Paris," the seraph said, apparently seeing no need to identify itself. "I trust that the required information has been obtained."

All the other gargoyles deferred to the gargoyle of Christ Church Cathedral, who shuffled forward a few paces and inclined his great gargoyle head.

"As instructed, Venerable," he said. "I and two of my colleagues carried out a personal investigation. We are able to confirm that the head of the crusader mummy at St. Michan's Church has not been stolen. There was interference with another head—that of a child—but it was recovered and has been restored to its proper resting place. Damage to that crypt seems to have been attributable to mere vandalism, and did not involve the crusader's body at all."

The seraph turned some of its many eyes on the Notre Dame gargoyle, who looked very relieved. It made Paddy wonder what made a long-dead crusader so important. Or had there been a complaint about the job they were doing here in Dublin?

"May one ask," Paddy said boldly, "why this was

deemed sufficiently important to send the two of you? We of the Dublin Watch do take pride in the way we guard our charges; and while it is true that an act of vandalism took place, I would point out that the location in question lost its gargoyle some years ago, as have several other properties. Nonetheless, the rest of us do continue to guard as best we can."

The Notre Dame gargoyle raised one elegant claw in a gesture intended to reassure his Irish brethren, for Paddy's remark had taken on an increasingly defensive edge.

"Please, no criticism is intended," he said. Though the language spoken among the denizens of heaven was no earthly tongue, the French gargoyle's words were tinged with the accent of the land where he was assigned. "We of the Paris Watch are hoping that the problem is largely one of our own jurisdiction, but it could have reverberations here. We still cannot be certain that it does not."

"What problem is that?" Audie asked.

"Simply this," the Notre Dame gargoyle replied. "Some nine centuries ago, there was formed among the sons of humankind an order of crusader monks called the Order of the Temple of Jerusalem, or the Knights Templar. Their ostensible mission was to guard the pilgrim ways in the Holy Land, and to make war against enemies of the Faith—which, for the next two hundred years, they did most admirably.

"I say 'ostensible mission,' because they also had a less public and far more important spiritual agenda which remains a vital bulwark in mankind's defense against evil— but this was known by only a few. What *was* known was that the order had amassed enormous wealth and power, because their military successes inspired generous donations from pious patrons. This led to envy and resentment and, eventually, to their official suppression. Among the many spurious charges brought against them was that of idolatry."

The word evoked a mutter of shocked indignation among most of the assembled gargoyles, for idolatry was a serious offense against God.

"But, they weren't idolators!" the Custom House gargoyle blurted. "I know they were accused of worshipping a head," he added, as all eyes turned toward him, "but it simply wasn't true."

A gargoyle from the Dominican Priory muttered, "Well, someone has finally mentioned a head," and the one from the Pro-Cathedral asked, "What does this have to do with any of the heads at St. Michan's?"

"With luck, nothing," the seraph said, rustling fiery wings as it took back the floor. "But heads are the key to the larger picture, because the charge of idolatry did, indeed, involve the alleged worship of a head, which was sometimes associated with the name Baphomet."

"Baphomet?!" the Leinster House gargoyle sputtered. "*That* old demon?!"

"I thought it was bound aeons ago!" the Trinity gargoyle chimed in.

"If you will allow me to finish . . ." the seraph said mildly.

Further speculation ceased at once.

"The charge that the knights venerated a head was always specious, but it did contain a grain of truth, for certain of them were, indeed, involved in secret activities surrounding a head associated with the name Baphomet. The Baphomet was and is a demon by that name; but the Templars were not worshipping it—they were working powerful magic to keep the Baphomet bound."

A collective murmur of consternation whispered among the assembled gargoyles, ceasing as the seraph flexed a fiery wing.

"It was, in fact, King Solomon," the seraph went on, "who, under instruction from Archangel Michael, trapped the demon and bound it in a head-shaped receptacle which he secreted underneath the Temple of Jerusalem. There it remained undisturbed for several millennia.

"But what man crafts is transient. The binding gradually began to weaken—and since its keeping had been delegated to man, in the person of Solomon, it could not be taken back. So Holy Michael instructed certain pious French knights to go to the Holy Land, where they would discover a sacred task to be accomplished.

"The founders of what was to become the Order of the Temple uncovered the relic during excavations beneath Temple Mount, along with other treasures of both the Seen and Unseen world. Again instructed by the archangel, they renewed the binding on the Baphomet and entrusted its ongoing maintenance to a secret inner cadre of the order they then founded. The worldly treasures they had found would provide a financial basis for their future success as a crusader order, and the treasures of the Unseen world gave them power to wage war against less palpable powers of Darkness."

"Would that the story ended happily," the Notre Dame gargoyle said, taking up the thread of the narrative. "Though the order earned a well-deserved reputation both for military prowess and financial acumen in the next two centuries, its wealth inspired jealousy, which led to its downfall. The fall of the Temple put its hidden work into grave jeopardy—so grave that scattered survivors of the order's inner circle undertook extraordinary measures to ensure the continuance of that work.

"This they did by inserting key survivors into some of the other religious orders of the time, especially the other crusader orders, so that certain common prayers and meditations could be channelled toward maintenance of the Baphomet's binding. This did not detract from the other work of these orders; it simply enabled the Temple's hidden work to continue, even though most of those performing it were not aware of the full scope of the benefits.

"That work continues to this day, in the hands of the descendants of these crusader orders—who, by extension, can be reckoned as the spiritual descendants of the Temple—little though most of their members have any real inkling what greater purpose is served by their prayers and meditations and even their good works, in the guardianship of this world against evil."

"Yes, yes, they are all faithful servants of the Light," the seraph said a trifle impatiently. "Unfortunately, the gradual dilution of their conscious focus has resulted in a weakening of the binding thus effected—a happenstance of which the forces of Darkness cannot be unaware, especially now, when the long nights hold their greatest potency and the cosmic resonances of the approaching millennium make many things unstable. Without reinforcement, the binding can be broken—which would loose the Baphomet upon the world."

"Things fall apart, the center cannot hold," the Trinity gargoyle murmured close beside Paddy, in an almost reverential tone. *"Mere anarchy is loosed upon the world.* Yeats," he added by way of explanation, at the seraph's look of faint annoyance. "He was a poet, a local chap—used to hang around at Trinity sometimes. I don't suppose he was one of your closet Templars, was he?"

The seraph merely flashed its many eyes in exasperation, perhaps considering whether the Dublin gargoyles had been stationed here too long, and were picking up quaint Irish attitudes. Paddy snorted.

"Forget about Yeats," he said. "I want to know what that head at St. Michan's has to do with anything."

"Perhaps nothing," his Parisian counterpart replied. "Or at least, not directly. The Baphomet is bound outside time and space, but the physical focus of its binding—the head-shaped reliquary—was taken out of Paris at the time of the order's suppression, along with many other treasures of the Temple. Most of these treasures were loaded aboard the galleys of the Templar fleet and dispersed to various locations thought to be safe—as, indeed, most of them still are."

"Except that, lately, certain signs have been detected to suggest a cautious testing of the bonds that bind the Baphomet," the seraph interjected, flexing a wing at its companion. "Concurrently, a number of known Templar sites have been disturbed—graves, in particular—and corporeal remains have been taken away. Heads, to be more precise.

"Given the Templar connection, and the fact that the Baphomet is bound in a head-shaped reliquary, we must consider whether, under direction by the minions of Satan, someone is searching for the remains of some Templar of the former inner circle, who knew the binding—and the unbinding—of the Baphomet. If one could be found, there are ways to summon back that man's soul and compel him to reveal how this can be accomplished."

"Just a moment, if you please," said the gargoyle from the Pro-Cathedral. "It sounds like you're suggesting that our crusader at St. Michan's is one of those Templars."

The Notre Dame gargoyle looked faintly embarrassed, and the seraph ruffled all six of its wings.

"I fear the threat is even more serious than that," the seraph said. "The principal Templar stronghold on this island was at a castle called Clontarf, not far from here—which, in case you had ever wondered, is why so many gargoyles were assigned to this city. The physical resting place of the Baphomet reliquary lies beneath the ruined church that served the castle."

Blank astonishment greeted this revelation, followed by a flurry of muttered gargoyle speculation that did not end until the Christ Church gargoyle drew himself to his full height and lashed his snaky tail.

"Someone should point out—and I guess I'm elected—that no one stole the head of our crusader mummy, even if he *was* a Templar. Which is not to say that there's no danger from someone else coming along with darker deeds in mind, but we can certainly assign rolling guard duty there, while we sort out the situation at Clontarf Castle." He nodded to the St. Audoen's gargoyle, who immediately headed off to do just that.

"What will that involve?" the gargoyle of the Four Courts asked. "Sorting out Clontarf, that is."

The Notre Dame gargoyle glanced at the seraph, but kept silent before the burning regard of its many fiery eyes.

"What is required," the seraph said, "is to reinforce what holds the Baphomet at bay; for that binding has decayed, and urgently needs reinforcement. Only a human can do this: a man of faith. Having delegated responsibility for that binding, we of the angelic orders cannot take it back. And best if he be a warrior such as those who served the Temple of old."

"But, it's been nearly seven hundred years since the Pope suppressed the order," said the gargoyle from the Dominican Priory—who had cause to know, since Dominicans had helped to torture and interrogate the knights, and had burned the last grand master at the stake. "They don't exist anymore."

"The Freemasons have Knights Templar," the Leinster House gargoyle said thoughtfully. "I've seen them going in and out of the Grand Lodge building in Molesworth Street, from up on the roof of the Dáil."

The Notre Dame gargoyle puffed out his cheeks and snorted. "No disrespect for Freemasons—they do many good works—but they really aren't quite the same. Oh, there may be a connection, way, *way* back, with renegade ex-Templars—but I'm given to understand that a better choice would be someone from one of the old crusader or-

ders: the Knights of Saint John, the Knights of Malta, Saint
Lazarus, the Teutonic Knights."

Mention of the Order of Malta made Paddy sit up
sharply—for Francis Templeton was a Knight of Malta.
But before he could speak, the seraph ruffled the fiery
feathers of all six wings.

"There is a further complication," it declared. "Authorization has been obtained from Very High Up—through
no little bending of normal rules and procedures, it should
be noted—to allow the summoning of your Templar to this
plane, since he knows the procedure for rebinding the
Baphomet. But the actual work must be done by a living
human, according to the covenant made with King
Solomon.

"This presents two distinct perils to any would-be human ally, both of them potentially lethal. First, there is the
danger inherent in the very act of rebinding the
Baphomet—for we already know that the forces of Satan
wish to see the binding broken and the Baphomet released.
It is certain they will detect and resist any attempt to reinforce the present binding.

"In our favor is the likelihood that any active assault on
their part will not occur for several more days, until the
time of the winter solstice, when darkness is most potent
and the binding is weakest. Hence, a preemptive strike by
our human ally, armed with the wisdom of Solomon, is
likely to succeed before Satan's minions can respond in
force—though he may well have to contend with at least a
token resistance. In that, at least, he can enlist both angelic
assistance and the aid of his Templar mentor."

The gargoyles were mostly nodding silent agreement as the seraph continued.

"Unfortunately, such aid presents its own dangers. Living flesh cannot long bear exposure to the glory whereby your ancient Templar is to be summoned and resurrected— yet bear it he must, if he is to achieve an effective partnership. And there is the further peril of prolonged close contact with our kind, which will be inevitable in the course of facilitating this arrangement. Even were he not to see your true forms with mortal vision, it is unlikely he could survive such exposure."

As the seraph spoke, all at once Paddy understood the greater purpose behind his encounter with Templeton, who had already seen him with mortal vision—and why he had let himself get careless. Once again, he stood in awe before the all-encompassing scope of the Master Plan.

"I may have just the man," he said, drawing himself up as every gaze turned toward him, including all the seraph's many eyes. "He isn't a Knight Templar, of course, but his name is Templeton—and he *is* a Knight of Malta. He's also basically a good man, a man of faith, who has lived a full life."

"Please elaborate," the seraph said.

Briefly Paddy told them about Templeton, and his assistance in recovering the silver stolen from St. Patrick's.

"It would seem," said the seraph, "that you have grown fond of this human."

Paddy inclined his great gargoyle head.

"I have."

"Yet you would condemn him to death."

"All humans die."

"But what you would ask of him almost certainly will hasten it."

"I have already hastened it," Paddy said. "He saw me."

"Ah."

"But he takes his knighthood seriously," Paddy went on. "He'd want his death to count for something. It *should* count for something." He paused a beat. "Maybe that's why he saw me."

"Perhaps," the seraph allowed. "How long was he with you?"

"All day—maybe eight hours. And Death has already sent a Deputy to take him, but I pled special circumstances and asked for a stay. I've been given until the end of the year."

"Then he has about a week," the seraph said. "Do you think he will agree?"

"I won't know until I ask, will I?" Paddy replied.

Chapter 14

Templeton's Sunday had started somewhat more auspiciously than the previous day, for he woke before the family started stirring, and had nearly finished a quick breakfast of tea and toast before he heard movement upstairs. Aisling usually did a somewhat truncated version of breakfast before the family set out for Mass as a family at the local church, but she and her husband had again been out late at a Christmas party, and the boys had spent the night with friends.

Nonetheless, he did not relish a repeat of the previous morning. By gulping down the last of his tea, he managed to get out of the house before anyone wandered downstairs, and decided to attend the eleven o'clock Mass at the Pro-Cathedral instead of his local parish. Hearing snatches of choir practice at St. Patrick's the day before had reminded him just how much he enjoyed hearing a good sung Mass—and it would postpone any further family rows, at least until the obligatory ritual of Sunday lunch.

Warmly dressed, for it looked like more snow, he caught a local bus and reached the terminal at Bus Áras with plenty of time to spare, hobbling a little as he walked the three brisk blocks to Marlborough Street, for his arthritis was acting up a little, with the cold.

It had been a while since he last attended "the Pro," as Dubliners called it. Its classical façade was very different from the dark Gothic tracery of St. Patrick's. Built in the Greek Revival style, less than two hundred years before, its imposing portico was said to be modeled partly on the Temple of Theseus in Athens. It all but overpowered its setting. (It had been intended for the site now occupied by the General Post Office, two streets away, but anti-Catholic sentiment following the rebellion of 1798 had relegated it to the less conspicuous location in Marlborough Street.)

Inside, all was white and gold and stucco and mosaic tile, airy and bright. Fluted Ionic columns marched down either side of the nave and continued around the apse, which was flanked by pedimented side altars to the Blessed Virgin and the Sacred Heart, each with its arched golden canopy. Above the apse, an expanse of quarter-dome bore a representation of the Ascension, its delicate stucco work picked out from a pale blue background.

It was a church of Templeton's own variety of Christian faith, and it never failed to move him; but as he passed down the tessellated center aisle this morning, between rows of light oak pews, he found himself scanning the classical splendor of the place through different eyes—and wondering whether the Pro, like St. Patrick's, had a resident gargoyle. Its sparser design provided no convenient niches or intramural passages that he could see, but the front of the altar did sport a pair of fairly respectable angels kneeling in adoration before a carved chalice.

He found a seat to one side, two-thirds of the way down the nave, and settled in to say his prayers, rising as the organ swelled and the entrance procession began. The Palestrina Choir was known and respected far beyond the shores of Ireland, perhaps most famous for having produced the famous Irish tenor John McCormack, just after the turn of the century. They performed even better than Templeton remembered from previous visits, singing the responses of the Mass in intricate polyphony, and interspersing traditional anthems of the season along with the familiar hymns.

Templeton decided that it had been a good day to come to the Pro. The readings for the Fourth Sunday of Advent had finally begun to foreshadow the great celebrations of Christmas to come, telling of John, called the Baptist, who had foretold the coming of the Messiah and preached baptism for the forgiveness of sins, also recalling words of the prophet Isaiah.

The great composer George Frederick Handel had enshrined parts of the Scriptures attendant upon this season in his immortal *Messiah*—written right here in Dublin, in the space of only six weeks, and first performed in nearby Fishamble Street. Dubliners annually commemorated that historic occasion, on its anniversary in March—sometimes to the accompaniment of sleet and hail and gale-force winds, for they performed out of doors, since the church of its first performance was no longer standing. As the Palestrina Choir sang an excerpt from that oratorio, it occurred to Templeton to wonder whether his gargoyle friend (assuming that he was, indeed, real) might even have heard that first performance, now more than two hundred years before.

The voice of one that crieth in the wilderness: Prepare ye the way of the Lord, and make way in the desert a highway for our God. . . .

The music never failed to move him; nor did it fail today, though he remained curiously restless as the Mass wound to its close. Returning to his place after Communion, he spotted Brendan O'Keeffe, a fellow Knight of Malta, who grinned as their eyes met and signalled that they should rendezvous afterward.

"'Morning, Frankie," Brendan said with a grin, as they came together in the broad queue filtering outside. "What on earth brings you all the way to the Pro? It's *snowing,* for God's sake, and there's Mass at the Nuncio's later this afternoon."

Templeton shrugged, mildly annoyed at the old nickname. He and Brendan had been friends for more than seventy years, since their earliest school days, and he had long ago given up trying to persuade his childhood confidant that he really did prefer to be called Francis. Brendan remained convinced that nicknames were friendlier and less formal—a safe enough supposition, since his own name did not easily lend itself to a nickname.

"That didn't keep *you* away this morning," Templeton pointed out.

"No, but I had to be here. I was ushering," Brendan replied. "Besides, hearing two Masses in the same day can only be to the good. What's *your* excuse?"

"Guess I just had it in mind to hear a really good choir this morning," Templeton said. "It *is* nearly Christmas, after all."

"Well, you got your wish," Brendan said. "You driving this afternoon?"

"Nope, I got my godson to play chauffeur. Thought it might be fun to be driven, for a change. Besides, it's hard to drive in spurs and a sword."

"That's as good an excuse as any *I've* heard." Brendan gave him a funny grin. "The word is that you had the Roller out a couple of days ago," he said. "Bertie Hanlon saw you talking away to an invisible passenger. Aisling'll be giving you a hard time on *that* one!"

Templeton rolled his eyes. "I wonder if there's anyone in Dublin who *didn't* see me on Friday," he muttered, though he knew there was no malice in his friend's comment. "I was finishing up the last of my Christmas shopping, and I bought myself a little cassette player. I was singing Christmas carols."

"Is *that* what it was?" Brendan said with a wink, then added, "Don't worry. *I* don't think you're going off the deep end. But we old fuddy-duddies have to stick together. My son's after *me* to stop driving—and I think this may be the year I do it. I'm younger than you are, Frankie—"

"By a whole six months!" Templeton interjected.

"Yeah, but my eyesight's not what it was. I think I'll

take a taxi today—though last time I did that, I managed to shut the end of my sword in the damned car door! It's *still* off being repaired at Wilkinson's."

"I guess chivalry isn't what it once was," Templeton replied with a grin, his humor restored. "You want us to swing by and pick you up instead? We've got room."

"Nah, it's out of your way."

"Not that far. Besides, it'll give me an excuse to escape early from the ritual of Sunday lunch. Don't get me wrong; Aisling is a great cook, but I'm sure I haven't heard the last of the haranguing about the driving. She and Kevin have been out partying the last two nights, but I got an earful over breakfast yesterday."

"Wants you to give up Phyllida, does she?"

Templeton returned a sour glance. "She sure doesn't want me to drive it. Maybe it's time to think about passing it on to Marcus. I think he may be getting married. . . ."

"*Is* he?"

"Well, he didn't say as much, but he's been seeing some lady doctor, over in Liverpool. He told me about her yesterday. Sounds pretty smitten . . ."

To Brendan's eager inquiries—for his nephew and Marcus had gone to school together—the two of them made their way back to the station at Bus Áras, where Templeton caught a bus that would take him nearly to his front door. He found himself wishing for his cane, but he climbed to his customary seat on the upper deck of the green double-decker bus and settled back to watch the snow flurries as they wound through the streets of Dublin. He hoped the weather didn't get much worse, or the snow would make driving that much more difficult for Marcus.

Sunday lunch was everything he had feared it might be. The boys were still at their friends' house, but both Asling and Kevin were ready to grill him more about his Friday escapades.

"I must've had half a dozen people ring me yesterday, Da, to tell me how they'd seen you talking to yourself in that old car," Aisling told him, as she passed him a plate piled with roast chicken, stuffing, two kinds of potatoes, and three kinds of vegetables. "And this morning at Mass, several more came up to me, wagging their fingers. You have to accept that you're eighty-two years old."

"What's this really about?" Templeton demanded. "Is it that you resent me spending money on Phyllida? It's mine to spend. I have my pension."

"Da, you know it isn't that."

"Then, is it that Marcus is to have the car when I'm gone?"

"Da—"

"You two have no interest in the car," Templeton went on, glaring at Kevin. "And the boys really don't. To them, she's just an old car. She should go to someone who'll love driving her, the way I have, and the way my father did, before me. I courted your mother in that car, Aisling, and while you were growing up, for many years, it was our only car. Don't you remember the trips to the seaside, when you and your sisters were just wee things? And the summer holiday trips, and the picnic hampers in the back—"

"Da, it isn't that. Of course I remember. But Marcus isn't even married. And when would he have time to spend on the car, with the schedule he keeps?"

"You might be surprised," Templeton said. "Apparently he's met someone."

"Oh, my goodness!" His daughter gave a little gasp of delight and reached across to clasp her husband's hand.

"Is it true? Is it serious?"

"I think so," Templeton said. "He sounded quite smitten."

"I don't believe it!"

"*I'll* believe it when we receive the wedding invitation," Kevin said, though he, too, was smiling. "I'd always thought he'd be the perennial bachelor. Can you tell us about the woman smart enough to catch Marcus Cassidy?"

Glad of the opportunity to divert conversation from himself, Templeton launched into a droll recap of what Marcus had told him about the delectable Cáit—which managed to get him through the rest of the meal without further reference to his own shortcomings. He fled before dessert, for he had to change clothes before heading off for his Malta event.

It was a Christmas diplomatic reception at the official residence of the Papal Nuncio, near Phoenix Park, with representatives invited from all the various chivalric orders and the diplomatic community—which meant full uniform. Accordingly, after he had put on a white dress shirt with French cuffs, Templeton then pulled on high-waisted black trousers with a stripe of gold bullion down the sides of the legs, shouldering into the braces that held up the trousers.

Well-polished black ankle boots provided the appropriate footwear—with the gilt box-spurs set into the heels that would have made driving tricky—and a heavy cardigan went over the whole, for he was not about to walk to Phyllida's garage wearing the double-breasted uniform tunic of scarlet, with its embroidered gold collar and white turned-back facings and fringed gold epaulets. That was already packed in its garment bag, his neck insignia neatly tucked into one pocket. The cocked hat that completed the uniform went into the bottom of the bag. His sword was already down in the hall, by the door.

"What time do you think you'll be home, Da?" his daughter called, as he paused in the hall to wrap up in a tartan scarf and pull on a heavy black overcoat.

"Why, are you going out?"

"Yes, Kevin's got his office party tonight." She came into the hall while putting on an earring. "It's a dinner dance over at the Shelbourne, so we'll be late. And Áine has invited the boys for a sleepover. Her mob are home from school, and all the kids are dying to see one another."

"Don't worry about me, then," Templeton said, putting on a furry sheepskin hat. "I suspect that a few of us will go for something to eat afterward, and probably a pint or two of Christmas cheer—though the Nuncio always feeds us well, at these receptions, so I don't know how hungry anyone will be. But with Marcus driving, you needn't worry," he added, forestalling an incipient lecture. "Have a good time."

She came to kiss him before he left, with garment bag over his arm and soft-cased sword in hand. As a concession to the formality of the afternoon, he had exchanged his usual furled umbrella for an elegant, silver-topped cane. A quarter-hour later, he was approaching Phyllida's garage.

The glassy stare of the car's big Marschal headlamps

met him as he turned into the alley, for Marcus had already brought Phyllida out of her garage and was pulling his own Honda into her place. He grinned and raised a hand in greeting as Templeton approached, and was waiting to help him finish dressing by the time his godfather joined him inside. Unlike the day before, he was wearing a dark three-piece suit with white shirt and conservative striped tie—appropriate both for the afternoon's diplomatic function and for going on to work later in the evening.

"Not the best day for it," Marcus said cheerily, as he helped the older man out of his overcoat. "That sky looks like it might have more snow."

"Dangedest thing I ever saw!" Templeton grumbled, as he shed hat and scarf and stripped off his cardigan, while Marcus took the scarlet tunic out of its zipper bag. "It almost never snows in December. But if you've got to wear a uniform, this is the kind of weather for it!"

"Isn't that the truth?" Marcus agreed. "I don't miss mine, but it did do a good job of keeping out the cold, especially with a couple of sweaters underneath. If I thought I could get away with it, I'd be wearing an Arran sweater under my suit. Out of deference to His Eminence, however, I've settled for a waistcoat."

"A noble sacrifice for sartorial protocol," Templeton said with a smile.

"Protocol is, indeed, the name of the game," said Marcus. "Later tonight, when I've finished with your lot, I'm on duty at a government function—a black-tie affair, as I only found out this morning. So I've got my own zipper bag in the back of my car."

"Well, you'll cut an appropriate dash in that," Templeton quipped. He had done up his collar, and now slipped into the red tunic Marcus held for him.

"Yes, and wasted on all those politicians," Marcus replied. "I'd rather have the fair Cáit on my arm, and dance the night away."

More of such banter continued while he helped Templeton put on the neck badge and button up his tunic. When they had buckled on the sword, Templeton retrieved his uniform hat and stood to attention.

"How do I look?" he asked, tucking his hat under his arm as Marcus backed off a few steps to survey him, head to toe.

"Like a *parfait* knight," Marcus said, gesturing toward the garage door with a flourish. "Come, good chevalier. Your carriage awaits."

Chapter 15

Knowing where Templeton kept his car, Paddy had a vague notion where the old man must live. After leaving the gargoyle conclave later that evening—which only went into recess pending his return, though their visitors departed once business was concluded—Paddy set out for the north part of the city.

Locating the actual residence was a matter of little more than half an hour, for even as gargoyles have an affinity for objects and, indeed, people associated with the buildings they guard—such as the silver belonging to St. Patrick's Cathedral, and Paddy's favorite verger—so is an even more potent bond established when a human looks upon a gargoyle's true form, for as long as that human lives.

Accordingly, it took Paddy very little time to zero in on

the rambling Victorian town house tucked away in the Phibsborough district. The declining state of the neighborhood and, indeed, the number of cars parked in front of the old house made it clear why Templeton chose to garage the old Rolls Royce elsewhere.

Nonetheless, Paddy was certain that he was in the right place. This late, none of the upstairs lights were on, suggesting that most of the household already slept, but light shone behind a fanlight above the front door, and a glow behind drapes in a downstairs window drew Paddy like a moth to flame.

He glided into the forecourt of the old building and approached the lit window, taking cover in the shadow of a prolific fuchsia bush that was nearly a tree. A gentle puff of gargoyle breath (which could pass through glass) parted the edges of the heavy damask drapes far enough in the center for Paddy to see that the room beyond was the formal library of the old house, with a cheery fire burning in the grate. To either side of the chimneypiece stood tall, glass-fronted bookcases, both of them full to bursting with books. More light came from a reading lamp at the elbow of a large leather easy chair set close before the fireplace, where a white-haired figure sat with head bowed over an open book.

Templeton, without a doubt, and alone, perhaps even dozing.

Slipping back around to the front of the house, Paddy compacted himself enough to squeeze through the brass-edged letter slot in the big front door, then ghosted across the tiled entry hall and under the door of the library like an ooze of ink, to materialize in the darkest corner of the room.

Templeton lifted his head briefly, looking around but not in Paddy's direction, then sighed and turned a page of the book in his lap. He was wearing a tartan dressing down and soft slippers, obviously in for the night.

Paddy let him settle for a moment while he surveyed the surroundings, deciding how best to make his approach. The room clearly was Templeton's private retreat, filled with prized collectibles and memorabilia of a long and contented life. Most of the wall space not occupied by bookshelves was hung with paintings, some of them depicting the religious themes Paddy might have expected, several of them oil portraits of a century past, their subjects bearing a family resemblance to Templeton himself. A competent watercolor near the door, of a storm at sea, was signed *M. Templeton*. Another, of four little girls with titian curls, bore the same signature.

Of far greater interest was a clutter of silver-framed photographs on a library table set into the front window bay, most of them black and white or sepia-toned, ranged two-deep in a ragged semicircle that left clear very little space for writing. The subjects were many and varied: weddings and christenings, first Communions and confirmations, interspersed with dog-eared snapshots of departed pets and old cars, with a few holiday postcards propped among them.

The one given pride of place, though it was not the largest, showed a much younger Templeton standing stiff but proud beside a smiling young woman in a hat and suit that would have been fashionable half a century before. Templeton wore a uniform, and the woman held a modest bridal bouquet. The sepia photo had been hand-tinted to hint at the red of the young woman's hair, the pale blue of her jacket and skirt, the khaki-green of Templeton's coat.

Nearby, a much more recent photograph in color showed a more traditional bride on the arm of a much older Templeton, standing beside the ribbon-festooned front end of the old Rolls Royce. In the photo and also holding down a stack of letters beside it was the silvery radiator mascot that had been supplanted by the little gargoyle: the graceful Flying Lady like those Paddy had seen on other old cars outside St. Patrick's.

Templeton coughed, stirring in his chair, and Paddy shrank back into the shadows again, watching as the old man rose and took his book back to one of the big, glass-fronted bookcases. He waited until Templeton was replacing the book in its slot on the shelf, the glazed door open (and hence at the wrong angle to reflect his presence), before gliding silently to within a few feet of Templeton's back. His reflection was gazing over the old man's shoulder, in all its angelic dignity and beauty, as Templeton gently closed the door.

"Francis," he said softly.

The sound focused Templeton's attention on what was actually being reflected in the glass behind him. Gasping, his face draining of all color, he whirled and did a double take, clutching at his chest as he staggered backward a step, for Paddy's gargoyle form was close enough to touch. A little strangled sound escaped his lips as, one hand up-flung in a warding gesture, he caught his balance on the edge of the bookcase, then glanced back at the black mirror of the bookcase door, half in disbelief. Paddy had neither advanced nor retreated.

"It's *you!*" the old man breathed. "It really is *you!* Jayzus, you gave me a fright! You'll be the death of me, if you keep that up—and me, with a dicky heart!"

"I'm afraid I already have," Paddy said. "Been your death. Or will be. You shouldn't have seen me, before. I didn't mean for it to happen, but it did."

Emotions ranging from astonishment through fear and denial to challenge flicked across the old man's face in rapid succession.

"What do you mean?"

"I mean that when humans look upon our true form, they die."

"Then, why am I not dead?"

"It doesn't always happen right away," Paddy admitted. "But it *will* happen—sooner, rather than later, I'm afraid. I know this is difficult to accept."

"You're damned right!"

Templeton eased back to his chair, feeling his way past other bits of furniture, glancing uneasily between Paddy's gargoyle image and his true form as an angel. Then before sitting, he deliberately turned the chair to face Paddy directly, very tense.

"All right, you say I'm going to die soon," he said, chin lifted a little defiantly. "Tonight? Have you come to take me?"

"No, not tonight," Paddy answered. "I've come to ask your help."

"My help. Right. You've just told me that I'm going to die because I've seen your true form—*again,* I might add!—and now you want *me* to help *you*?"

"I'm sorry," Paddy said, a trifle uncomfortably. "You weren't meant to see me. I didn't think about the side of the car being a black mirror. I was concentrating on the little gargoyle."

Templeton snorted, casting a glance at the Flying Lady hood ornament weighting letters on the table.

"Humph. I suppose I shouldn't have changed the mascot. But who'd have thought that my little dragon would catch the fancy of a gargoyle, fer Chrissakes?" He cocked his head at Paddy. "Well, it's done now, and it can't be helped, I suppose. Anyway, what's this help that you say you need? Why me, and what did you have in mind? And could you—hunker down or something, so you aren't looming over me? I'm getting a crick in my neck!"

"Sorry," Paddy murmured. Even folding himself to a crouch, his head was at the same level as Templeton's. "Is that better?"

The old man only gave him a somewhat wary nod, stiffly setting both hands on the chair arms.

"All right," said Paddy. "I told you that my fellow gargoyles and I guard the city. Almost always, we work alone. That is, we only work with other gargoyles and with the Watchers I told you about. That's fine, for most things. We're given a lot of latitude in what we can and should do, and there's a fair amount of power delegated to us from Upstairs. But sometimes, only human action will suffice to accomplish what needs to be done."

"But, why me?" Templeton asked.

"Because what's needed will require great courage and great faith—in short, it will require a true knight."

"A knight?"

Paddy nodded.

"You need a knight," Templeton repeated. "What for?"

"A quest to strike a blow against evil."

"But you're an angel. I don't see how I could possibly help you."

"It's—a little complicated, but remember that angels were created as helpers of various sorts. Mankind's salvation must be achieved through human efforts as well as Divine."

"Isn't that Christ's job?" Templeton retorted. "No offense intended."

"None taken. But that kind of salvation is on a much larger scale. You humans have to take responsibility for the day-to-day process of salvation. That's why I've come to you on this particular item."

"And what, precisely, would that item be?"

"Well. What do you know about the Knights Templar?"

"The Templars?"

Paddy nodded.

"Uh, they were a crusader order, like the Knights of Saint John, the Hospitallers. That's where the Order of Malta come from, you know. . . ."

"Yes. Go on."

"Well, they got in trouble with the Pope. He had their grand master burned at the stake. They were heretics, weren't they?"

"No, they were set up by the King of France, who wanted their wealth," Paddy replied. "But he didn't get it.

Key Templars in Paris received advance warning that the king was planning a coordinated swoop—simultaneous mass arrests of every Templar in France—so they got their treasures out ahead of time; packed them aboard their fleet at La Rochelle. These ships dispersed the treasures to various safe locations and then were never seen again."

"So?" the old man said, when Paddy did not immediately continue.

"So, the Templars had holdings in various countries all around Europe. Their main outpost in Ireland was right here in Dublin, out at Clontarf Castle. Not the one that's there now; an earlier one on the same site. One of the treasures was hidden there—and it's still there. We . . . think that the men who broke into St. Michan's may have been looking for it."

"Aha!" Templeton said. "Hunting for buried treasure!"

"After a fashion," Paddy replied. Unless there was no other way to secure the old man's help, he was determined to avoid specific mention of the Baphomet for as long as he could. No point in needlessly adding to Templeton's anxiety.

The old man's expression suggested that he had quite missed the implications of Paddy's side-step. His next question confirmed it, as he fastened, instead, on something he had some hope of understanding.

"Then—are you saying that your crusader mummy was a Templar?"

"He was."

"But—that just isn't possible," Templeton said flatly. "I don't see how he could even have been a crusader. We talked about this before, and I didn't believe it *then*. Wishful tourist claptrap and fact are two entirely different things."

"I assure you, he's a Templar."

"But, St. Michan's can't be more than three or four hundred years old."

"The present *church* is only that old," Paddy agreed, "but it was built on foundations of earlier churches going back nearly a thousand years—and that includes some of the vaults. Believe me, I watched them being built. And he is, or was, a Templar. Maybe it's stretching things a bit to say that he was a crusader," he conceded. "The crusades were mostly over by the time he joined the order."

"Right," Templeton said, looking a little dazed. "So . . . this—Templar mummy was disturbed when vandals broke into the vaults, and . . ." He shook his head impatiently. "Paddy, this doesn't add up. You said before that they were lager louts, that they busted up a lot of coffins. At worst, that suggests that they were maybe looking for valuables they thought had been buried with the bodies."

"That's far from the worst," Paddy said, "though we're hoping that there's no direct connection between what happened there and any danger to what's buried at Clontarf."

"And what *is* buried at Clontarf?" Templeton demanded. "What is it you're not telling me?"

"I'm afraid that most of it will have to wait until you've agreed to help," Paddy replied. "I don't want to scare you off."

"Don't you think I've been scared before?" the old man blurted.

"There's scared—and there's *scared*," Paddy pointed out.

"Nope, scared is scared," Templeton said stubbornly. "I fought against Hitler, more'n fifty years ago. Now, *that* was scary! People shooting at you, throwing hand grenades at you, trying to blow you up or stab you . . .

"Nope, I figure that if you guys are asking for my help, you'll do your best not to scare me too much, if you can avoid it."

"That's true," Paddy agreed.

"So, what's at Clontarf?"

"I'd really rather not be too specific just yet."

"Then tell me in general. Give me a hint!"

"All right," Paddy said, choosing his next words carefully. "For now, let's just say that not all of the treasures of the Temple were conventional riches of gold and jewels and plate."

"Okay . . ."

"Some of them were religious artifacts, relics, even some items relating to the control and subjugation of— let's call them negative forces, though I can assure you that no involvement of yourself in dealing with these items would endanger your immortal soul."

Templeton's mouth opened and closed several times without anything coming out, his eyes round and wide, and he rubbed a somewhat shaky hand nervously over his lower jaw.

"Guess I asked for that," he finally murmured. "Talk about getting in over my head . . . And you *have* scared me. But if I believe in any of this, I guess I've got to accept what you've just said." He grimaced and glanced aside briefly, still obviously trying to make sense of it, then looked back at Paddy, though he was much paler than he had been only seconds before.

"All right, say that everything you've told me is true— and I have no reason to doubt your word. Let's go back to what happened at St. Michan's, since I'm not sure I want to speculate further about whatever's buried at Clontarf—at least not now. Even if your man *was* a Templar, there's no way those lager louts could have known that. Most people wouldn't even believe he was really a crusader. And out of the five million or so people who live on this island, how many do you think are likely to know that Clontarf was a former Templar site? That doesn't even address the odds against anyone making a connection between the two. Couldn't it be just a coincidence?"

"It was no 'coincidence' that you saw my true form in the car door, " Paddy replied, "even though *no one* has ever seen me that way unless I planned for it to happen—and then, only if I intended that they should not survive to tell of it. That certainly wasn't my intention with you. Angels don't make careless mistakes. But neither do we have all the pieces of the Master Plan, the way *He* does."

Templeton swallowed noisily, obviously struggling to take it all in.

"So, are you saying that, uh, *He* made the lager louts mess with your Templar mummy, in order to bring the situation at Clontarf to your attention?"

"That may or may not have been an active part of the overall Plan," Paddy allowed. "What seems more certain is that you're being given an opportunity to assist the work of Heaven in a very important mission. Will you do it?"

Templeton briefly closed his eyes, wetting his lips with a nervous flick of his tongue.

"I dunno," he said very quietly, after a pregnant pause. "What would I have to do?"

Paddy restrained a relieved sigh, for now it was almost certain that the old man was going to agree.

"First of all," he said, careful to keep his explanation hypothetical, "I'm to assure you that you wouldn't have to do it alone. A human has to be the key player in this, but if things get nasty, you'd have all of us to back you up."

"All the gargoyles."

"Yes. All the ones in Dublin, at least. And remember that we *are* all angels."

Templeton only nodded, clearly overwhelmed by the prospect.

"They'd want to meet you first," Paddy went on. "Now. Tonight. In fact, my boss insists on it. If you agree to help."

"Your boss? Not—?" Templeton pointed upward, with a queasy expression on his face, but Paddy shook his head.

"No, not Him. The senior gargoyle here in Dublin. But one of His big deputies could show up, it's that important. One was here earlier this evening. Well, not *here,*" he amended, gesturing around the library. "In the place where we meet in conclave. I have permission to take you there. I should warn you, however, that you could find it kind of . . . *intense,* with that many of us around."

"If you're saying I'd be scared, I told you, I've been scared before."

"I think it's safe to say that this will be different from anything you've experienced," Paddy said confidently.

"Yeah, I guess you're right about *that.*" Templeton

cocked his head at Paddy with a strained little grin. "Back to this business about dying. How long have I got?"

"Well, in general, if the first glimpse doesn't kill you, you get about a day for every hour you're with one of us."

"Then, I've got about a week?"

"Hard to say. It isn't exact. And helping us could extend it by a bit—or not."

"By a day for each hour?" Templeton asked. "Remember, I was a banker. We like things to be precise."

"Like I said, it gets complicated. I frankly don't know what it will do to you, to spend time with more than one of us."

"Is *that* apt to kill me?" Templeton said.

"I don't think so. But it won't stave off death indefinitely, either."

"There's no way out of the dying part, is there?"

"No."

"I thought not. Can I think about it for a minute?"

"Of course."

"Could you—uh—go away for a few minutes, give me some space? You're kind of—uh— overwhelming."

"Sure," Paddy said. "Just don't watch while I'm coming and going. I don't want to scare you any more than you are already."

"Well, I'm not exactly scared of *you*. . . ."

Paddy only nodded, lest his gargoyle smile be taken for ferocity.

"You wouldn't be human if you weren't," he said softly. "Turn your head."

Templeton obeyed, and Paddy slipped back under the door to crouch in the shadows under the stair. All the house was quiet, except for the ticking of a fine Victorian grand-father clock over in the tiled entry hall.

The clock struck two. When it chimed the quarter-hour, Paddy slid tentatively back under the door. Templeton was standing beside a handsome Georgian secretary desk, holding a photograph of his wife.

"I can give you more time, if you need it," Paddy said softly.

Templeton briefly stiffened, then gently set the photo back on the desk and moved back toward the bookcases.

"You've already said you can't do that," he whispered. With steady hand, he reached out to slightly open one of the glass-fronted bookcase doors, so that he could see Paddy's true form reflected in the dark glass. He caught his breath as their eyes met, for even avenging angels are achingly beautiful. Then he managed a faint, brave smile.

"I think I'll be ready to go. I told you, I've got a dicky heart. I've been expecting to go for a while now. They tell me it will probably be quick. I wasn't looking forward to some long, drawn-out affair that would beggar my family. After all, everybody has to die of *something*. When I do go, will I see my wife again?"

"I think so."

"Then, it sounds okay to me." Templeton gestured around the room. "It isn't as if I'll be that much missed. Most of the people I love are dead, and most of those left just don't understand. I'm eighty-two years old. Maybe I can spend Christmas with my wife. . . ."

Chapter 16

Paddy left ahead of Templeton to await him at the garage. After he had gone, Templeton sank back into his chair for a long moment—the chair that he and Maeve had bought together for their first anniversary—and gazed about him at the memories of a long and mostly contented life.

It was coming to an end. Like all men, he had known this in a theoretical sense from a very early age, made aware of it increasingly as the years passed and his contemporaries dropped by the wayside, one by one. Maeve's death had underlined it. He had come to know it more specifically as his own health began to wind down—and when his doctors cautioned him about the increasingly fragile state of his heart.

Now he knew it with a certainty not ordinarily vouchsafed to mortals—and had learned it by way of an angel!

Well, a gargoyle—which he sensed, to the very depths of his being, was essentially the same thing. That his "angel" had come to him in a guise not anticipated in any of the teachings of his faith oddly gave him little anxiety.

Nor was he even much frightened. Now possessed of angelic corroboration concerning his imminent demise, he also owned an unswerving conviction that, when an ending came to this life, it was, indeed, but the beginning of a new life, a new adventure. As a knight dedicated to the service of the Light, what better quest could one ask, than to pass to that other shore in the service of the One True Light, as Christ's vassal? Was this not what his knightly vows had always meant to him, first as an ordinary soldier of Christ, sealed before the bishop in the sacrament of confirmation, and later reiterated as he made his vows before the Prince-Grand Master of the Order of Malta and pledged himself to more specific service as a knight of that order, following in the footsteps of Christ's knights who had served Him for two thousand years?

The light of adventure was in his eyes as he got up from his chair, and a spring was in his step as he went quickly upstairs. He must dress and leave before Aisling and Kevin came home, for he could never explain to them what he was doing, going out at this hour and in this weather. At best, they would shake their heads in indulgent forbearance, chalking up his behavior to yet another mild eccentricity of age; at worst, they would have him committed. He paused at the top of the stairs to look out at the darkened forecourt below, but he could see no sign of Paddy. Nor did he expect to.

Switching on his bedroom light, he threw open the wardrobe doors and began rooting through his closet for something to wear, for he was still half dressed in his Malta uniform underneath his dressing gown. He had shed his scarlet tunic and exchanged the spurred black boots for soft slippers, and eyed these thoughtfully, but instinctively he sensed that an altogether different uniform was required for whatever extraordinary work he must perform tonight: warm and rugged, somehow linked symbolically with his knighthood, but nothing to do with earthly trappings.

All at once, he knew what would be fitting. Rummaging far back in his closet, he pulled out the plain black boiler suit that Knights of Malta sometimes wore as an undress uniform. He had last worn his on one of the order's annual pilgrimages to Lourdes, when many of the knights served as attendants to the sick and crippled seeking healing at that holy shrine—pushing wheelchairs, helping the handicapped, feeding invalids and the like. The zippered boiler suits bore no insignia of rank; only a red-and-white-embroidered sleeve-flash on the left shoulder, declaring *Knights of Malta, Ambulance Corps,* with the order's white cross and *Ireland* below.

He tossed it across the bed while he stripped off his dressing gown and exchanged black dress trousers for a pair of heavy black sweat pants, his white shirt for a black polo-necked sweater. Then he stepped into the black boiler suit and zipped it up. For shoes, he laced on thick-soled boots lined with sheepskin, also fetching the black beret that went with the undress uniform, with a *Malta-Ireland* insignia pinned to one side.

This he folded and stuffed into one pocket of the boiler suit. Into another went his neck decoration as a Knight of Malta. As an afterthought, he tucked a dog-eared favorite snapshot of Maeve into an inside pocket. Then, taking up his cane and his sword in its soft leather case, he gave the room a final look and went hurrying back down the stairs.

At the garage, Paddy sensed him coming. Snow was falling, but the old man had bundled up warmly in overcoat and scarf and sheepskin hat, with heavy boots on his feet and leather driving gloves. He was using a cane from time to time and carrying something of similar size cased in leather: his sword, Paddy realized with a faint smile. The old man's footsteps crunched on the snow as he approached the garage doors, but Paddy had made certain that no one would remark at any sound in the deserted alley, briefly passing over the nearby residents as an angel of sleep, as once he had passed as an angel of death, during his avenging days.

"Paddy, you in there?" the old man called softly, fumbling at the padlock on the door as he sorted through his keys—though, for answer, Paddy willed the lock to fall open in the old boy's hand.

"Guess you are," Templeton murmured, unlooping the lock from the hasp and cautiously easing the door open far enough to slip inside. To his surprise, it did not squeak on its hinges as it usually did.

"D'you do that, too?" he asked, casting a wary glance around the dim garage.

For answer, Paddy brought the lights to life, bright enough so the old man could see. He was waiting in the shadows at the rear of the car, watching to see how Templeton was holding up.

"I'm not sure how you plan to get out of here at this hour without anybody noticing," Templeton said, as he pulled off his furry hat and came over to the car. "I've got nosy neighbors here. Rolls Royce cars are quiet, but so is this neighborhood, and it *is* nearly three in the morning."

"You'll be amazed at how quiet it is," Paddy replied. "Just get in the car and let me worry about that."

"Whatever you say," Templeton said.

He opened the front passenger door and tossed his hat onto the front seat, sliding his cased sword underneath and propping his cane in the passenger foot-well, then shut the door as quietly as he could and went around to the driver's side to slide behind the wheel.

Even as he was closing the driver's door, Paddy streaked past him and into the back seat, taking up his watch-position underneath the red tartan blanket, as he had two days before. With the door already in motion, Templeton's little gasp coincided with the muffled *thunk* as the driver's door closed, but then his startlement was redirected to the sight of the garage doors slowly and silently opening outward.

"Are you planning to do a lot of this sort of thing?" Templeton whispered, with a glance in his rearview mirror at the tartan lump behind him.

"'Fraid so," Paddy replied. "We'll operate outside time for part of what we have to do tonight, but we've still got a lot to do. Ready to drive?"

"Ready as I'll ever be," Templeton said.

"Good. But don't start the engine until we're clear of the alley. We're running silent tonight."

As he said it, the big car began to roll slowly toward the parting garage doors. Templeton caught his breath again, but then he applied himself to carefully navigating the Rolls through the garage doorway and out into the alley. As Templeton glanced back at the doors in his side mirror, he could see them silently closing again.

"How do you do that?" he murmured.

"Trade secret," Paddy said breezily. "You can start the engine when we get to the end of the alley—and turn on the headlamps. We don't want to attract undue attention."

"Oh, and this car isn't going to attract attention?" Templeton muttered.

"It's a little far to walk," Paddy said. "Besides, on a night like this, there aren't too many people out."

"You've got *that* right," Templeton agreed.

Letting the big car roll to a halt at the end of the alley, he switched on the ignition, set the choke, and pressed the starter button. The engine rumbled to life with nary a cough or sputter, settling into a quiet purr.

"Okay," Templeton said, switching on the big Marschal headlamps. "Where to?"

"Dublin Castle."

"You're joking. That's where you meet?"

"Well, not *in* the castle. Under it. They'll be getting anxious. And then we'll need to make another stop before we head out to Clontarf."

"The gargoyles meet under the castle," Templeton repeated, grinning with unexpected delight. "Boy, if the government only knew. Talk about breaches of security . . ."

"Just drive," Paddy said with a smile. "We haven't got all night."

Ghostlike, the big Rolls Royce glided through the silent streets of Dublin, threading its way down O'Connell Street, across the Liffey, and along the quays. Ahead and to their right, behind a veil of gently falling snow, they could see the domed lantern of the Four Courts, aglow in golden floodlights, with snow mounded along its front stairs, that faced the river. When they turned left up Parliament Street, City Hall loomed against the starry sky, obscuring the castle beyond.

"Go right and head around the back," Paddy said, as they approached the junction. "You can cut through Castle Street."

The old man said nothing as he maneuvered the turns, taking care where slush had turned to ice, passing the ceremonial entrance to the castle to skirt along its length before turning left again into Werburgh Street. The big car was nearly silent on the snow-muffled cobblestones, its tires only hissing softly on the wet. As they cruised slowly past the boarded-up bulk of the ancient church for which the street had been named, Templeton glanced at the tartan lump in his rearview mirror.

"St. Werburgh's is pretty old," he said. "So is Christ Church Cathedral. I suppose they've both got gargoyles. I know you aren't supposed to tell," he added, "but what difference does it make, if I'm going to die, anyway?"

"None, I suppose, since you're apt to meet them in a few

minutes," Paddy replied, to Templeton's astonishment. "The one from Christ Church is our spokesman, when we need one—first among equals, you might say; goes by the name of C.C. Go left here at Ship Street, and continue on past the entrance to the castle. I can get *you* past the guards, but it's easier if we leave the car out here."

"Will it be safe?" Templeton asked. "This doesn't look like the best neighborhood for parking a nice car."

"No one will bother it," Paddy said confidently. "Trust me."

"Oh, I do," Templeton said in an undertone. "It's the street gurriers I don't trust. But I suppose they're mostly tucked up in their beds, on a night like this."

"You can depend on it," Paddy replied, knowing that other gargoyles had done as he had done in the vicinity of the garage, making sure that the neighborhood slept.

Quietly the old car glided past the back entrance to the castle, which was open twenty-four hours a day because of the garda station just inside the castle precincts. Templeton parked beside a warehouse and switched off the ignition and headlamps.

"We're really going into the castle?" he said.

"Well, into the castle grounds," Paddy replied.

"And no one is going to see us?"

"They won't see *me*," Paddy said. "And they won't pay any attention to *you*."

"That's a pretty good trick," Templeton said, easing the driver's door open.

"Yeah, it's one of my better ones," Paddy agreed. He was out of the car in a streak of shadow, molding his gargoyle form along the curve of the big car's swooping front fender, so he could cup his taloned claws around the little gargoyle perched atop the radiator cap.

"You should at least let me take that off," Templeton said worriedly, also getting out of the car. "Mascots are usually the first thing to be nicked."

Between Paddy's claws, the little gargoyle was stretching stubby dragon wings, its ruby eyes aglow as it turned its head this way and that to survey its surroundings.

"Don't worry," Paddy said as he stepped back. "Junior will guard the car. Now, just walk right in as if you owned the place, and don't stop. I'll take care of the rest."

Clearly dubious, Templeton retrieved his cane and his fur hat from the passenger seat, jammed the latter on his head—and locked up the car before heading back toward the rear entrance to the castle. Paddy scuttled on ahead, keeping to the shadows, and had dealt with the guards by the time Templeton trudged the fifty snowy yards from car to arched entryway.

The red-and-white striped barrier was raised, a white garda car parked just inside the entrance, but the guards inside the security shack barely looked up as Templeton approached, only nodding vaguely in his direction before returning to their newspapers. Following instructions, Templeton just kept walking, resisting the impulse to glance over his shoulder.

Passing the towers of the castle's south range and then the garda station, he kept his head down and rounded the dark bulk of the Chapel Royal, which looked onto the upper castle yard. There, faced with the empty expanse of car park that served a long, modern office complex—annoyingly incongruous in the historical setting, Templeton had always thought—he paused in the chapel's shadow and glanced around.

"Uh, Paddy?" he called softly.

Instantly Paddy was right beside and behind him, a darker shadow-shape than that cast by the stone buttress.

"Go across the yard to the Powder Tower," Paddy said. "There are steps going down. The door will be open by the time you get there."

Even as Templeton nodded agreement, Paddy was streaking across the yard, between one blink and the next. As Templeton followed at a more sedate pace, he noticed that the gargoyle's passage had left no evidence on the virgin snow—though his own footprints and an occasional coin-sized pockmark from his cane stretched back behind him, shadowed and glittering in the yellowy illumination cast by the occasional security light. He shook his head as he wondered yet again how Paddy did that.

There was no snow on the steps at the foot of the old Powder Tower, which were sheltered by the bulk of the tower itself, but the steps were wet and slippery. Templeton clung to the iron handrail and felt his way with his cane as he carefully descended. The door at the bottom was cracked open, just far enough for him to enter, and swung silently closed as soon as Templeton had slipped inside. Paddy was waiting beneath a green-glowing emergency exit sign that made him look even more eerie than he usually did.

"You did that very well," he said. "Believe me, no one will remember seeing you."

"Easy for *you* to say," Templeton muttered. "What next?"

"Follow me," Paddy said.

Turning, he led the way down a series of steel steps and metal-grilled ramps descending to the original level of the river, where parts of the medieval castle's outer wall had been uncovered during archaeological surveys. Templeton groped his way after, feeling for his footing with cane and booted toe, straining at the darkness, for the only dim illumination now was the occasional red-gleaming eye of a security light. He had been here once before, on a tour of the castle, but that had been years before, and there had been proper lighting. Noticing his difficulty, Paddy caused a soft bluish glow to radiate from all the iron—a feat which elicited a soft gasp of wonder on Templeton's part.

"An easy party trick," Paddy said, making light of the act, for the old man did not need reminding that he was dealing with something beyond his ken—and humans were sometimes wont to mistake mere angelic intervention for the Hand of the Divine. "Can't have you tripping and breaking your neck."

He oozed over a guardrail to the ground level several feet below and indicated a gap where Templeton could wriggle through to join him.

"This used to be a water gate for the castle," he said, as Templeton eyed the gap uncertainly. "I usually come a different way, but it isn't exactly accessible to humans. Mind your step."

Saying nothing, though a little apprehension was starting to show on his face, Templeton maneuvered himself through the indicated gap and eased down onto the stony floor of the excavation beyond, wondering how he was going to get back up. But Paddy was already heading off down a low passageway leading back under the castle wall.

Following somewhat less confidently, for the walls were glowing now instead of the ironwork, Templeton concentrated on his footing and tried not to think too much. But when the passageway turned a corner, then narrowed and simply ended, after a dozen yards or so, he drew up in confusion. The gargoyle nearly filled the end of the passageway, even hunkered down, and the old man could see nowhere to go.

"What now?" he asked, looking bewildered.

"Now you make your next demonstration of faith," Paddy replied. "As you've undoubtedly noticed, this doesn't seem to lead anywhere. Not very far on the other side of this wall, however, is another series of tunnels that very much lead somewhere. To get to them, however, I'll have to take you through solid rock. Fortunately, that isn't a problem."

Templeton looked at the wall, mouth agape, then looked back at Paddy.

"You're going to take me through solid rock," he said. The statement was also a dubious question. Paddy only nodded his great gargoyle head.

Templeton drew a deep breath and let it out with a whoosh.

"Right. Okay, what do I have to do?"

"For a start, I'd suggest closing your eyes," Paddy replied, moving around behind Templeton. "Actually, I don't think you're going to mind this at all."

As he said it, he enfolded the old man in his gargoyle embrace, at the same time moving forward. Templeton momentarily sagged against his chest, suspended in contentment—and heaved a little sigh as Paddy gently released him on the other side of the wall, both astonished and quite blasé regarding what had just been done to him. He blinked a few times as he opened his eyes, reorienting himself to his new surroundings, but a part of him simply put aside the wonder, aware that this was but another taste of wonders yet to come.

"You don't need light, do you?" he asked, glancing at Paddy.

"No."

"So, this is for me?" Templeton said, indicating the glowing walls.

Paddy gestured toward the corridor before them.

"People tend to put a great deal of faith into what they can see," he replied. "I have to warn you that you're apt to see a great deal that's hard to believe, but at least if you can see the things that seem—well, normal—that should make it easier to deal with some of the other stuff."

"Thank you—I think," Templeton said. "So, where are we going now?"

"To meet some of my colleagues," Paddy replied. "Just follow me."

Chapter 17

They went at a pace to accommodate Templeton's human form. Paddy kept his wings carefully furled, lest their tips strike sparks from the low ceiling, for the old man would be finding it disconcerting enough that the walls to either side of them were glowing with a soft blue light—and he was going to see enough incredible things in the next few hours without straining his credulity prematurely.

Light they must have, nonetheless, to accommodate human vision, and there was none in these tunnels save what Paddy summoned up. Indeed, though gargoyles could function well enough without it, even they preferred at least some trace of light, for light was of God, Who had pronounced it Good.

Ahead, as they rounded the final bend, the line of brighter light around the distant door confirmed to Paddy that the others had reassembled, and had sensed their approach. As they came nearer the door, however, Templeton hung back just a little, clearly apprehensive.

"Paddy," he said softly.

"Yeah?"

"I really am going to die, aren't I?" he said. "I mean, I'm not supposed to see any of this—you said so yourself."

"You aren't going to die yet, I promise you," Paddy replied. "I've already interceded for you, and you've been given the time you'll need, so that you can help us out on this. Otherwise, you would have croaked when you were climbing those steps in my bell tower."

"You knew I was there?" Templeton asked.

"Of course. I know everything that happens in my cathedral—though I confess, I didn't sense you coming. I would have expected you to bring the big car."

"I came with my godson," Templeton responded, almost without thinking. "You say I would have died then, but you interceded?"

"Yep."

"But—why did you do that? You didn't know about this, did you?"

"No, not then. But I knew it wasn't right for you to die in any ordinary way, just because I'd gotten careless and you'd seen me."

Templeton glanced warily at the door. "And now I'm going to see more of you," he said apprehensively.

"Yep. But that doesn't affect the clock that's ticking. Within limits, I've been given permission for you to decide when's the right time. I think that . . . when you've done what needs to be done tonight . . . you'll be ready to go. It seems your wife would like to have you Home for Christmas."

"Maeve . . ." Templeton whispered, his whole face suffused with a look of poignant yearning. "You've talked to *Maeve*?"

"No, but she apparently put in a word Upstairs. She must be quite a woman."

"She was," Templeton responded, almost automatically. And then: "No, she *is!* Dear Lord, she *is!* Paddy, do you realize what you've just told me? That there really *is* something afterward!"

"Well, of course," Paddy replied. "You didn't ever *really* doubt it, did you?"

"No—yes—how should *I* know?" Templeton shook his head, briefly closing his eyes. "Sometimes, maybe. But—"

He shook his head again and looked back at Paddy, a faint smile stirring in his white moustache, new confidence in his gaze.

"All right," he whispered. "We'd better do this, if we're going to do it. Will I—be scared?"

"Not *too* scared," Paddy assured him. "Just stick close by me, and don't let anyone bully you."

"Do gargoyles bully?"

"*They* wouldn't think so—but you might."

The room beyond was circular and dimly lit from everywhere and nowhere, something like a small amphitheatre with tiered benches running around the perimeter and a sheen of standing water in the center—in essence, a black mirror, for Templeton's benefit.

Going in first, one scaly gargoyle arm curved protectively around his charge's shoulders, Paddy breathed a silent thanks to whichever of his colleagues had thought of the water. Though the forms ranged around the tiers were a rather ferocious-looking assortment of quite amazing gargoyle forms, the images dimly reflected in the black mirror of the central puddle were those of princely warriors clad in glowing armor, with bright swords belted at their waists and stars bound across their brows. The dark wings folded back from each set of broad shoulders trailed rainbows and starlight.

Templeton's face drained of color and he swayed on his feet, gloved hand clenching the head of his cane. Then he sank trembling to his knees, sweeping off his fur hat to clasp it to his heart, averting his eyes. A mild ripple of consternation whispered through the assembly, and the Christ Church gargoyle moved a little apart from the others.

"You must not kneel to us," he said gruffly, with a concerned glance at Paddy. "We are servants like yourself. If anything, we should kneel to *you*. Please get up."

Cautiously, Templeton lifted his head, his gaze darting between the princely reflections and the more solid-appearing gargoyle forms crouched on the tiers. Apparently he found the latter less daunting than the former, for he showed no hesitation in accepting Paddy's offer of a scaly arm to lean on as he got back to his feet. He seemed not to know quite what to do with his hat and his cane as he lifted his gaze to the gargoyle who had spoken. Paddy, sensing that his friend perhaps had been overwhelmed by the sight of so many angels, willed the water away. Best, perhaps, if he simply helped Templeton deal with gargoyles.

"Thank you," C.C. said, inclining his great gargoyle head. "You have shown yourself a man of great courage by even coming here. Has our brother from St. Patrick's told you what is needed?"

Templeton swallowed awkwardly and fiddled some more with his hat.

"Not a lot," he admitted. "He dropped hints about something creepy buried at Clontarf—something to do with the Knights Templar. Scared the hell out of me! He said that you need a knight to do something about it, something that . . . even angels can't do."

"That is true," C.C. agreed. He nodded toward Gandon, the Custom House gargoyle. "Please tell our friend about the 'something creepy' buried at Clontarf."

Paddy could sense Gandon restraining a smile as he moved a little nearer, but an earlier disclosure by the more junior gargoyle had made it clear why his particular expertise was being tapped.

"Before I tell you *what* it is," Gandon said, "allow me to tell you how it came to be there. Forgive me if I repeat things you already know. You will have been told that all of us formerly served as avenging angels. In a previous assignment, before coming here, I was given the task of wreaking God's vengeance in the Holy Land. Often I was with the crusader armies, of which your Knights of Malta are descendants.

"In that sense, you, too, are a crusader—and you, too, are now being called upon to execute a task given to some of your crusader predecessors: to assist in reinforcing the binding on a demon first subdued by King Solomon the

Wise, who had been instructed by an angel. It was the Knights of the Temple of Jerusalem who were given this task, and who executed it faithfully for many years, until their order was betrayed and they were forced to disperse."

Templeton's jaw had dropped at the mention of a demon, his gloved hand crushing the fur hat against his breast, and he glanced to Paddy for reassurance.

"The demon was bound in a head-shaped reliquary which the Templars had brought out of the Holy Land," Gandon went on. "They possessed several such artifacts and treasures, all of which were taken out of Paris just ahead of the mass arrests and dispersed to places of safety. The reliquary containing the bound demon came to this land, and was hidden at the site of their largest stronghold on this island. It lies there still, but the binding has weakened over the centuries, and must be reinforced."

When he did not go on, Templeton glanced at Paddy, then said tentatively, "What makes you think that I can possibly help you with this?"

"It is man's privilege," said C.C., "to share and assist in God's work on earth. But when a work has been delegated, He does not take it back. The binding of the demon Baphomet was delegated to King Solomon and the sons of humankind, and passed to the Knights Templar and their heirs. We can and will assist such heirs, but it is human faith which must provide the focus of the actual working."

"But—I don't know how to do that," Templeton said.

"If you are willing," said Gandon, "you will be shown."

"I *am* willing," Templeton said, ducking his head, "but

I—don't think I'm worthy." In his distress, he had twisted his fur hat into a shapeless ball.

"Nonsense," Paddy said lightly. "I've seen your courage."

Templeton had looked up at the sound of the more familiar voice, and slowly shook his head, though a faint smile was curving at his white moustache.

"That was never courage. It was sheer desperation. You scared the shite out of me!"

"Shite," Paddy pointed out blandly, "is not one of the requisites for the task at hand, so that won't make a difference." He glanced around at the others, folding his wings protectively around Templeton. "I think we may take that as an acceptance. We'll need the car for this. The two of us will meet the rest of you shortly at St. Michan's."

"If I'm dreaming all of this," Templeton said, as he and Paddy made their way back through the underground tunnels, "it's one hell of a dream."

"It isn't a dream," Paddy said, "and it's got nothing to do with hell unless we really screw up."

"What do you mean?" Templeton replied, in some alarm. "I thought someone was going to show me what to do."

"They are," Paddy said. "It's just that when you're messing with the forces of Darkness, nothing is absolutely certain, at least in the short term. Oh, everything will work out all right in God's time," he added, at Templeton's shocked look, "but in finite terms, we could cause a lot of people a lot of grief in the short term."

"*Now* you tell me," Templeton muttered, as they approached the end of the tunnel system, where Paddy would have to take them back through solid stone. "You know, it *has* occurred to me that you could have been lying to me all along. I mean, you *say* you and your buddies used to be avenging angels, and that you're doing God's work—but what if you were actually *fallen* angels, trying to trick me into serving Satan?"

"*What?!*"

"Well, you *could* be . . ." Templeton said stubbornly. "After all, the Bible says that Lucifer was the most beautiful of all God's angels before his fall—and it's well known that Satan is a master of deception. . . . Maybe you aren't trying to keep a demon bound after all," he blurted. "Maybe you're trying to get me to help you free it!"

Paddy stopped dead and sat back on his haunches, propping himself with his tail, to stare at the old man incredulously.

"*That,*" he said emphatically, "is about the most ridiculous thing I've ever heard you say! You don't really believe that, do you?"

"Well, no," Templeton admitted uncomfortably. "But I thought it. I had to consider it. And I'm none too happy about that hint that hell could be involved, if we were to screw up. What did you mean by that?"

Paddy heaved a relieved sigh. "Oh, that. You needn't worry. What has to be done is not without a slight risk, but we'll all be there to back you all the way. Unless this were to turn into a major confrontation, a new war in heaven, I think the chances of screwing up are minimal."

"You *think*?" said Templeton.

"Francis. Trust me on this one," Paddy replied, as he swept his wings around Templeton and took him through the wall.

They spoke but little as they made their way back toward the surface, threading along the steel ramps and stairs that honeycombed the excavations of the castle's medieval foundations to emerge in the base of the Powder Tower. Outside, under a canopy of frost-brittle stars, a pristine layer of new snow blanketed the upper yard.

After a quick scan, Paddy darted on ahead, skirting the wall and arched gateway that divided the upper and lower yards. Templeton followed at a more sedate rate. They had rounded the Chapel Royal and were heading back toward the security checkpoint before Templeton spoke again, after glancing back at the single set of footprints in the snow behind them.

"Uh, Paddy?" he said softly.

"Yeah, what?"

"Uh, you don't leave any footprints. If you were talking to me while we were passing those guards, could they hear you?"

"No, but they could hear you," Paddy said testily, "so please shut your gob until we get to the car."

"Sorry, just checking," Templeton muttered.

He did, indeed, keep his mouth shut for the next five minutes, only nodding with what he hoped was confident nonchalance when one of the guards looked up at his approach and then went right back to his newspaper. When he and Paddy were back in the car and he was going through the procedure for starting the engine, he glanced in his rearview mirror. His gargoyle companion was, once again, a tartan lump in the back seat.

"Just for the sake of curiosity, did he really not see me, or will he just not remember that he saw me?" he asked.

"Maybe a little of both," Paddy replied.

"You're no help at all," Templeton grumbled.

"Does it matter?" Paddy asked.

"No, I suppose not. Where to now? St. Michan's, I assume?"

"That's right."

"May one ask what happens when we get there?"

"One may ask . . ."

"But one won't be told. Is that it?" Templeton said with a raised eyebrow.

He imagined he could see the great gargoyle shoulders shifting in what, in a human, would have been a noncommittal shrug.

"Okay, I can take a hint," Templeton said, as he pushed the starter button and the big Rolls Royce engine rumbled to life with a purr. "St. Michan's it is."

Chapter 18

" S o, tell me why we're going to St. Michan's," Templeton said, as they emerged into Dame Street, heading west, after he threaded the big Rolls Royce through a series of back lanes that circled behind Dublin Castle.

"We—ah—need to get some information before we head up to Clontarf," Paddy replied, declining to provide specifics just yet that might alarm Templeton.

"But not from another gargoyle," Templeton ventured.

"What makes you say that?"

"Because I had the impression they were all there at the castle. If they'd had the information, they would have given it to us then."

"That's true," Paddy said. Clearly, Templeton was no

slouch, when it came to putting pieces together. "We're—ah—meeting someone else whose help we're going to need, before we go off to Clontarf."

"I see," Templeton said. "And when you say 'we,' does that mean you and me, or you and me and all those other gargoyles?"

"There'll be a lot of us," Paddy admitted.

"In the car?" Templeton asked, in some alarm.

"Not exactly. But don't worry about the details. Go right, as soon as you pass Christ Church."

"I *do* know how to get to St. Michan's," Templeton said a little testily, under his breath.

When they had passed beneath the arched overpass that joined Christ Church Cathedral with its former synod hall—the latter housing the Viking heritage center called Dublinia, so detested by several of Paddy's colleagues—they motored across the bridge that spanned the Liffey, around behind the Four Courts, and along a road that made a T with Church Street. The signal stopped them there, but off to the right Templeton could see the dark bulk of St. Michan's looming just on the other side of the street. As the signal changed and he made his turn, he heard Paddy stir behind him.

"Turn left into that first little lane past the church," the gargoyle said. "We'll park around behind."

"You're in charge," Templeton said in an undertone, casting his gaze across the front of the church and along the shuttered shop-fronts of the deserted street. "I have to tell you, though, this looks even less like the kind of place I want to park a car like this."

"Quit worrying about the car," Paddy said. "Turn left

again, when you get to the bottom of the street, and then go really slow."

Templeton complied, craning his neck to gauge the clearances as he hauled the big car around the corner into Bow Street, for passage was tight because of the cars parked along both sides of the street, and the Rolls was very wide. Halfway down the block, however, he was hardly surprised to find a parking space big enough for *two* Rolls Royce cars the size of Phyllida, just outside a modest two-story apartment building that butted up to the burial ground of the old church. Without comment, he pulled into the space and brought the big car to a halt, setting the brake and then switching off the headlamps and ignition.

"All right, try to be really quiet when we get out," Paddy whispered, the tartan lump of him suddenly looming right behind Templeton's head. "Everybody's pretty much asleep at this hour, but we don't want to roust any of the local dogs. They can see us; and there's already been a lot of coming and going."

"Will I need my sword?" Templeton asked.

"No, not until later."

Nodding taut agreement, Templeton quietly eased the door open on the driver's side and slipped out of the car, cane in hand, gently pushing the door closed instead of slamming it. Between one heartbeat and the next, Paddy slipped out, too, though Templeton didn't actually see him move. The gargoyle simply was in the passenger compartment one instant and beside Templeton the next.

"I wish you wouldn't do that!" he whispered.

"Sorry," Paddy replied. "Come this way now."

Quietly he beckoned Templeton through an iron gate

that should have squeaked but didn't, then through a small
patio-courtyard that led past the building's entrance and up
a short run of concrete steps to the level of the old burial
ground, the back of which served as a quiet and pictur-
esque garden for the local residents.

Templeton hesitated at the edge of the snow-powdered
grass, prodding with the tip of his cane, for the streetlights
on the road they had just left did not penetrate this far, and
he guessed that the ground would be very uneven in such
an ancient graveyard. But as he watched Paddy set off
along a narrow tar macadam path that meandered in the direction of the old church, he noticed that, unlike at the castle, this time the gargoyle left faintly luminescent
footsteps. The glow was just enough for Templeton to see
his footing as he followed carefully after, casting furtive
glances back the way they had come and peering ahead
with even greater concern, for the main façade of the
church was quite well illuminated by the street lamps on
Church Street beyond.

But they did not go that far. Skirting the west end of the
church, beneath its stubby, battlemented bell tower, they
passed close along the south side of the nave, keeping to
the shadows, until they came to the angle it formed with
the south transept.

There, faintly illuminated by spill from the distant
streetlights that reflected off the snow, Templeton could
just make out the darker shapes of two pairs of steel doors
that, presumably, led into the vaults in the church's foundations. Set almost parallel to the ground, they reminded him
of pictures he had seen of storm cellars built in parts of
America that were prone to tornadoes. Each pair of steel

doors had a length of heavy chain strung through its metal handles, secured with a hefty padlock.

"So," he whispered to Paddy, crouching down beside him and lifting one of the locks. "Am I supposed to pick this, or do you make the chains fall away?"

"Neither," Paddy replied. "Why, can you pick a lock?"

"No. But it seemed like one of the options."

"I have a better one," Paddy said. "Just give me a second . . ."

As he had at the castle, he folded his wings around Templeton and took him through, ignoring the steep steps beyond and dropping to the floor of the vault below. It was crowded with gargoyles, most of whom were clustered outside the last vault on the left, where the crusader mummy lay in his moldering casket. A soft bluish glow filled the place, emanating from the brick-lined walls and the iron grillwork across the fronts of the vaults.

As the old man realized where he was, now in the shelter of one of Paddy's scaly gargoyle arms, he looked momentarily startled, but the procedure was beginning to be routine enough that he quickly recovered. The other gargoyles drew back to either side of the passageway as Paddy directed his human charge between, to where a brighter light was spilling from the vault where their long-dead Templar lay.

Templeton didn't know what he had expected to see, but it was not the small grey and tan tabby cat crouched on the lid of a coffin set against the wall on the right—or the very handsome man standing amid the four open coffins in the little chamber, who was dressed in a dark three-piece suit of exquisite cut, and looked like he could have stepped from the boardroom of some major financial institution.

"It's fortunate that I let myself be persuaded from my original intentions," said Death's Deputy, with a nod to Paddy. "The seraph informed me regarding what's required, and confirmed authorization." He shifted his gaze to Templeton. "I do hope you'll not be frightened by what you're about to see, Francis—for there's truly nothing to be frightened of. You will have heard or read the Latin phrase *Mors non dominabitur*?"

Templeton's surprise that the man knew him by name was quite overshadowed by those last three words. Voiceless, he could only nod.

"And would you speak their meaning aloud?" the man gently urged. "I wish to be reassured that you truly understand."

Somehow Templeton managed to find his voice.

"Death shall have no dominion."

"Precisely. Humans fear that this may be but a hope, a dream; but I tell you in the name and in the power of the Holy One, whose servant I am, that all things are possible. You require instruction for the task set before you. Instruction you shall have, from one who, in his mortal span, also served this task."

Without further explanation, he turned to face the open coffin set along the back wall of the chamber, stretching forth a powerful yet graceful hand over the crusader's mummified remains. As he did so, Templeton caught a faint impression of silvery wings trailing from the shoulders of this very solid figure in a three-piece suit, and knew that he was in the presence of yet another angel.

"I shall speak aloud for your sake, Francis Templeton," Death's Deputy said, "and in words that will be familiar to you from holy writ. I come at the will of the Logos, ever present, Who said to the daughter of Jarius, who was dead, *Talitha cumi,* which is, Damsel, arise; and Who likewise commanded Lazarus to come forth from the grave. In similar fashion, and in His name, do I now summon this man, known in earthly life as Richard of Kilsaren, to return to this mortal plane and arise and come forth."

The faintest breath of breeze seemed to quicken within the dusty confines of the burial chamber, fresh with the tang of the sea and a heady hint of wildflowers washed by a summer's rain. The little cat stood up and lifted her head to sniff the air, ears pricked and whiskers all a-tremble. The gargoyles bowed their heads. Templeton seemed to feel a deep vibration stir beneath the soles of his feet and creep up his spine. His knees went a little wobbly, but Paddy braced him from behind. Even so, he actually stopped breathing for a few seconds.

For a silvery mist was gathering in the crusader's coffin, rising up from deep within, curving tenderly around the mummified corpse it contained and gently shrouding a miraculous transformation. In the space of scarcely half a dozen heartbeats, before Templeton's awestruck and fascinated gaze, the ravages of nearly eight centuries reversed themselves, the corpse's leathery skin and shrunken flesh regaining the color and contours of mortal life. Even the cere brown of the rotting graveclothes gave way to raiment of a soft white.

As a restored hand stirred, lifting to rest on the edge of the coffin, Templeton gasped—which started him breathing again—and backed off an involuntary pace as a bearded, white-clad figure smoothly sat up to turn a piercing blue gaze first on the angel, to whom he nodded, then on Templeton himself. He appeared to be in his vigorous forties, and in the peak of health.

"So, we are to be brothers-in-arms," the man said with a faint smile.

The voice was deep and vibrant, confident. A detached part of Templeton caught traces of an unidentifiable accent to the man's speech, but he had no difficulty understanding him. It occurred to him to wonder if the man was even speaking English—or, for that matter, whether Paddy and the other gargoyles had been speaking English. Not to mention the elegant angel, who clearly commanded the power of life and death.

Templeton gave a cautious nod.

"And your name, I am told, is Francis," the man went on. "In mortal life, I was known as Brother Richard. Our orders, I believe, were rivals in those days. But we shall be allies now. You are of the Order of Malta, are you not, who descend from the Knights of the Hospital of Jerusalem."

"You know about the Knights of Malta?" Templeton blurted, astonished at this revelation.

Inclining his head in answer, Brother Richard heaved himself forward and stood up in the coffin, keeping his head ducked in the low space as he stepped out of it. His fair hair was clipped close to his head, in contrast to his wiry and rather shaggy beard. His raiment was the long white mantle and tunic of the Order of the Temple, with a red cross *moline* broad across the left shoulder and the breast. A goodly sword was girt at his waist, and long-shanked spurs adorned the heels of his boots, in token of his knighthood.

As he straightened as much as he was able in the low vault, he spied the little cat—and smiled as he reached out to fondle an ear and then run a gentle hand down her back. When the cat arched against his hand, purring audibly, he picked her up and cradled her to his chest as he glanced at the angel and the gargoyles ranged behind him.

"We had best be about our work," he said to them, glancing then at Templeton. "Please understand, Brother Francis, that I have come willingly, and freely offer such assistance as I may render, but I cannot say it pleases me to be here. In due time, you will know the supreme contentment of the next life. Were it not for your great need, I would not have chosen to return."

Templeton managed to make his dry throat swallow, glancing at Paddy for guidance.

"An appropriate response would be 'Thank you, Brother Richard,'" the gargoyle said. "He has left the Presence to come here. We should not keep him from It any longer than is necessary."

"Th-thank you, Brother Richard," Templeton stammered, then looked again to Paddy. "Uh—what do we do next?"

"We take ourselves off to Clontarf Castle," Paddy replied.

"Let me come!" said the little cat, from within Brother Richard's embrace—much to Templeton's astonishment.

"That's most irregular," said Death's Deputy.

"No, 'tis fitting," Brother Richard said. "Besides," he added, with a glance at Templeton and Paddy, "I think her presence may be welcome, later on."

Templeton didn't know what that was supposed to

mean, but the angel inclined his head and Paddy nodded. The cat burrowed her nose harder into Brother Richard's white robes, purring and kneading his arm with her white-mitten paws, clearly elated.

"And you'll see about that other matter we discussed?" Paddy said to Death.

Death nodded.

"We'd better go, then," Paddy said, urging Templeton back toward the steps leading up to the closed steel doors. "We have only a few hours until dawn."

Chapter 19

Templeton still wasn't sure how the gargoyle did it, but one second he and Paddy were standing on the vault's dirt floor, next to the steep stone steps; the next, the pair of them were back outside, sheltering in the angle of the church's transept. Brother Richard and the cat were already there, the latter perched happily on the big crusader's shoulder, and the doors to the vault were still firmly closed, the chain wound through the iron handles. Templeton wondered about the other gargoyles—and that angel in the three-piece suit!—but Paddy set off immediately across the old burial ground, the afterglow of his footprints clearly heading for the car.

Quickly, lest the footprints fade before he could follow, Templeton set off after the gargoyle. New snow had begun to fall during their interval underground, crunching underfoot, but he could hear no other sound save a very occasional car passing on Church Street—and Brother Richard's footsteps, as he followed close behind. Glancing over his shoulder, it occurred to Templeton that if anyone saw the white-clad Templar moving through the churchyard, they would be quite justified in thinking they had seen a ghost.

Phyllida was exactly as they had left her. The little gargoyle on the radiator cap watched with beady ruby eyes as they approached, but craned over its shoulder and started flapping its little wings when Templeton started to put the key in the lock to the front passenger door.

"I think Brother Richard maybe ought to ride in the back," Paddy said, staying the old man's hand. "Junior has pointed out that the white robes would be somewhat conspicuous, if anybody should see us driving along. He can shelter under part of the tartan rug with me."

Glancing at the crusader, Templeton realized that Brother Richard was far larger than he had appeared down in the cramped vault. (Indeed, few men looked very big beside a gargoyle.)

"Right."

Nodding, he moved to the rear door instead, opening it wide so that his knightly companion could get in. Brother Richard seemed quite unabashed at this introduction to a mode of transport that had not been conceived in his own time, and folded himself gracefully into the rear compartment, settling on the carpeted floor with his knees drawn up and the cat cuddled close to his chest.

Gently Templeton closed the door, pushing it until it

latched with a muffled click. But when he would have gone around the rear of the car to get to the driver's door, Paddy stopped him just abreast of the boot, motioning for him to open that as well.

Templeton dared not ask why, for he knew his own voice might carry, even if Paddy could not be heard unless he wanted to, but he gave the gargoyle a questioning look. Paddy merely touched the latch, then turned the handle and lifted the boot lid a few inches.

Immediately, a dark rush of shadows surged down from the ancient churchyard and across the concrete terrace, flowing upward like a dark tide to fill the boot to brimming. Templeton gave a little gasp, for he sensed that, in some inexplicable way, it was the essence of all the other gargoyles, but Paddy only shook his head and gently lowered the boot lid, closing its latch with a soft click before motioning Templeton to get into the car.

The low rumble of the big Rolls Royce engine starting up sounded like thunder to Templeton's tight-wound senses, but nothing stirred as he switched on the headlamps and guided the old car out the end of the street and into Hammond Lane. From there, it was a matter of two quick jogs to get back onto the quays, heading eastward along the River Liffey. In the headlamps' twin beams, it was evident that the snowfall was increasing.

"Can we talk now?" Templeton asked, when they had crept past the Four Courts and were approaching O'Connell Street.

"Sure," came Paddy's muffled voice from behind the seat, under the tartan rug. "What do you want to talk about?"

"Well, for one thing," Templeton said, "I want to know if I have a bootful of gargoyles."

"Yeah, you do."

"But—how do they all fit?"

"Ever heard of that old debate about how many angels can dance on the head of a pin?"

"Yeah. . . . ?"

"Well, I can't imagine why any of us would want to do such a useless thing, but the answer is, As many of us as wanted to."

"Then . . . as many of you as wanted to could fit in my boot," Templeton said.

"That's right. We—uh—haven't exactly got physical bodies. Brother Richard knows what I'm talking about. Oh, we can be quite solid when we need to be. But we can also expand or shrink, according to need. This morning, we all need to come with you and Richard, to make sure everything goes smoothly."

"I see," Templeton said. They were cruising past the Custom House, heavily veiled behind falling snow. Once the hub of financial dealings for the port of Dublin, it now housed civic offices—and, he suddenly realized, a gargoyle.

"So, who's guarding the city, if all its gargoyles are in the boot of my car?"

A low gargoyle chuckle rumbled from behind Templeton.

"We can sort of be more than one place at a time," Paddy said. "Kind of like the way Junior can deputize for me. Don't worry about the details and don't worry about the city. Just concentrate on getting us to Clontarf. How long do you suppose it will take?"

"Maybe another ten minutes or so," Templeton replied.

"More, if the snow gets worse. It's only a couple of miles from the city center—I've been there for weddings—but I don't want to bounce us off a curb or put us into a ditch."

"There are *weddings* at Clontarf Castle?" came Brother Richard's surprised question from under the tartan rug.

"Well, not the weddings themselves, but the celebrations for weddings—the wedding feasts. It's a hotel now. It's—uh—changed a lot since you Templars were there."

"So it would appear," the Templar replied. "We were warrior monks, you know, under strict vows of celibacy. Once we had entered the order, we were forbidden contact even with sisters and mothers."

"Well, a lot of things about the Church have changed, too," Templeton replied. "I can't say I like all the changes, either. Do you keep up with these things—uh—Upstairs? Do you know about things like the Reformation?"

"You mean Luther, and Cranmer, and Wesley, and people like that?" came the reply.

"Guess you do. What do you think?"

"Well, a few of them got it mostly right—and some of them have totally missed the mark. But you'll see for yourself."

"Yeah, I suppose I will," Templeton replied, with a quick, queasy little twinge in the pit of his stomach. It had suddenly occurred to him that this was not simply a casual conversation with an interesting new acquaintance, but commentary on things he was, indeed, going to see for himself—and rather sooner than he had hoped.

But he found he really wasn't scared. A little apprehensive, yes, because he didn't know what was going to happen, or how—but after everything else that had happened in the last two days, he had already decided he would do his best to simply take things as they came. Not that he really had much choice in the matter.

And not that he really minded, when it came to that. Actually, he was quite enjoying himself. Aside from knowing that there was a gargoyle and a resurrected Templar in his back seat—not to mention an unknown number more gargoyles in his boot—it was a grand night for motoring, even with the snow, with the silent city sleeping all around him and the streets not yet gone icy and no traffic to impede progress. And he had to admit that his companions were more·fun than he'd had in a very long time, not since Maeve died. . . .

With a soft scuffling sound, Brother Richard poked his head out from under cover and rose up onto his knees, so he could peer out over the gleaming bonnet of the big Rolls Royce. It occurred to Templeton to wonder whether Brother Richard's resurrected body maybe wasn't as warm as a normal person's, because the little cat took that opportunity to wriggle from his arms and onto the back of the seat, from which she jumped down onto the seat beside Templeton to curl up in front of the blowers from the heater.

Of course, cats always sought out the warmest place, so that didn't mean Brother Richard's body was cold; just that it wasn't as warm as in front of the heater. But as Templeton absently gave the cat a scritch—which elicited a contented wiggle of pleasure—other questions regarding the Templar's body popped into his mind.

Just how alive was he? Was his heart beating? Did he need to breathe? The big knight did seem to be properly

resurrected—though Templeton sensed that much of what
Paddy and his angelic colleagues made possible owed as
much to illusion as to reality.

Not that Templeton had any notion what reality was, after the past few hours. Looking in the rearview mirror at
Brother Richard's bearded face, Templeton decided that,
with the rest of him still covered by the tartan rug, the Templar probably wouldn't even arouse a second glance should
someone happen to see him now. The car itself was far
more likely to attract unwelcome interest.

"Interesting," Brother Richard said after a few minutes,
as they negotiated a roundabout at the Eastlink Bridge and
headed north, leaving the river behind. "In my day, all of
this was open, much of it marshland—and beyond the Pale,
of course. Everything north of the Liffey was, other than
our compound at Clontarf."

"I suppose things *have* changed a bit," Templeton
agreed. "Even in my time they've changed a lot."

"Can you speed it up?" Paddy said suddenly. The gargoyle atop the bonnet had begun flapping its wings wildly,
its blunt little dragon snout outthrust like a pointer dog.
"There's something not right at Clontarf. We may be not a
bit too soon."

Templeton pushed up their speed as they passed the entrance to the Port of Dublin and doglegged back along the
Royal Canal, cutting north again through a park and rolling
through the red traffic signal at Clontarf Road as they
turned east. Fortunately, there was no traffic, though the
streets were getting more treacherous from the snow. A
cautious dash along the bay shore brought them to Castle

Avenue, where they turned north into a heavily residential area. A sign pointed to Clontarf Castle ahead.

Templeton had to slow down then, for parked cars lined both sides of the snowy street, and there had been little traffic in the last few hours to disturb the snow. Behind him, still kneeling on the floor in the rear, Brother Richard was leaning on the back of the seat, the tartan rug around his shoulders, peering ahead in wonder; the trailing edges of the rug still mostly sheltered Paddy. The little cat had gotten up and stretched and was reared up on her hind legs to follow the Templar's gaze, white front paws braced on the burled walnut dash. Beyond an ornate pedestrian gate set into a handsome stone wall, they were beginning to catch glimpses of floodlit towers behind a range of modern houses in a gated close called Knight's Wood.

Brother Richard made a little sound of dismay as they headed east to skirt the wall, formerly the boundary of the castle grounds.

"Are you sure this is the right castle?" he asked.

"It's the only Clontarf Castle *I* know," Templeton said, a little defensively.

"It's been rebuilt a couple of times since the old days," Paddy pointed out. "This one is less than two hundred years old."

"Dear God, will *anything* be the same?" Brother Richard whispered to himself.

As they came abreast of the entrance to the castle grounds, which was guarded by a tiny Gothic gate lodge, Templeton slowed to a halt, himself craning his neck to look around as his passengers did the same. Beyond the gate lodge and a run of very upmarket modern terraced houses, they could just see the main tower of the castle itself. The sign at the entrance said Clontarf Castle Hotel, and the name of the housing estate surrounding it seemed to be Castle Park.

"Any suggestions?" Templeton said.

Brother Richard shook his head. "Everything is so different. In my day, this was all open country, and the sea came much closer to the castle."

"So, where would the head have been hidden?" Paddy asked.

"In the vaults beneath the church that served the castle," the Templar replied. "Somewhere beyond here, I think. Can we go closer to the castle?"

"We won't dare park in there," Templeton replied, "but I think it's safe enough to make a pass through the car park, at this hour. But be ready to duck down behind the seat, both of you. There could be a security guard, and there're probably a few security cameras as well. Don't ask," he added, at Brother Richard's look of inquiry.

"Do it," Paddy said.

Templeton put the car back into gear and turned in through the castle's entrance, eyes fixed on the castle as he eased his way down the narrow, curving avenue. He could remember a time when the castle at least had been surrounded by parkland, before its owners had sold off its land to developers—as his own father had done on a smaller scale at the Templeton family home. What Clontarf had retained was only enough for the car park, a tiny garden, and the castle itself—which, in fact, was more of a castellated country house than a true castle, though several towers poked up from behind.

They cruised along the length of the car park to gauge the size of it, noting a modern accommodation wing grafted onto the back, then made a second, closer pass as they headed back out. The Gothic front was pretty much as Templeton remembered it, but the main tower and most of the right-hand side had been encased in a modern façade that tried to keep the feel of a proper castle hall while still answering the needs of a four-star hotel.

"Even the most stalwart of my brethren," said Brother Richard, "would be hard-pressed to defend such a place." As they glided past the entrance porch, he gestured toward the expanse of wide leaded windows at ground level and gave a contemptuous snort. "This is no proper fortification! What has happened to the goodly castle that used to guard this strand?"

"Some of the foundations may be left," Templeton said, as Paddy lifted his head seemingly to sniff the air. "Can I take us out of here now? If someone comes to check us out, I can hardly claim to be a lost wedding car at this hour."

"Go ahead," Paddy said. "Brother Richard, have you found your bearings yet?"

"Let us see if we can circle the castle," Brother Richard said. "The church that served it may well be long gone—everything else is—but I sense that we are near what we seek."

They followed the road's curve around to the left as they cruised back past the gate lodge. The stone wall delineating the former bounds of the castle grounds gave way to another cluster of modern terrace houses, with the castle's silhouette behind. Off to the right, down a junction road, Templeton pointed out a largish church, but Brother Richard shook his head.

"It wasn't that far from the castle," he said, returning his gaze to the glimpses of castle that were still their reference point. "It was just outside the bawn wall—there! What's that?"

Just beyond the houses they had been skirting, behind a lay-by to accommodate local buses, a lone streetlight illuminated an ornate stone gateway piercing a formidable stone wall. Through the iron bars of the arched gate, they could just make out the irregular shapes of tombstones.

"Cripes, that's right!" Templeton murmured, pulling to the curb. "There's an old cemetery back in here. Look! The castle's right behind the back wall. And I seem to remember the ruins of an old church."

"Park the car!" said Paddy.

"You mean, right here? Leave it in the bus bay?"

"The buses don't start running for hours—and by then, we'll be long gone. Don't waste time!"

"Okay," Templeton said doubtfully. "But it's right under a streetlight. If the guards drive past, they'll see it."

"They'll figure you had a breakdown, or ran out of petrol," Paddy said. "They won't expect you to be in the vicinity. You'll have gone for help. Besides, Junior will guard the car."

"But—"

"Are you going to argue with me every time I tell you to do something? Bring your sword and come on—both of you!"

Panic seized the old man for just an instant—for suddenly, abruptly, the moment was upon them to actually *do* whatever it was that needed to be done, something that could well expose him to the forces of hell—but he found himself pulling the door handle nonetheless. Instantly Paddy was through the widening door-opening, circling to the rear to open the boot for the other gargoyles to emerge. The little cat bounded after.

By the time Templeton could get out and release Brother Richard from the back seat, the gargoyles had streaked into the old cemetery in a shifting of shadow-shapes. As Templeton retrieved his sword from under the seat, fumbling it from its soft leather case and unwinding its belt, Brother Richard, too, headed for the arched gate, his white mantle flaring behind him as he strode across the snow-covered pavement—leaving footprints, unlike the gargoyles. Glancing after him as he belted the sword under his overcoat, Templeton found himself flashing on images of Darth Vader stalking the corridors of the Death Star, in the film *Star Wars*—Vader, who had served the Dark Side of the Force, personifying one of the most potent symbols Templeton could imagine for the embodiment of evil and menace. He prayed that he had not misjudged the Templar or their gargoyle companions; that all of them were, indeed, on the side of the angels—as they *must* be, if Paddy was, indeed, what he said he was. Because if he wasn't . . .

"Francis!" came the Templar's urgent whisper, as he beckoned for Templeton to hurry up.

Templeton hurried as best he could, finally getting the clasp on his sword-belt to catch. Then he exchanged his sheepskin hat for the plain black beret he had stuffed into the pocket of his black coverall, pulling it down low on his brow as the Special Forces wore them—which certainly seemed appropriate to his brevetment for tonight. He started to lock up the car, but then decided that if any of this was true, it *all* must be true—and merely tossed a salute to the little gargoyle on the hood, before heading after Brother Richard. As he went, he also put on his neck insignia as a Knight of Malta, fastening it up under his scarf, so that the cross hung against the black of sweater and boiler suit and overcoat.

The Templar was waiting under the arch into the graveyard, peering through the tall barred gate, his white robes giving him the appearance of the ghost that, in a sense, he was. Stern and tense as he drew Templeton closer into the shadows of the arch, his visage softened as he noticed the old man's neck-cross, and he blessed himself and then touched the first two fingers of his right hand to his lips and to the white enamel at Templeton's throat.

"I thank you for this, Brother Francis," he whispered. "Now we are, indeed, brothers under the Cross. Come!"

The gesture set the old man's mind at ease, that Brother Richard was, indeed, both who and what he said he was: no Satanic impostor, but a true knight in the service of the same Lord. Hand braced on the hilt of his sword, Templeton banished any lingering uncertainty and leaned down to inspect the padlock on the barred gate.

"You would've thought they'd leave this unlocked," he said under his breath, lifting the lock in one gloved hand and peering beyond for some sign of the gargoyles.

"They did," Brother Richard replied, "but *they* are the caretakers of this place, not our gargoyle allies. Look." For as he pushed at the gate, it swung easily and silently, demonstrating what had not been evident before: that the chain was merely looped several times through two of the bars and kept there by the lock snapped through, not serving any useful function at all, save to *appear* locked.

"Come," he said eagerly, pressing through the opening and into the shadows behind the wall, where they could not be seen from the road. "This will be where it was."

Off to the right, the dark bulk of a roofless building blotted out a portion of the frosty, star-speckled sky, framed by the brighter snow at ground level. Immediately the Templar strode out in that direction, threading his way unerringly among the gravestones and monuments. In the dark, Templeton could see no trace of Paddy or the other gargoyles, and had to follow close behind the white-robed specter of Brother Richard—who, unlike Paddy, left no helpful glowing footprints. They rounded the end of the ruined structure to be brought up short by a barred screen of fretted ironwork that completely filled the broad arch that otherwise would have given access to the interior of the derelict church.

The gargoyles were already inside, but Paddy came up to the bars and offered a taloned, faintly glowing claw to Brother Richard, who clasped it and simply walked through the bars. The gargoyle turned then to Templeton, whose jaw had dropped in astonishment.

"He—walked right through those bars," he whispered.

Paddy inclined his great gargoyle head. "Yeah, come on. We haven't got all night."

"But—"

"Just gimme me your hand," Paddy said, clicking his claws impatiently, as he had at their first meeting.

Templeton felt a little lightheaded, but then he screwed up his courage and thrust his hand between the iron bars, at the same time closing his eyes. A part of him reasoned that Paddy had already taken him through several solid walls and steel doors tonight, so passing through mere metal bars was not likely to feel appreciably different; but somehow, the prospect had seemed less daunting when it happened while enfolded in the gargoyle's angel wings.

In fact, he could discern no real difference. He felt the cool, strong clasp of the gargoyle's talons around his hand and wrist, moved forward in answer to the powerful tug against his apprehension—and opened his eyes as he was released, to find himself on the other side. The other gargoyles were hunkered around a bit of gently glowing stone curbing shaped like an upside-down U, the white-robed Brother Richard crouched in their midst, with his hands laid flat against the ground that the U enclosed and the cat perched on his shoulder.

"Is this where it's buried?" Templeton asked, coming to crouch warily among them.

"Not buried; hidden," Brother Richard said. "There is a vault below, and I think it likely that no one has passed this portal since my brethren closed it, many centuries ago." He glanced at the gargoyles. "Brother Francis and I will require your assistance to gain access, my friends. Can you do it?"

"Can we *do* it?" the Christ Church gargoyle muttered indignantly. "Of course we can do it!"

Motioning the two humans back from the U-shaped curbing, he and Gandon, the Custom House gargoyle, took up positions to either side of the U, mantling their great wings up and over them like a dark canopy. At once, a faint rumbling stirred underfoot, causing Templeton to catch at Brother Richard's sleeve for balance and in some alarm as the earth within the curbing belched upward, spattering damp earth on the snow all around and opening a stone-lined stairway into darkness.

The silence in the aftermath was profound, relieved only as the gargoyles cautiously surged forward to peer downward, hesitating but a moment before plunging down the stairwell like oily water eddying down a partly clogged drain.

A faintly phosphorescent glow remained where they had passed, like the glimmer of fireflies. Only Paddy hung back for Brother Richard and Templeton, craning after his fellows. The cat crept to the edge of the curbing and peered down with cat aplomb, back and tail faintly bristled and whiskers all a-quiver, before bounding in to follow the other gargoyles.

"Come on," Paddy said. "Everything's quiet for now, but it might not stay that way for long. Something still doesn't feel right. . . ."

Chapter 20

Boldly Brother Richard led the way downward—he knew the place, after all—and the cat jumped down to scamper on ahead. Templeton followed with somewhat less confidence, keeping well back from the Templar's trailing white mantle—which, if he trod upon it, could trip up both of them. He could feel grit underfoot as he tried each uneven step before putting his weight on it, one gloved hand keeping balance against the side of the stairwell, for a misstep could also send both of them tumbling.

With the other hand he managed the sword at his side—always awkward on stairs—pivoting the sheathed blade forward, so that the tip preceded him and *that* didn't end up tripping him. Quite incongruously—for he was mostly worried about what might lie ahead—it occurred to him that not many people knew how to wear a sword, these days. Notwithstanding the experience of his friend Brendan, who had closed the end of his in the door of a taxi, Knights of Malta were among the few who did know how.

Of course, wearing a sword and actually *using* one were not necessarily the same thing. He hoped Paddy wasn't expecting him to go whacking away at anything. . . .

The stairway made several turns as they descended, the greenish glow growing steadily brighter, until Brother Richard and then Templeton himself at last emerged into a level, almost cavernous space, Paddy bringing up the rear. Giving it a hurried glance, Templeton thought it looked more like the undercroft at Christ Church than the crypts at St. Michan's, with thick, heavy pillars supporting a barrel-vaulted ceiling.

But like St. Michan's, it appeared to have mummies—maybe half a dozen or so—not coffined, but laid out on low stone biers set along the brick-lined walls. Brother Richard paid them no mind as he continued on through the chamber, toward the source of brighter light spilling from an arched doorway ahead, but Templeton found himself pausing beside the nearest, hand on the hilt of his sword as he leaned down for a closer look.

The form was more skeletal than Brother Richard's had been, held together by little more than the cere, disintegrating rags of what once might have been a white habit and mantle like the ones that Brother Richard now wore. Splayed across the chest, Templeton could just make out the faint suggestion of an eight-pointed cross—what color was impossible to say. The hilt of a broadsword lay beneath the skeletal hands still crossed piously on the breast, its blade shrouded along the length of the corpse's legs by more rotting cerements and a veiling of ancient and dust-laden spider webs.

"A brother Templar," Paddy said close beside him.

"*Jay*zus, don't do that!" Templeton blurted, even as he recoiled and recovered.

"Sorry."

Impelled back into motion, and muttering under his breath, the old man hurried on after Brother Richard, who was just disappearing through the green-glowing archway. As he, too, came abreast of it, he stopped dead, causing Paddy to nearly tread on his heels and mutter his own muffled expletive.

Templeton's jaw dropped. The other gargoyles had ranged themselves around the outer edge of a stone-girt room that was at once too small to contain them and too large to sense its boundaries, webbed wings spread to enclose the space. Here, however, their varied and fantastical gargoyle shapes were overshadowed by a hint of their true angelic forms, so that each seemed veiled by a semitransparent image of the princely armored warriors they truly were, worn like a cloak of glory.

But the gargoyles themselves were not what at once drew Templeton's closer regard, magnificent though they were. It was what lay in their midst: an object of dreadful beauty that fairly took Templeton's breath away.

Catching sight of it, he had no doubt why the Templars had been accused of worshipping a head—and it was an exquisite piece of workmanship, so lifelike that he almost expected the golden lips to part in speech. Encrusted with gems both precious and semiprecious, and set upon a

plinth of banded chalcedony, its sightless eyes gazed out
in a blaze of jasper and peridot from atop a chunk of
stone shaped like two cubes set side by side, as high as a
man's waist. Its crafting appeared to be Persian or
Mesopotamian—or perhaps Egyptian—conjuring images
of ancient Babylon, and Luxor, and Ur of the Chaldees.

Guarding either end of the stone were golden pairs of
child-sized kneeling cherubim, also with an Oriental look
to them, their upraised arms and angular wings overarch-
ing the jewelled head like a protective canopy—or a restraining dome for whatever was within. To Templeton's
awestruck gaze, the overall effect resembled nothing so
much as biblical accounts he had read describing the Ark
of the Covenant—though the head was wrong, all wrong,
and did not belong on this mortal plane.

"Thank God, we are in time," Brother Richard said,
shouldering between the gargoyles to approach the thing.
"The binding has, indeed, grown weak, but it still holds."
He circled the double cube, closely inspecting what it held,
then beckoned to Templeton.

"Come. I must prepare you. We should waste no time.
Give me your sword, and then kneel."

Not inclined to question, Templeton did as he was told,
drawing his sword and then dropping to his knees with the
sword across his gloved hands. All around him, the gar-
goyle/angels had also drawn their blades, which shone like
sunbeams lancing through cloud.

Brother Richard took the sword from him, smiling
faintly as he hefted it experimentally.

"It is not the blade I would have chosen for slaying
Saracens," he said, "but it is a goodly weapon in the service

of the Light, and I sense it has served your purpose well." He reversed it to extend the cross-hilt before the old man, his big hand holding it under the quillons.

"Lay your hands upon this cross and swear that you are God's, unto death and beyond," Brother Richard commanded, locking eyes with Templeton. "Swear that you will stand against whatever may come in the next hour, all for His sake. For He is that Lord before Whom every knee should bend and every head bow down."

Hurriedly baring his head, the blood singing in his ears, Templeton stuffed the black beret into the front of his coat, then used his teeth to help pull off his gloves, shoving them into the coat pockets. Only then did he place his trembling hands on the quillons of the sword. Brother Richard's words had not been specific to any particular order of chivalry, so far as he could tell, but they seemed to embody the very essence of Christian knighthood, resonating with the oath he had sworn at his dubbing as a Knight of Malta. He need have no reservations about swearing as Brother Richard asked.

"I swear by almighty God that I am His man, unto death and beyond," he said steadily. "Before God and this company, I offer my sword and my strength in His service, and will stand as I must against whatever may come. Amen."

"*Selah,* so be it," Brother Richard said, withdrawing the sword and reversing it, the hilt now in his hand. "And accordingly, I do confirm your service as a brother knight, *in nomine Patris, et Filii, et Spiritus Sancti.* Amen."

As Templeton bowed his head, the blade descended on his right shoulder, then left—and at the same time, he sensed the swords of all the surrounding gargoyle/angels briefly extending to touch his head. Their touch was like a benison, washing peace and new strength through his weary bones. In that instant he became certain that he would know what he must do, when the time came. It was Brother Richard's hand that clasped his and helped him to his feet.

"Well done, my brother," the Templar said, letting him put his beret back on before handing back his sword. "Now, we have work to do." He drew his own weapon, a heavy broadsword, and moved around to the other side of the jewelled head. "Thrust your sword into the ground as I do, about an arm's length from the edge of the platform. This will be your anchor point. Do not abandon it."

Watching Brother Richard, Templeton attempted to follow suit, but the ground was hard, and his lighter blade resisted, bending, until Paddy assisted him. The gargoyle/angels were echoing the action all around them, spiking their angelic blades into the ground like so many bars of a glowing cage. But before they could complete their circle, the chamber suddenly was filled with a glare of tawny radiance and a stinging wind that roared like a blast furnace.

"Stand fast!" Brother Richard shouted, bearing down on the quillons of his sword, as the ground around them bellowed forth dozens of terrible, misshapen fire-forms wielding spears and scythes and jagged tridents. "Do not despair, for God is with us!"

Templeton was already following the Templar's example, though a glancing buffet from one of the demons—for such they must be—made him stagger, with one elbow hooked around the blade of his sword and the other hand locked over the hilt. The sudden invasion of demons had also overturned one of the golden cherubim, and another was teetering under the assault of several of the fiery attackers—hateful imps and demons, who struck sparks from the settings of the gems as they prodded at the head with pitchforks and spears, keening and cackling with malevolent glee. The gargoyles had swarmed in at the first sign of trouble, and were beating off some of the demons, but more kept coming, and the assault went on.

"They seek to shatter the head, to free the Baphomet!" Brother Richard cried, hurtling around to try to raise the fallen cherub. "If they succeed, the Baphomet will be free!"

In that instant, one of the imps noticed that two of the defenders were merely human. A swipe at Brother Richard had no effect, for he was immune to injury in any mortal sense, but Templeton was more vulnerable. Under a piercing glare from the imp's burning eyes, he felt something tighten in his chest like the clench of an iron fist. A cry escaped his lips, and he would have crumpled, had not the Templar caught his weight and borne him to his feet, with a grip on the old man's forearm as icy as the grave.

"Do not give in!" Brother Richard implored, tugging Templeton toward the toppled angel. "You must help me right the cherub! Mortal life is worth nothing, if they free the Baphomet—and Satan's minions have already breached one of the defenses!"

Staggering, pain throbbing down his arms, Templeton went willingly nonetheless, for the hatred radiating from the fiery demons left him in no doubt of the evil present. So malevolent were these servants of Darkness that the very air seemed to reek with their defiance and frenzied intent to free what lay imprisoned within the golden head—an entity that, if once released, would wreak untold havoc upon the world.

"Non nobis, Domine!" Brother Richard shouted, as he seized a wing of the toppled angel, grunting as he tried to heave it back into position. *"Non nobis . . . sed nomini tuo . . . da gloriam!* Help me, my brother!"

"Non nobis, Domine!" Templeton gasped, silently finishing the response in his heart as he ducked his head and shouldered his way to Brother Richard's aid. Somewhat oddly, he could not seem to feel the touch of any of the demons as he passed among them, though his movement clearly pushed them aside, and seemed to be strengthened by the ancient Templar motto, which had also been their battle cry.

Non nobis, Domine—Not to us, Lord, not to us but to Thy name be the glory! His own order had used another battle cry, but they had all fought the same good fight, all those centuries ago in the Holy Land. And Paddy and the others had warned him that it was a battle he was being called to wage.

Setting his hands on one of the golden wings of the toppled angel, he cried out as the gold seared his hands, but in that instant he knew that to falter now was to die in spirit as well as in body. He could feel the buffeting of darker wings as he and Brother Richard heaved the guardian angel back into position, but he could sense, also, the fiercely benign protection of Paddy and the others, mostly shielding the two human knights from the fury of their fallen brethren. His hands felt like the very flesh was melting from the bones, and pain was pounding behind his eyes, clenching his chest, but surrender to the pain was not an option.

"Move around to the end now, and set your hands on the wings!" Brother Richard ordered, himself advancing as if against a heavy wind toward the golden angel at the other side of the stone plinth.

In a daze that somehow began to distance him from the pain, Templeton did as he was bidden, a part of him amazed that the flesh did not slough off his hands as he shifted his grip. The burning touch of the gold had become icy cold, hardly less painful, but now he became aware of gigantic, armored arms enfolding him from behind and clasping gauntleted hands over his, where they clung to the golden wingtips—part of Paddy, for the first time directly visible, without a black mirror, solid and reassuring. More important than mere sight, he fancied he could feel the peace of that powerful embrace as a shielding mantle, somehow insulating him from the evil maelstrom all around.

"Now avert your eyes and pray as you have never prayed before," Brother Richard cried, "as I reconstruct the bindings!"

Templeton obeyed, lips moving in recitation of the time-honored prayers of his faith, but he could not resist stealing an occasional glance from beneath lowered lashes. Though he had a vague notion that the Templar's next words were in Hebrew, he could not be sure.

That mattered little, however, because whatever the language, the power in the words became physically visible, like gossamer rainbow bubbles streaming from Brother Richard's lips. They seemed simply to dissolve away at first, dispersing aimlessly like tiny, localized firework displays—dancing pinpoints of red and blue conjoined. But then, a few at a time, some of the bubbles began to attach themselves to the golden cherubim and to the be-gemmed head—much to the fury of the milling denizens of Darkness.

Templeton cringed from their anger and frustration, that battered at his very soul, but he did not allow his hands or his prayers to falter. Calling on the Blessed Virgin and all the saints to protect him and to strengthen Brother Richard in the work they shared, he prayed that whatever evil threatened here might be driven back, in the name of God.

"Ave, Maria, gratia plena!" he whispered under his breath, which now was coming hard. *"Pater Noster, qui est in coelis . . ."* And then, repeating again the ancient Templar motto: *"Non nobis, Domine! Non nobis, sed nomine tuo da gloriam."*

The words and the prayers interwove with the iridescent bubbles still streaming from Brother Richard's lips. The prismatic array reminded Templeton of the promise symbolized by God's gift of the rainbow, after the Flood, and suddenly he knew that they would succeed.

Slowly the bubbles obscured the features and then the very form of the golden head, each succeeding layer damping the strength of what was contained therein and rendering it impotent. The rainbows glinting on the four cherubim, rather than obscuring them, united in a single shimmering veil of unquestionable power and goodness that reinforced the binding contained within the span of the four sets of wings.

Templeton could feel the power vibrating up his arms and resonating deep in his diaphragm, numbing him to the tips of his toes. Where his hands still gripped the cherub's wingtips, he could see the edges of the rainbow veil wrapped around his wrists like multicolored gloves. A tension building in the very air around him made it hard to breathe, constricting his chest like tight bands.

But though the sweat was pouring off him, he did not loosen his death-grip on the golden wings. Nor did his prayers cease. A part of him was still aware of Paddy looming right behind him, enfolding his soul in angelic protection, even if the strength of his body was slowly ebbing; and all around, as the minions of Darkness began to abandon this foothold on physical creation, the other gargoyles streaked after, to harry and pursue them from this place.

All at once, with a vast subterranean rumbling, the entire stone plinth upholding head and golden cherubim began to sink into the earth. This movement brought a cry of triumph to Brother Richard's lips, and he released his death-grip on the golden wings. Templeton, too, drew back his hands, sinking wearily to his knees as the Templar stabbed both arms toward the golden head in a final gesture of command, consigning the Baphomet to its prison once again as it sank from sight beneath the earth for another thousand years. In an instant, even the opening had disappeared, leaving only a sheen of heavy dust on the floor of stone and earth.

The silence that followed was broken only by the old

man's ragged breath as he sagged to the floor on hands and knees, distantly concerned about the continuing tightness in his chest, though he felt no pain. Only gradually did he become aware that the surrounding murmur of the gargoyles' voices had become a wordless paean of victory interwoven with the murmured thanksgiving offered up by Brother Richard.

But when he managed to lift his head, the gargoyles' angelic trappings had vanished and the illusion of mortal life was draining away from his Templar companion, now leaning heavily on the taloned arm of the Christ Church gargoyle. The little cat was crouched on C.C.'s shoulder, gazing down on the failing knight with wise cat compassion.

"My brother, forgive me," Brother Richard whispered, in a voice as cere as the graveclothes already growing visible beneath the semblance of life he had assumed. "The ending of this task I must leave to you, for I can no longer stay in this long-spent body. But very soon we shall meet again."

With that, the light of intelligence drained from the hollow eyes, ancient flesh withering and shrinking once again under leathery skin as the body seemed almost to collapse in on itself. Even as Templeton gasped with the shock of it—and knew the portent of the pressure still clenching his own chest—the last vestiges of the Templar's pure white habit melted away like the snow outside, leaving only a mummified corpse in C.C.'s tender embrace.

This the senior gargoyle gently gathered to his massive gargoyle chest as Paddy hunkered down beside Templeton. The old man grimaced and rubbed at his left arm, a wary look of apprehension tightening his face, but Paddy only shook his great gargoyle head.

"Not yet, friend Francis," he said gently. "And not here."

"Then, I'm *not* having a heart attack?"

"Like I said: not yet and not here. You need to take Brother Richard back to St. Michan's."

"And then?"

"Don't worry," Paddy said. "I've called someone to come along with you."

"But—"

"Come on, get your sword. We need to get Brother Richard back to the car. And you don't want *it* found *here*, do you?"

"I guess not . . ."

Still rubbing at his arm, Templeton dutifully hauled himself to his feet and staggered over to pull his sword from the ground—there was no sign of Brother Richard's—following a little woozily as the other gargoyles streamed back into the corridor and started toward the stairs, the cat leading the way and C.C. bearing what remained of Brother Richard.

Chapter 21

In something of a daze, the old man managed to follow them up the stairs and into the still darkness outside. The stairwell sphinctered closed with a faint sucking sound as Paddy followed, the last of them to exit. Templeton turned to look, but the opening was gone, as if it had never existed. The snow had stopped.

"Don't worry, it's secure for another millennium or so," Paddy said. With Paddy's arm around his shoulders, Templeton hardly even noticed that they walked right through the iron bars to leave the ruined church. "And it's all thanks to you and Brother Richard. You did a great job. You were really brave."

"I don't feel brave, I feel scared," Templeton said dully, as they trudged back along the path toward the graveyard gate and the street lamps beyond. "I'm so tired, Paddy. I don't know if I can do this."

"Of course you can," Paddy replied. "This will be a piece of cake, compared to what you've already done. Besides, there's your help," he added, just as Templeton set his heavy hands on the gate. "She's waiting for you beside the car."

Caught in the process of shouldering the gate wider, Templeton stopped dead in his tracks to stare, clutching at the iron bars for support. For he knew that slender figure communing with the little gargoyle on the radiator cap of the old Rolls Royce, one hand tracing the line of a stubby chrome wing. He knew that mane of fiery hair blazing under the streetlights—the glory of County Kildare!

"Maeve!" he cried.

Her smile, as she turned at the sound of her name, was like sunlight flooding his darkness, bespeaking the profound affection that had sustained and enriched their lives together through more than half a century of marriage. A strangled little cry caught in his throat as she lifted her hand in an oh-so familiar gesture both of greeting and of longing.

He had no memory of crossing the twenty feet or so of paving that lay between them; only that, all at once, he stood breathlessly before her, weaving a little on his feet, not daring to touch her for fear of shattering the illusion— for, illusion it surely must be! How could it be his own darling Maeve, standing here before him with snowflakes tangled in the fire of her hair?

"Maeve," he said again, this time breathing the name almost as a prayer—for, illusion or not, she was so very beautiful—even more beautiful than he remembered.

"Aye, and you are my own dear love," she whispered, smiling—and lightly brushed the knight's cross at his throat with a trembling feather-touch.

And the touch was real! With a sob, he caught her hand in his and pressed it to his cheek, feeling the sweet caress of her other hand against his cheek.

"Maeve," he whispered a third time, drinking in the measure of every well-beloved feature.

"Happy Christmas, Francis," she said softly. "How I *have* missed you! But we must not linger here, my love. You must take Phyllida back—and Brother Richard. . . ."

He heard her speaking through a haze of pressure at his chest—but no pain—and he caught his balance against the car door, suddenly lightheaded, afraid that his knees would cease supporting him.

"Sweet Jesus, I'm tired, Maeve—so tired!" he murmured. "I don't know that I can drive."

"Of course you can, you silly man!" she said. "I shall help you." Her blue eyes danced, teasing, laughing, blue as the sky—Patrick's blue!—eyes for a man to drown in. "Let me sit close beside you, as I did for all those years, with my arm through yours and my hand on yours, and help you shift the gears. . . . May I not do that?"

Wordlessly, wonderingly, he nodded, groping past her for the door handle. He opened it and handed her in—as he had done for all those years—then pushed it gently closed. A tartan hillock already loomed in the back seat of the car, the little cat hunkered down on its summit, and somehow he knew, as he made his halting way around the boot to the driver's door, that the rest of the gargoyles were already inside. He shed his sword as he went, furling its belt around the scabbard, and fumbled it into the passenger foot-well before he eased into the driver's seat. Sitting seemed to revive him a bit. If only he could have a little nap . . .

"Francis, we must go," he heard her say, the words jarring him back to his last remaining obligation.

With a faint sense of curious detachment, he found himself mechanically going through the proper sequence with hands and feet to start the car and get it into gear.

"How I did love this old car," Maeve said, as the engine rumbled to life. "Is it Marcus who'll be driving her next?"

Nodding, he released the brake and let the big Rolls Royce creep forward, hauling at the steering wheel to make the U-turn back in the direction they had come an hour before.

"I wouldn't trust her with anybody else," he said. "He drove her today . . . no, yesterday. . . . Didn't miss a shift. He knows how to treat a lady. . . ."

"He does," she agreed. "Such a fine young man. And I'm glad he loves our Phyllida. I like to think that she helped him turn out the way he did. He's been a good son to us, Francis. Do you think he'll ever find some lovely girl to share her with, the way you shared Phyllida with me?"

"I think maybe he has," Templeton replied.

"Has he really?" she said, with a little coo of pleasure, her hand resting lightly on his on the shift knob. "Tell me, Francis, tell me!"

"Well, her name is Cáit. She's a doctor."

Talking about Marcus and the fair Doctor Cáit helped

him concentrate on his driving as they drove the two miles back to St. Michan's. It also helped take his mind from the growing numbness in his hands and feet and the pressure in his chest—still not pain, for which he supposed he had Paddy to thank, but an almost overwhelming weariness. The gargoyle said not a word, but Templeton knew he was there behind the seat.

By the time they had crossed the Royal Canal and headed off along Parnell Street, Maeve was helping him to steer as well as shift, because he couldn't really feel his hands anymore. Fortunately, there was almost no traffic. His vision had started to go a little funny as they made the turn into Capel Street, and the sweat was pouring off him as, together, they hauled the big car around the turn into Mary's Abbey and Chancery Street, which skirted the back of the Four Courts.

"We're nearly there," Maeve whispered, as he braked for a red light at Church Street. "I know you can do it."

"Just run the light," Paddy said quietly, from the seat behind. "There's nothing coming and no one watching."

Though Templeton had never been inclined to break traffic laws—the big Rolls was too conspicuous—he was too tired to argue. Though he did slow almost to a stop, casting a look in both directions, the road was clear as Paddy had promised—and St. Michan's was just ahead.

"The gate just past the church is open," Paddy said, pointing with a scaly arm between the seats as Templeton made the turn into Church Street. "Just pull in there and park."

Nodding, Templeton did as he was told, concentrating hard to navigate the very wide Rolls Royce through the very narrow gate. The cat jumped onto the back of Maeve's seat to watch. He could hear her purring in the utter silence that settled on the car after he had switched off the ignition. He was shivering as he fumbled blindly with the headlamp switches.

"Well done, Francis," Paddy said, touching his shoulder. "Just one last thing. You needn't get out of the car, but I do need you to open the sunroof for me. I've got to put Brother Richard back."

Just how the gargoyle planned to get the crusader mummy's body out through the sunroof remained to be seen, but Templeton lifted a hand that felt like lead and slowly cranked the sunroof open. Maeve helped him, her hand on his, and slipped her arms around him as his hand fell back heavily into his lap.

"So cold," he whispered, turning his face into her shoulder. "Hold me, Maeve."

"My dearest love, I will always hold you," she said.

Vaguely he was aware of her lips against his cheek, of the comforting softness of the tartan rug being laid around his shoulders and tucked around him. He felt the buffet of Paddy's wings as the gargoyle surged upward through the sunroof, taking Brother Richard back to his resting place.

And then, quite inexplicably, he was standing hand in hand with Maeve beside the car, watching the wind lift her flaming hair against the glare of a streetlight.

"Dear God, you are so beautiful," he whispered. "If you knew how I've missed you . . ."

"I know," she replied. "But that's past now. Look."

Jutting her little pointed chin, she indicated the shiny black door of the old Rolls Royce, polished like a mirror. It reflected Maeve herself, the breeze lifting her glorious red hair and molding a flowered summer frock to her slender figure, but it also reflected a young and dapper Francis Templeton, dark-haired and handsome, wearing the scarlet dress tunic of his knighthood.

And even as Templeton gaped, Paddy's angelic form appeared behind them, looking over their shoulders—a dark, winged prince in rainbow-glinting armor, with a filet of stars bound across his brow. At Templeton's awed look of inquiry, Paddy inclined his noble head.

"All is well," he said quietly, "and now it's time for you to go Home. You're a true knight, Francis Templeton, and it's been a pleasure and a privilege to work with you."

"But—am I dead?" Templeton asked.

For answer, Paddy gestured toward the driver's seat of the old Rolls Royce. There, with the tartan rug wrapped close around his shoulders like a shawl, the spent form of the old man's human shell sat slumped peacefully behind the wheel, the little cat snuggled close beside his thigh.

Astonished, Templeton glanced back at his wife in wondering question as she slipped her arm through his.

"Darling, shall we go?" she said, her adoring gaze upturned to him.

Even from where they stood, outside the car, he could hear the little cat purring in the predawn stillness, singing him Home. . . .

Chapter 22

Paddy lingered after the two of them had gone. C.C. and the other gargoyles had seen that the crusader mummy got safely back where it belonged, in its vault beneath St. Michan's, and soon dispersed to their various assignments, via the passage under the Liffey. Paddy knew that he should return to St. Patrick's as well, but he wanted to make certain that nothing went amiss when Templeton's body was discovered. He had grown fond of the old man in the three days of their acquaintance.

Ascending to a vantage point behind the parapet in the church's bell tower, where another gargoyle once had kept guard over this part of Dublin, he watched the waking city come alive. In light of what had happened here, and the convenience of the connection from the vaults below to the passages that crisscrossed beneath the rest of the city, he decided he would recommend permanent reinstatement of a gargoyle post at the ancient church. In the interim, maybe a part-time gargoyle would even be sufficient. He thought the Phoenix Park gargoyle might be persuaded to divide his time between the two locations, since he occasionally grumbled that little of real interest ever happened in the park.

Meanwhile, the bell tower was an ideal place from which to keep watch over the old Rolls Royce. Through the open sunroof, Paddy could see the bright swath of tartan around Templeton's shoulders, the black beret on his bowed head. The little cat stayed beside him until the first pedestrians started passing on the sidewalk outside the church wall, well before the sun actually rose, curled up in the sheepskin hat the old man had left on the passenger seat. Paddy watched the cat trot off through the graveyard, leaving little cat paw-prints in the snow, her striped tail carried like a question mark.

One of the ladies who ran the gift shop in the church foyer was the first person to take more than casual notice of the old car and its occupant, when she came to open up for the day—and called Emergency Services. The street-lights were just going off when the ambulance arrived, its flashing lights casting blue glints against the grey of the building and the snow all around. A garda car arrived a few minutes later, and stayed when the ambulance had gone.

Very shortly after that, a small red Honda pulled in behind the garda car and the old Rolls Royce. It was Templeton's godson who got out. The garda sergeant who walked back to meet him inclined his head sympathetically as the two shook hands.

"Sorry to be the bearer of bad news so close to Christmas, Marcus," he said. "If it's any consolation, he probably went very peacefully. He looked like he'd just gone to sleep. Paramedics said it was his heart."

Marcus continued past him to the old car, trailing a gloved hand along a rear fender.

"I'm not exactly surprised," he said. "We'd known for months that he had a dodgy heart. I didn't expect it so soon, though. I saw him only yesterday, and he was in grand form."

"I guess you never know, do you?" the sergeant said.

"I guess you don't. Still, I suppose it's as well it happened this way. He lived with his youngest daughter and her family, and lately they'd been pressuring him to give up driving. Seems he'd begun talking to himself while he drove around, apparently chattering like a magpie. At least that's what *she* said. In my opinion, he was as sharp as ever; just getting a little lame. But he was afraid he wouldn't be allowed to drive anymore. *That* would have killed him just as surely as his heart. He loved this old car."

"Well, it's good that he wasn't driving when it happened," the sergeant said. "But I wonder what he was doing out so early? And what made him stop here at St. Michan's? It can't have been easy to maneuver through that narrow gate. It would've been much easier to just pull to the curb."

"I dunno," Marcus replied. He bent to look through the passenger window, gloved hands resting on the windowsill. "Did you guys open the sunroof?"

The sergeant shook his head. "Nope. Wouldn't know

how. The ambulance guys said it was open when they got here. But I don't suppose it can have been open for long, because there wasn't any snow in the car. I suppose he wanted a breath of fresh air."

"Yeah, I suppose so."

"One other odd thing, though," the sergeant said, as Marcus opened the passenger door and stretched inside to close the sunroof, reaching across the passenger seat, where the tartan rug lay neatly folded beside Templeton's sheepskin hat. "He was wearing a black boiler suit under his overcoat, and a black beret—though I don't suppose those were the accouterments of a cat burglar, at his age."

Marcus managed a grin as he cranked at the sunroof. "Not bloody likely. He was a Knight of Malta. They wear those as an undress uniform when they go on pilgrimage to Lourdes. Can't imagine why he would have been wearing it here, and in the middle of the night—or so early in the morning," he added, as he finished with the sunroof and extricated himself from the open doorway. "He did go to a Malta affair yesterday, though. I drove him and a couple of other old duffers over to the Nuncio's, yesterday afternoon—but that was in full dress kit: red tunic, sword, spurs on the boots—the whole lot."

"A sword, you say?" the sergeant said. "That explains the one we found in the front seat. Almost forgot to tell you about that."

"You're joking!"

"Nope. See for yourself. We put it in the boot for safe-keeping. It's a pretty thing, probably worth a few bob. Boot's unlocked," he added, gesturing in that direction.

Somewhat bemusedly he watched as Marcus went back

to open the boot lid and peer inside, brow furrowing as he propped it open on its stops and lifted out the sheathed sword with belt wound round.

"That *is* odd. He always kept this in a soft leather case. . . ."

"Actually, it was leaning against the passenger seat when he was found," the sergeant said, as Marcus turned the sheathed sword in his hands, looking puzzled. "Looked like he might have been wearing it, and took it off in a hurry. Any idea what he might have been up to?"

"I have no idea . . ."

"Beats me, then." The sergeant shook his head as Marcus put the sword back in the boot and closed the lid. "Ah! Just remembered one more thing that you might find interesting, since we're talking about strange things. You see that tartan rug, up in the front seat?"

"Yeah?"

"Well, when the ambulance guys found him, he was sitting slumped over the wheel, and he had it wrapped around him like a shawl, all cosy-like."

"*Did* he?"

Coming back to the open passenger door, Marcus leaned in to pull out the folded rug. As he did so, a faint scent of roses came and went. Going very still, he held the rug briefly to his face and tried to catch another whiff, but it was gone. But he was smiling faintly as he breathed out with a sigh and gathered it to his breast, one hand caressing the bright wool.

"His wife gave him this, when they were courting," he said. "For just a moment, I thought I caught a hint of her perfume. They were married for more than fifty years, but I don't think they ever exchanged a cross word. She and my mother were best friends, so she helped raise me. When she died, a few years ago, he never really got over it."

"Well, it looks like maybe his last thoughts were of her, then," the sergeant said.

"I think perhaps they were," Marcus replied. He replaced the tartan rug on the seat, gently smoothing it a few times with his hand, then closed the passenger door with a decisive *thunk* and glanced around with a sigh, even casting his gaze up toward the battlement where Paddy watched—though, sun-dazzled, he did not see the gargoyle.

"I think I'll take the Rolls now, and come back later to get the other car," he said.

"I guess that's all right—seeing as it's you," the sergeant said.

Marcus quirked him a faint smile. "Don't worry; it's mine now, anyway. Francis wrote me into his will on my twenty-first birthday. He wanted someone to have the car who would appreciate it the way he did, and his father before him." He trailed a gloved hand along the curve of the fender as he went around the front to the other side, a caress lingering on the red and white shield held by the little dragon mascot on the radiator cap.

"If this old car could only talk," he said, as he opened the driver's door, "I expect she'd have a few fine stories to tell, over the years. Phyllida, he called her. I'd give a lot to hear the true story of what happened last night, though—not that we'll ever know."

"I don't suppose we will," the sergeant agreed.

As the two exchanged a few more words, Marcus glanced back at the little gargoyle. Something in his gaze made Paddy wonder whether the day might just come when he and Marcus would find themselves thrown together for a partnership not unlike the one Paddy had briefly enjoyed with Francis Templeton—though, hopefully, more in the nature of their first adventure than their second. Breaking in a new partner took so much time and effort. . . .

But Paddy had all the time in the world and then some, for he was, after all, an angel, and among the first-born of God's creation. Patience was a part of his very makeup—though he had to admit that his long sojourn among humans sometimes tried that patience just a little.

After a few minutes, Marcus got into the old car and started the engine. From up in the bell tower, Paddy watched the garda sergeant stop traffic so that Marcus could reverse the car carefully out of the driveway and then head slowly up Church Street. When it had disappeared, he made his way around to the most sheltered angle of the tower and waited until passing clouds briefly deepened the shadows before he plummeted to the snow-covered churchyard. (In fact, he gave the clouds a little nudge.) No one saw him as he streaked into the vault that connected with the passage underneath the Liffey.

A quarter-hour later, he had briefly bent the local weather again, this time obscured by briefly flurrying snow as he launched his shadow-essence up the side of cathedral and tower to his post behind the crenellated battlements.

Home at last. It was not the Home to which Francis Templeton had now returned, but it was the home ordained for the gargoyle known as Paddy by the will of the One Who had sent him, from which he might best serve the purpose for which he had been created. Since it was their nature, angels desired nothing more than this, and Paddy was well content.

Under the brightening sun of a brilliant winter's day, as the light glistened on the stones of the Irish battlements of the cathedral's tower, he settled back and listened to the sweet treble voices of the boys from the Choir School lifting in pure praise, as Choral Matins wound to an end. Very shortly, the clock in the tower below began striking the hour of ten, its sound ringing reassurance and continuance all across the streets and rooftops of Dublin. He had guarded the city for a thousand years, and by the grace of God he hoped to guard it for at least another thousand.

And as Paddy turned his keen and ever-vigilant gaze out over the city—*his* city—he decided that on a day like this, after a night like the one just past, it really was great to be a gargoyle!

Afterword

Alas, there are, in fact, very few gargoyles in Dublin—at least that can be seen. The Georgians are, indeed, to blame for this unfortunate state of affairs, though it must be said that, in compensation, the city of Dublin boasts some of the finest Georgian architecture to be found anywhere. As for positing that gargoyles (or at least the mystical essence dwelling within their carved stone shells) are actually former avenging angels, I make no apologies for undoubtedly shaky theology in this regard. Besides, it was fun taking a few playful pokes at some human institutions, as Paddy himself does from time to time.

The short story from which this book was expanded, "The Gargoyle's Shadow," was triggered by an act of vandalism that occurred at St. Michan's Church several years ago, somewhat different from that described in this story. Also, since moving to Dublin some fifteen years ago, I had been hearing references to the mysterious underground passages that may or may not connect various key buildings in the older parts of the city. Some swear blind that they don't exist; others are dead certain they do—and based on what I was able to uncover, the jury is still out. And of course, readers familiar with my previous work know that I just can't leave the Knights Templar alone.

So what has emerged in *St. Patrick's Gargoyle* might well be described as "Katherine at play." Historians rarely need an excuse to poke around in beautiful and historical places, and Dublin has beauty and history in ample supply: all of it fair game for exploration, with the very legitimate excuse that I was actually working. A great many wonderful Dubliners allowed themselves to be caught up in my enthusiasm, and graciously shared their knowledge and expertise. The things I got right, I owe to their generous assistance; the things I got wrong are my fault entirely.

Following are some of the good folk of Dublin, by no means all of them, who gave me a hand and shared the *craic,* without whom this book could not have been written:

Nicole Arnould, Royal Society of Antiquaries, for helping ferret out information on Clontarf Castle and its Templar connection;

The Reverend Peter Campion, Dean's Vicar, St. Patrick's Cathedral, for clarifying how the cathedral operates, especially at Christmas time;

Michael Casey, The Irish Georgian Society, for insights on those elusive underground passages;

Mary Clark, Dublin City Archives, who finally identified the puzzle of St. Nicholas Without—which is (or was) without, or outside, the walls of Dublin;

Peter Condell, guide at St. Michan's Church, who knew which of its six vaults probably connects with the tunnel under the Liffey, and showed me its entrance;

David Griffin and Simon Lincoln, The Irish Architectural Archives, for helping point me toward additional information about Clontarf Castle;

Chevalier Dáithi P. Hanly, former Dublin City Architect and Knight of Saint Lazarus, who has the Abbey Theatre's entrance in his garden, and who carved two real gargoyles;

Mrs. Pat Kane, chairperson of the Flower Guild, St. Patrick's Cathedral, who told me about the Christmas decorations at the cathedral;

John Kealy, caretaker for Clontarf Cemetery, whose brain I picked regarding the burial vaults under its ruined church;

Geoffrey Kennedy, son-in-law to Anne McCaffrey (yes, *that* Anne McCaffrey), who has actually seen the entrance to one of the underground passages (it runs from behind O'Connell Street, under the Liffey, to somewhere under Trinity College);

Scott MacMillan, for heraldic, chivalric, and vintage car expertise above and beyond the call of duty or matrimony;

Charlie Reed, tower-captain of the St. Patrick's Society of Change-Ringers, who let me sit in on several ringing sessions at both St. Patrick's and St. Audoen's and even ring a bell, albeit badly;

Chevalier Patrick White and Senator Donal Lydon, K.M., both of them Knights of Malta, who unravelled the mysteries of the order's uniforms.

To these and all the others I've inadvertently omitted, my profound thanks.

Katherine Kurtz
Dublin, Ireland
May 1999

Turn the page
for an exciting preview of

In the King's Service

the newest Novel of the Deryni from
Katherine Kurtz

Prologue

"I hear that you have a son at last," Dominy de Laney said to Sir Sief MacAthan, as she settled beside him at the heavy, eight-sided table in the Camberian Council's secret meeting chamber. "Congratulations are surely in order."

Across the table from them, Vivienne de Jordanet was absently twirling a dark ringlet around one forefinger as she read over the shoulder of the man to her right: Lord Seisyll Arilan, one of the Council's two co-adjutors. Both of them looked up at the other woman's comment, and Vivienne gave the new father an indulgent smile.

Sief's face brightened, a boyish grin creasing his still-handsome features as he basked in this affirmation of his male potency. After nearly thirty years of indifferent marriage, four living daughters, and several stillborn or short-lived sons, he had all but given up hope of a male heir. The birthing had been difficult, for the child was large and his wife was no longer young, but the new babe was hale and lusty, if disappointingly unlike Sief in appearance. Of course, most infants were inclined to look like wizened little old men so soon after birth. Hopefully, the pale eyes would darken—and as yet, the babe had too little hair to tell what color it would be.

"I must confess that I am pleased," Sief allowed. "I've decided to call him Krispin. There was a Krispin MacAthan a few generations back. His sisters adore him already. I suppose it is a natural reaction of young girls, anticipating children of their own."

Dominy de Laney smiled and patted his hand, kindly mirth in the sea-green eyes. "Young boys, as well, Sief. In truth, most children seem to like babies. My own are constantly begging for another sister or brother. And well do I remember when Barrett was born. I've always wondered whether our poor parents had him to achieve some respite from me and my sisters. Especially after Cassianus died, we were determined that there should be another boy for us to pamper."

The comment elicited a chuckle from Vivienne, who sat back in her chair just as the great doors to the chamber parted to admit the scarlet-clad subject of Dominy's comment, one of his graceful hands resting on the arm of Michon de Courcy for guidance. Barrett de Laney's hooded robes were those of a scholar at the great university of Nur Sayyid, but his emerald eyes gazed into eternity, sightless—not through any infirmity of age, for he was only two-and-thirty, but through blindness, incurred when he was hardly grown to manhood, willingly accepted in exchange for the freedom of several dozen children.

Those who had taken his sight had intended to take his life as well—a probability Barrett had been well aware of, when he submitted to the hot iron that bought the children's release. In memory of that day, he still wore his thinning hair sleeked back in a soldier's knot that was faded red, where it was not streaked with white. He had not expected to leave that place alive, or that another would lay down his life instead, to secure his escape.

The man who guided him now, of his father's generation, had fostered him as a child of promise, helping to hone his natural talents, and had taught him to adjust to his lack of physical sight—a task made far easier by the powers they shared in common with the others in the chamber. For all of them were highly trained Deryni, members of that long-vilified race of sorcerers and wise men who must coexist with mortals not so gifted, in whom fear and perhaps even jealousy bred intolerance that often killed.

Even other Deryni did not know the composition of this elite and highly secretive body now gathering under the purple dome of the Council's meeting place, though most with any formal training had at least some inkling of its existence and the policing function it carried out for the good of all their race. A few individuals were believed by some to have the Council's ear, but none would ever confirm or deny. Only rarely did it intervene directly in the affairs of other Deryni, and even less often were its rulings challenged.

Mostly, its guidance was more subtle: the hidden hand working through others, behind the scenes, to discourage and hopefully prevent wanton use of Deryni powers. And while rigorous discipline and the mutual intent of its members gave it access, as a body, to power not generally available to any single individual, the Council's greater power lay in the speculations of other Deryni about what the Council might actually be able to do, and apprehension regarding what force it could bring to bear to enforce its rulings and to discipline those who strayed from responsible behavior.

For the Deryni in Gwynedd were few, and always had been so, regarded by the much larger human population with varying measures of awe, respect, wariness, and outright fear—which, in reaction to Deryni abuses, whether real or imagined, could shift all too swiftly to hostility and mindless violence. Once that occurred, sheer numbers could overwhelm even the mightiest of magical defenses—and had done so, more than once, in rampages of wholesale slaughter that had decimated the Deryni population in Gwynedd.

It had not always been thus. Early in the previous century—and still, in many of the lands neighboring Gwynedd—humans and Deryni had cohabited in relative peace, mostly to the mutual benefit of both races. But there had always been those who harbored an uneasy mistrust of the Deryni and their sometimes startling abilities, and feared the possible misuse of powers not accessible to ordinary men. Some said that such powers were too near that of gods, or at least of angels; others were convinced that such powers could only be demonic, corrupting not only the wielders of those powers but those touched by them.

Such hostility, born of fear of what was not understood,

had finally come to a head in the previous century, triggering a period of persecution akin to a religious crusade that had decimated the Deryni population of Gwynedd. Now a rigid and restrictive code of laws regulated the existence of those remaining, barring them from holding public office or owning property above a certain value and excluding known Deryni from many occupations, under pain of fines, imprisonment, or worse. And the discovery of one's power being used, even with the most benign of intentions, was apt to trigger a killing rampage by frightened and irate humans—and was given legitimacy by human law.

With care and cunning, those laws could be circumvented, as all of the members of the Camberian Council were well aware, though even those who lived beyond the borders of Gwynedd mostly maintained a low profile, for magic could make one a target as well as giving one a tool or weapon.

Only Sief had managed to carve out a secure public position within Gwynedd itself, at the king's court in Rhemuth, as had his family for many generations. Seisyll and his extended family lived outside the capital. Neither was known to be Deryni. Michon owed fealty to Gwynedd for his ancient barony, far to the west, and made periodic appearances at court as he was able, but he mostly kept far from the court and its scrutiny, as his family had for generations.

The others lived beyond the borders of Gwynedd, where those of their kind could live more openly, though even they were circumspect. Barrett, perhaps, had the greatest freedom, being currently in residence at one of the great Torenthi universities. A seventh member of the Council likewise lived outside Gwynedd, but had sent apologies for non-attendance, being currently engaged in a diplomatic mission away from Portal access.

But six were more than enough to transact informal business; five of the seven would have been sufficient to uphold any serious ruling of the Council, though no capital matter was under discussion on this night. When possible, the Council met fortnightly, to brief one another on affairs in the areas where they lived. In the past three decades—longer than any member's span of service save Sief himself—there had been no serious demand on the Council's powers of arbitration. Though all of them were well aware how precariously the plight of Deryni in Gwynedd still stood, slow gains had been made in the past several generations, and the future was beginning to look hopeful.

"We should begin," said Seisyll Arilan, when Michon had led Barrett to his seat between them and taken his own. "Doubtless, Sief will wish to return to his new son. My congratulations," he added, inclining his head in the new father's direction. "Your lady wife is well?"

Sief gave a nod, still looking pleased. "Weakened somewhat, which is to expected with an older mother, but I am hopeful that the child will show more of its paternal heritage than its maternal. I never forget that she is the daughter of Lewys ap Norfal."

"You did agree to marry her," Michon pointed out.

"It was that, or have her killed," Sief said lightly, though all of them were aware that he meant precisely that. "We could not have trusted Lewys' daughter to a nunnery."

"Yet you have trusted one of her daughters to a nunnery," Dominy de Laney reminded him.

"She is my daughter as well," Sief replied. "And each

child is different. But I would have smothered Jessilde at birth, had she shown the wayward potentials of her grand-father—or her mother."

Vivienne rolled her eyes heavenward, then glanced at Dominy, a mother like herself.

"Let us please have no more talk of smothering babies," she said emphatically. "Especially not Deryni babies. It's bad enough that poisonous priests like Alexander Darby continue to spread lies about us. Have any of you actually seen that scurrilous piece of tripe that he published at Gre-cotha last year? *De Natura Deryniorum*, indeed!"

"Scurrilous or not," Sief said, "I hear that it's to become required reading for every seminary in Gwynedd."

Barrett was nodding, fingers steepled before his sight-less eyes. "It's been making the rounds at Nur Sayyid. Well written, they say, but utterly lacking in scholarly integrity."

"Lacking in scholarly integrity?" Dominy blurted. "Is that all you can say? Barrett, the man's a monster!"

"Yes, and he's a monster with a growing following," Seisyll pointed out. "And I can understand why. I heard him preach a few months ago. A very persuasive speaker, and a very dangerous man."

"I've heard him, too," Michon said. "It's a pity that a timely accident can't be arranged. A fatal one. Actually, it could. But given the public profile he's already established, I suppose the authorities would quickly draw the right con-clusion regarding who was responsible—and that would spark the very kind of reprisal that we try to avoid."

Seisyll Arilan gave a disgusted snort. "We should have taken care of the problem long ago. Now it's too late for the more obvious solutions."

"It's never too late to stamp out pestiferous vermin," Vivienne said coldly. "I'm sure one of my brothers would be happy to oblige."

"No, we'll not risk losing one of them for the sake of the likes of him," Michon said.

"Sometimes risks are necessary," Sief pointed out. "You are aware, I trust, that the bishops already have an eye on him?"

"For what, chief inquisitor?" Seisyll muttered.

"Actually, for a bishop's miter," Sief replied. "I have that directly from the Archbishop of Rhemuth. Unless Darby puts a foot seriously wrong, it will happen, mark my words."

"But—he was only ordained last year," Dominy said, sounding scandalized.

"Yes, but remember that he is hardly your typical green young priest," Sief said patiently. "He's a very fine scholar, but he also lived in the world before he took holy orders. He trained as a physician, and they say that he has all the arrogance that sometimes comes of both disciplines. That's a dangerous enough combination in a priest who also hates Deryni. In a bishop—well, I don't think I need to spell it out."

"He isn't a bishop yet," Michon said, in a darkling tone that suggested the matter might not be the foregone conclusion everyone else was assuming.

"Nonetheless, we do have other things to discuss this evening," he went on. "The Darby situation will require further consideration." He jutted his chin toward the document lying between Seisyll and Vivienne. "Meanwhile, am I correct in assuming that the two of you have been reading

Ptolemeos' report regarding the young Duke of Corwyn?"

As Seisyll nodded, prodding at the document with some indifference, Vivienne sat slightly forward in her chair.

"I found it interesting that Ptoley thinks that he might do well squired to one of the Forcinn courts," she said, glancing at the others, "at least so long as his father is alive."

"How old *is* he now?" Barrett asked.

"Young Ahern? Eleven," Michon replied. "You'll recall that after his mother died—oh, six or eight years ago, by now—Keryell sent all the children to the Orsal's court for a few years. Sobbon probably hardly even noticed, among all those von Horthy children, and Keryell had quickly taken a new wife."

"There are several more daughters by that second marriage, aren't there?" Dominy said thoughtfully.

"Yes, but the mother is human," Michon replied. "Which makes the daughters of little interest to us," he added, "or to those who are nervous about a Deryni duke in Corwyn—whether merely as a regent, as Keryell is, or as duke, as Ahern will become. In any case, Keryell brought the older children home right after Twelfth Night. For the past several months, Ptolemeos has been pressing him about Ahern's squiring. The boy will be in a unique position when he comes of age: a full Deryni on a ducal throne within Gwynedd. It's important that the right decisions are made about his future."

"I'll be glad when he's grown and married and has an heir," Seisyll muttered. "It's a pity that the male line in Corwyn has proven less than hardy. At least Stevana had a boy, God rest her soul, and blood *is* blood. . . ."

Chapter One

Far from where the Camberian Council sat in secret session, crafting their careful, deliberate plans for the future of their race, the wife of one of its members lay propped amid the pillows of their curtained and canopied bed and waited for the nurse to bring her infant son for feeding. Two days after his birth, Lady Jessamy MacAthan was feeling far stronger, but both the pregnancy and the delivery of this latest bairn had taken more out of her than any of her previous children, even the stillborn ones.

Of course, she was older than when she had birthed any of the others—past forty now, and with a growing history of miscarriages and stillbirths. She had not even been certain she could conceive again, much less carry a child to term.

But this child was important, destined for a secret but

very special role in the future unfolding for Gwynedd and
its kings to come. It was too soon to tell precisely what
young Krispin's magical potential would prove to be, but
his parentage ensured that he would be no ordinary boy.

The nursery door opened, and Mistress Angelica
brought in the fretting, wiggling bundle that was her son,
shushing and cooing over him as she laid him in his
mother's arms.

"He's very hungry, milady," the woman said, as Jessamy
put him to her breast.

"Yes, I can see that," Jessamy replied, smiling. "And
greedy, too. He's like a wee limpet. Thank heaven he
hasn't any teeth! But you needn't sit with me. I know you
must have things that need doing. Are the girls asleep?"

"Yes, milady."

"Good. I'll call you when we're finished."

She readjusted the child in the hollow of her arm and
settled back to let him feed as the nurse retired, allowing
the sweet lethargy of his suckling to drift her into idle remembrance, wondering what Sief would say, if he were
ever to penetrate past her shields to learn the truth—though
Jessamy would resist him to the death, were he ever to try.

She had never wanted or intended to marry Sief, who
was sixteen years her senior. But her mother had died when
she was but ten, and the loss of her father the following
year had left her in the hands of guardians who insisted on
the match: powerful Deryni, who had feared what Lewys
ap Norfal's daughter might become, and had sought to
minimize the danger by seeing her safely wed to one of
their own. Though she had never come to regard Sief with
more than resigned acceptance, she loved the children he

had given her; and she had learned to live with the arrangement because she must, and to wear the façade of a dutiful wife, because outward compliance allowed her at least an illusion of freedom here at the Court of Gwynedd—if only Sief knew *how* free. Her love of her children was one of the honest things about her life, as was her affection for the queens she had served here in Rhemuth for the past thirty years.

By now, memories of any other home had mostly receded to a distant blur, dangerous though it was to be Deryni in Rhemuth. Even before Rhemuth, her parents had never stayed long in one place, lest their Deryni nature be discovered—and Lewys ap Norfal had never been good at hiding what he was for long. Had they lived in Gwynedd those early years, she now thought it unlikely that Lewys would have survived long enough to sire any children. Even so, he had been notorious among his own kind, and had met his end attempting magic usually deemed impossible even among the most accomplished of their race.

Putting an end to that nomad existence, Sief had brought her to Gwynedd's capital immediately after their hurried marriage, giving the care of his frightened child-bride into the hands of the king's daughter-in-law, the gentle and sensitive Princess Dulchesse, who had been the wife of then–Crown Prince Donal Blaine Haldane.

The two women had liked one another from the start. Dulchesse, but twenty-one herself and already six years married, had yet to give her husband an heir, but she had taken the orphaned Jessamy under her wing and assumed the role of elder sister and surrogate mother, giving her the fierce protection of her royal station as the still-hopeful mother of kings. Indeed, in all but name, the princess had been functioning as Gwynedd's queen for all her married life; for Roisian of Meara, King Malcolm's queen, had withdrawn to a convent the same year Dulchesse came to court, after Malcolm was obliged to lead an expedition into rebellious Meara and execute several members of Roisian's family. One of them had been Roisian's twin sister.

Alas for Sief, placing his young bride in the household of the Crown Princess had not turned out at all as he had expected; but by the time he realized that he had become the victim of feminine solidarity. The rift had come the previous year, it was too late to change his mind.

"I shall school her to be a wife you may be proud of, my lord," Dulchesse had told the disbelieving Sief, on learning that he planned to allow Jessamy but a year's grace before consummating their marriage, "but you shall not touch her until her fourteenth birthday. She's but a child. Give her the chance to finish growing up."

"Your Highness, she is a woman grown," Sief had protested. "She has begun her monthly courses—"

"Yes, and if she should conceive so young, you are apt to lose wife *and* child. You shall wait."

"Your Highness—"

"Must I ask the king to tell you this?" she retorted, stamping her little foot.

Before such fierce determination, Sief had been left with no recourse but to back down.

Accordingly, Jessamy had been allowed to spend those stolen days of extended girlhood as a pampered pet of the princess's household, mastering the gentle accomplishments expected of a knight's lady and carefully beginning to weave the façade that she hoped would protect her in the future. Though her brother Morian technically lived at court, having been squired to Prince Donal's household before their father's death, they saw little of one another. Whether that was by chance or by design, she did not know; but on those rare occasions when they did meet, she sensed that he was bowing to the secret direction of those who had surrounded their father.

Fortunately, her own magical studies had been sufficiently advanced that she was able to shield her smoldering resentment both from him and from Sief, though she knew that she needed to know more. Unfortunately, she was still a child, albeit an exceedingly well-educated one for her age and sex. But at least Sief mostly left her alone for those next three years.

Once she had settled into the routine of the royal household, she had started looking for ways to further her education—at least the conventional part of it. When she let it be known that she possessed a fair copy hand and read and spoke several classical languages, she soon found herself being summoned to the royal library to assist in cataloging the king's manuscript collection. There she came to the especial attention of Father Mungo, the princess's aged chaplain, who was taken with her learning and her willingness to learn (and most assuredly did not know that she was Deryni), and soon began giving her private tutorials. She soon discovered that both the king and crown prince frequented the library on a regular basis—and thereby gained permission to spend time there whenever her duties permitted. Further honing of her esoteric talents would have to wait until she could figure out a way to gain access to teachers, or at least to texts, but in the meantime, Father Mungo's lessons and her own explorations in the royal library filled the time and gave her more tools for later on.

But she had known that her reprieve must end. On the day of her fourteenth birthday, on a sunny morning in early autumn, she was obliged to stand before the Archbishop of Rhemuth with Sief and reaffirm her marriage vows, in the presence of Malcolm and his new queen, the Lady Síle, Donal and Dulchesse, and all the royal household, for Sief was well regarded at court, and all agreed that he had shown remarkable forbearance in waiting three years for his bride. Reassured by Dulchesse, and gently briefed regarding what to expect when Sief finally came to her bed, Jessamy had endured her wedding night with reasonable grace.

She had conceived within months, shortly after the new queen was delivered of a prince christened Richard. Her own firstborn would have been a playmate for the new prince, a boy also named Sief, but the infant died hardly a week after birth. She had not yet turned fifteen.

More pregnancies had followed at barely two-year intervals after that: a succession of mostly healthy girls, stillborn boys, and early miscarriages. The ones who did not survive were allowed burial in a corner of the royal crypt, for the childless Dulchesse began to regard them as the children she would never have. Queen Síle had also come to mourn Jessamy's losses—and Dulchesse's barrenness—and buried several children of her own, in time. The three women had visited the little graves regularly until Queen Síle's death, the same year as King Malcolm. Dulchesse, finally queen at last, had died but two years ago. Now Jessamy laid flowers on the other women's graves as well as those of the children, sometimes in the company of the new queen, Richeldis, who had quickly borne King Donal his long-awaited heir.

There had been only a few pregnancies after the birth of Jesiana, her nine-year-old, and only one brought to term until Krispin: yet another girl, now four, called Seffira, whom Jessamy loved dearly. Though Sief was mostly indifferent to his daughters, his desire for a son was still strong, and he continued to visit her bed on a tiresomely regular basis, despite the apparent waning of her fertility. Sometimes she wondered whether her own antipathy had kept her from quickening—especially when this latest child had been so easy to conceive. Young Krispin, however, had been greatly desired—though not in the sense that her husband supposed.

His very begetting had been profoundly different from any of the others—no resentful and resigned yielding to marital duty, but welcome fruit of a well-planned series of quick, focused couplings that were timed to the most propitious few days of her monthly cycle, accomplished quite dispassionately amid briefly lifted skirts in a shadowed upper corridor of the castle, where others rarely went—or bent over a library table, or braced against a hay bale far at the back of the royal stables, surrounded by the warm, dusty fragrance of lazing horses. Her pulse quickened at the very thought of those days, though it was the daring of what she had done rather than lust that excited her.

Within days she had known she was with child, and thought she could pinpoint exactly when conception had occurred, though she let Sief think that it had come of their usual, more conventional conjugal encounters. The memory stirred a pleasant aching in her loins, quite apart from the soreness after birth, intensified by the sweet suckling of the babe at her breast.

A tap at the room's inner door announced the intrusion of the babe's nurse, white-coifed head ducking in apology as she eased into the light of the candles burning beside the curtained bed.

"You have a visitor, milady," the woman said. "The king has come to pay his respects. Shall I take the baby?"

"No, show him in," Jessamy replied. "Then leave us."

"Alone, milady?" Angelica said, looking faintly scandalized.

"Angelica, he's the king."

"Yes, milady."

The woman withdrew dutifully, unaware that her compliance had been encouraged by Jessamy's deft reinforcement. Very shortly, the king peered around the door and then entered, closing the door behind him and grinning. Jessamy smiled in return, inclining her head over the baby's in as much of a bow as could be managed from a mostly reclining position. As she looked up, she saw a flicker of pleased amusement kindle behind the clear gray eyes.

He did not look his age, though she knew that she looked hers, especially after the rigors of late pregnancy and childbirth—and she, more than a decade his junior. Now past fifty, Donal Blaine Aidan Cinhil was still the epitome of Haldane comeliness, fit and dashing in his scarlet hunting leathers. Gold embroidery of a coronet circled the crown of his scarlet hunting cap, and a white plume curled rakishly over one eye, caught in place with a jeweled brooch. While his close-clipped beard and his moustache were acquiring decided speckles of gray, hardly a trace of silver threaded his black hair—unlike her own once-dark tresses. The loosely plaited braid tumbling over one shoulder was decidedly piebald.

He took off his cap as he came farther into the room, tossing it onto a chest at the foot of the great bed with easy grace. He had been born in the halcyon years shortly following Gwynedd's costly victory at Killingford in 1025, the only surviving son of Malcolm Haldane and Roisian, Princess of Meara, whose marriage was to have cemented a lasting peace between the two lands. Instead, it had spawned a new dispute regarding the Mearan succession—and launched a series of periodic Haldane military incursions back into Meara.

The succession, even in Gwynedd, had remained precarious in the years that followed, for Donal was the only male heir Malcolm had produced by his first marriage, despite several sons and daughters by a well-loved mistress, legitimated shortly before his death but without dynastic rights. Donal's two half-brothers had made good marriages and served him loyally, and their father's second marriage to Queen Síle had produced another true-born prince in Duke Richard—until the birth of Prince Brion, Donal's heir presumptive, little though he aspired to the crown. Though trained from birth to rule after Donal, if need be, none had rejoiced more than he when, within a year of his brother's new nuptials, Queen Richeldis had presented Donal with a son: Prince Brion Donal Cinhil Urien Haldane, born the previous June.

"Good evening, Sire," Jessamy said to the father of that prince, as he moved closer beside the bed. "How fares the son and heir?"

"He flourishes," Donal replied, smiling. "When I put a sword in his hand, he doesn't want to let go. I expect he will be walking soon. He pulls himself up already. And how fares *your* son and heir?"

"He suckles well. He knows to reach out for what he wants. His father has reason to be proud of him."

"May I see him?" Donal asked, craning for a closer look.

"Of course."

Gathering the infant's blankets around him, and carefully supporting the tiny head, Jessamy held out the bundle to the king, who took the babe in the crook of his arm and proceeded to inspect him thoroughly.

"He appears to have the correct number of fingers and toes and other appendages," Donal declared. "And those are warrior's hands," he added, letting the infant seize one of his fingers and convey it to the tiny rosebud lips. "He will be a fitting companion for a prince."

"One had hoped that would be the case," Jessamy agreed good-naturedly.

"Brothers—that's what they'll be," came the reply. "He's perfect. His hair will be like yours, I think," Donal went on, gently cupping the child's downy head. "But those are not your eyes, or Sief's."

"No," was all the child's mother replied.

Chuckling softly, Donal let himself sit on the edge of the bed, and was carefully giving the child back into its mother's keeping when the bedroom door opened and Sief entered.

"Ah, and here's the proud father now," Donal said, twisting around to greet the newcomer. "I'd come to congratulate you, Sief, and to inspect the new bairn. And to cheer the mother in her childbed, if the truth be known. My queen tells me that a new mother appreciates such things. Not that she speaks to me overmuch, of late. The morning sickness is a trial she would liefer have foregone for a few more months."

Sief found himself smiling dutifully in response to the king's boyish grin, though he could not say why he found it unsettling to find Donal here.

They had long been friends beyond mere courtier and prince. He had served Donal Haldane for most of his life— had been assigned by King Malcolm as the prince's first aide, when Sief was a new-made knight and Donal was but ten—and been his confidant and brother-in-arms through many a campaign and court intrigue. The young prince had guessed that Sief was Deryni, very early on—and Sief knew that Donal possessed certain powers of his own that were somewhat similar, somehow related to his kingship. Malcolm had possessed them as well, and had also recognized Sief for what he was, though they had never spoken of it.

Sief had never spoken of it to the Council, either, though privately he had vowed to Donal that certain of his not inconsiderable powers were at the prince's service. Part of the reason for the Council's very existence, after all, was to safeguard the Haldane line on the throne of Gwynedd; for the Haldanes knew, as other humans did not, that the Deryni, properly ruled, posed little threat to the human population.

In practice, his direct service as a Deryni had been limited, and private. Those of his race were able to determine when a person was lying—a talent of undoubted use to a king. In addition, a trained Deryni could usually compel disclosures when a person attempted simply to tell part of the truth, or to withhold it. With care, the memories of a person subjected to such attentions could even be blurred to hide what had been done—though such investigations were always carried out in private. The court was only aware that Sir Sief MacAthan was an extremely skilled interrogator. More often, he merely stood at the king's side and observed, only later reporting on the veracity of what had been said.

Over the years, such attention to nuance of truth and falsehood had become second-nature when in the king's presence. Why, then, were Sief's senses suddenly all a-tingle at the prospect that the queen was once again with child?

"Then, the palace gossip is correct," Sief said tentatively.

"Palace gossip," Donal said, standing up with fists set to hips. "Surely you don't pay any mind to *that*."

"I do, when it may pertain to the welfare of the kingdom, Sire," Sief replied. "Prince Brion is still shy of his first birthday. It is still very early for a new pregnancy for the queen. Self-restraint, my lord," he added, trying not to sound self-righteous.

"A king needs an heir and a spare," Donal said breezily, "and good men to guard them and guide them as they grow. You know the heartache of losing sons. I must make certain that Brion has brothers."

Suddenly Sief caught just a flash of subtle evasion: not a lie, but a truth not fully divulged. To his consternation, it sparked a dread possibility that had never come to mind before, but which might make sense of several things in the year since the prince's birth; but he put such thoughts aside as he forced an uneasy chuckle.

"Just now, methinks Prince Brion needs his mother more than he needs brothers," Sief said. "Have a care for *her*, at least. People would talk, were you to take a third queen."

Donal shrugged, and his next words again left Sief with the impression that all was not being said.

"People will always talk about kings. I little care, so long as the succession is secure."

"There *is* Duke Richard, if all else were to fail," Sief pointed out.

"True enough. But my brother Richard aspires to a warrior's fame—and he has the sheer ability to excel at it. He little cares for the finer diplomacies of the council chamber—or even of marriage, at least thus far," Donal added with a shrug. "Besides that, he is the fruit of my father's loins; not mine."

"Aye, but blood *is* blood, Sire," Sief said, echoing the words of the Council not an hour earlier. "Richard is as much a Haldane as you or the new prince."

He thought he saw Jessamy stiffen slightly at those words, though her dark head was bowed over the infant in her arms.

"Indeed," the king said mildly. "I trust you aren't presuming to instruct me in my duties as a husband?"

Sief raised a placating hand, hesitant to even consider pursuing the subject; but Donal's manner seemed increasingly evasive, making Sief wonder whether he had, indeed, stumbled on something he would be happier not knowing.

He ventured a cautious probe, but Donal was tight-shuttered against even a surface reading. That was hardly unusual for the king, for Sief had long ago realized that Donal had shields as good as any Deryni's—though whether they would stand up to any serious attempt to force them remained an unknown question. What alarmed him was that Jessamy likewise had retreated behind shields far stronger than he had believed her to possess.

Chilled, he turned to look at her sharply—and caught just a hint of something in her eyes. . . .

With a little sob, she turned away from him in their bed, shielding the infant Krispin behind her body. In that instant, in an almost blinding flash of insight, Sief *knew* what more she was hiding—and Donal, as well.

"You!" He whirled on the king, fury and betrayal in his dark glare. "He's *yours*, isn't he? You've made me a cuckold! Was it here, in this very bed?"

Even as he said it, his clenched fist lifted and he lashed out with his powers, fully aware that he was threatening violence against the king to whom he had sworn fealty—and not caring, in his rage. To his utter astonishment, Donal Blaine Haldane answered with like force: potent and altogether too focused for what Sief had always imagined was the limit of the king's power. Before he could pull back, power slammed against his own closing shields and reverberated to the deepest core of his being, forcing a breach and starting a tear in his defenses that gaped ever wider, the more he tried to seal it.

With that realization came fear and pain—more pain than he had ever experienced in his life or even imagined he could feel. It began in his brain, exploding behind his eyes, but quickly ripped downward to center in his chest, like a giant fist closing on his heart. At the same time, he felt his limbs going numb, losing all sensation as his legs collapsed under him and his arms flailed like the arms of a marionette with its strings cut. Through blurring vision, he could just see Donal, right hand thrust between them with the fingers splayed in a warding-off gesture, and Donal's lips moving in words whose sense he could only barely comprehend.

"Listen to me, Sief!" Donal's urgent plea only barely penetrated the scarlet agony blurring his vision. "Don't make me kill you! I need the boy. I need *you*!"

"Lies!" Sief managed to whisper, from between gritted teeth, as the child—*Donal's bastard!*—started wailing. "Faithless, forsworn whoreson! I'll mind-rip you!—kill the bastard!—kill . . . *you* . . . !"

Enraged beyond reason, Sief tried again to launch a counter-attack against the man who had betrayed him, bucking upward from his slumped position and dragging himself to hands and knees, clawing a hand upward to help him focus—but to no avail. To his horror and dismay, the other's might was crushing him down, smothering the life from him—but he was too proud to yield, and too stubborn. All his life he had been so careful in how he used his powers, taken such pride in his abilities. He had always known that the Haldanes had powers that were akin to his own, but now, in extremis, he had not the strength or the abandon to turn his own powers to the wanton response that might have saved him.

He could feel his mind ripping under the onslaught of an attack he wondered if Donal even comprehended. (*Where* had he gotten such power, and the knowledge of how to use it?)

Hardly a whimper could he manage to force past his lips—nor could it have been heard, over the child's bawling!—but he could feel himself being dragged toward oblivion, all too aware that the damage only worsened as he struggled—and he couldn't *not* struggle! But somehow he had known, from that first flare of Donal's mind against his own, that there was neither any turning back nor any defense against this.

His last coherent thought, just before the darkness claimed him, was regret that he would leave no son from this life—for Krispin was *Donal's* son.

Yet still he tried to cling to that final image of the infant's puckered little face before his vision—the son that should have been his—as pain dragged him into an ever-darkening spiral downward and the last vestiges of awareness trickled into oblivion.

New York Times Bestselling Author

KATHERINE KURTZ

KING KELSON'S BRIDE
A novel of the Deryni

As a rival monarch takes his rightful place on the throne of a nearby land, it becomes more imperative then ever that King Kelson produce a long-awaited heir. Love is set aside for duty—and Kelson the king must make the choice that Kelson the man can not.

0-441-00827-5/$7.50

Fantastic stories from *New York Times* bestselling author

ROBIN McKINLEY

Paul Kearney

<u>Hawkwood's</u> <u>Voyage</u>

Book One of the Monarchies of God

0-441-00903-4/$6.50